TWO
MOONS

BY
STRUAN
FORBES

Cover Art by Jesse Malone
Layout and Design by The Author's Press
First Printing: March 2006

Library of Congress Catalog Card: Pending

US ISBN 10: 1-933505-05-2
US ISBN 13: 978-1-933505-05-3

TWO MOONS

The Author's Press

Atlanta Olympia Los Angeles

DEDICATION

For Ian Emery Rose, with love and hope.

PROLOGUE

Kathleen and Hans Gunderson patiently waited their turn for transport to the new colony, excited beyond words to be among the chosen. For more than three years they had endured the selection process that brought them to this moment, a chance to be among the first to found an experimental colony on another world.

They carried little of a personal nature. The government had already provided necessities such as clothing, shelter, and household goods, a complete array of what would be needed to survive in a hopefully benign environment for more than three generations. Between them, they carried only three small pieces of luggage containing the limited collection of objects that would connect them with their past on Earth. They looked down at the largest of the cases, thinking of the harmless contraband that they had been able to smuggle past the gatekeepers. It was such a small thing. Surely no one could object to one small divergence from the rules, and they simply could not bear to leave this particular pair of possessions behind.

"May I have your attention please?" said the uniformed man standing at the transport threshold. "May I have your attention? You are about to depart on the most historic journey in the history of mankind. Of all the millions who volunteered for this project, you are among the ten thousand who have been chosen to colonize one of a dozen terra class planets in nearby planetary systems. Your new homes have been prepared for you. Your environment has been cleansed of any immediate threat from local predation and the terra-forming of the surrounding countryside is complete. You will have everything you need for your success that we can provide, from energy to technology, to food to livestock and seed. We have done all in our power to give you a good start. The rest is up to you.

"As you know, what you do from this moment on will affect the entire human race and determine its future. Only by establishing and observing small groups of settlers in the process of developing such colonial communities can we determine how best to expand into the universe. Your success will provide for an end to massive overpopulation, to famine, and to a choking pollution and critical shortage of resources that now threaten to destroy our civilization. It will ensure that humans will be more than a mere footnote in the history of the galaxy. I wish you luck and look forward to observing your progress and your success. The World Community salutes you!"

With this, there was the sound of wild applause from the room's sound system, as if a vast crowd was present in the plain, featureless terminal. In spite of himself Hans stood a little straighter, filled with a pride at what they had accomplished through the years of training. They were going to take part in man's greatest migration and they were going to be among the first! Who could ask for more of life? Who could dream of a greater purpose?

"Please secure your luggage and prepare for departure," a mechanical voice bellowed and with a flurry of excitement, the thousands of people in the terminal began to gather their things for the jump. Kathleen and Hans moved forward with the line, grateful to be a mere thirty places back from the chamber in front of them. On either side, fifty gates just like this one were feeding emigrants through artificial wormholes to their new homes. Hans patted the case in his wife's right hand affectionately and waited. When their turn came, they stepped into the chamber together and as quickly as the door closed behind them it opened again, revealing a lush green valley punctuated by a large lake and freshly cleared and leveled site on which to build the colony. They stepped out, inhaling the crisp clear air which was heady with the spice of a new planet and its array of familiar and totally foreign odors.

They were quickly ushered clear of the chamber's door and out onto the plain by program directors, who signaled them to join the other colonists further out on the cleared land. They moved quickly, infected with the contagious sense of urgency that others exhibited ahead of them. Kathleen hesitated and pulled Hans to one side, pointing with a nod toward the group ahead. Hans followed her gaze. Directly in front of them were two project men, who were inspecting the luggage of the new colonists one last time, opening and rummaging through the small cases to be certain that no unauthorized items had arrived with the colonists.

"What do we do?" she whispered.

"Stumble," Hans snapped.

"What?"

"Stumble," he repeated. When you fall, I'll kneel to help you."

Kathleen took a quick step and pitched forward on her knees. Hans bent down, dropping his suitcase beside the ones she was carrying and pretended to examine her ankle. He drew the largest of the three cases forward, pretending to use it as a prop for his wife's supposedly wounded ankle. As he did so, he released the catch on the bag and opened it slightly. Two tiny black noses poked their way into the sunlight and sniffed. He pried the bag open a bit more and two heads, their pink eyes blinking in the light, now protruded from it. Hans pitched the case sideways and with an encouraging thump to its side, the two tiny lab rats to leap from their prison and scurry away into the grass. He closed the case with one hand while rubbing Kathleen's ankle with the other, then stood and helped her to her feet.

"Everything okay here?" asked the project agent who was now approaching.

"It's okay. My wife just stumbled. There doesn't appear to be any damage."

"Okay then," the man said kindly. "Let's move along. We've got hundreds of others to process, you know."

Quickly the couple picked up their bags and began walking toward the inspection station.

Kathleen stole a glance at her husband and whispered. "Do you think anyone saw?"

"I don't think so. Those two scampered away so fast, I hardly saw them myself."

"A shame to let them go," she said.

Hans shrugged. "It was far from a sure thing that we'd be able to keep them anyway. I guess no pets means no pets after all. Besides, how much trouble can two very small, irradiated white mice be on a virgin planet? Hell, they can't even copulate. It is a shame though. I'd have liked to have them with us.

In the high grass, two small white rodents made their way toward the smell of water, scurrying through the covering foliage. They came to a small puddle from which they drank and then began the process of looking for a nest site. After all, it was a genetic predisposition to establish a territory, particularly for the female who was already swelling with the gestating offspring in her womb. In a few weeks, the litter of some twenty kits would be born, and a safe haven would be necessary until they could survive on their own.

CHAPTER 1

It was early morning. Caleb Grant and Chandy Crone lay sprawled on the side of the escarpment, panting from their run. Chandy looked over his shoulder at the rising sun, ruddy in the early morning light, and then laid back, eyes closed, and soaked in the warmth of the soft feather grass on which he lay. This was his favorite time of day. The exertion always gave him a feeling of unbounded energy and he was getting better at the run. Today he had kept up with Caleb all the way through the forest and up the slopes of the high hill. As he caught his breath, he thought about the lessons he had been learning.

"Caleb," he said.

"Hmm?" answered the hunter.

"When will I be ready?"

"When will you be ready for what?" the hunter said sourly.

"Ready for my hunt. All the other boys my age had their first hunt two or three years ago.

They're beginning to look at me like I'm some kind of straw man."

Caleb chuckled softly. "You're no straw man, Chandy. If anything, you're more real and more man than they."

Chandy let out a low groan. "You didn't answer my question."

Caleb opened his eyes and glanced over at his young apprentice. The young man beside him lay sprawled out, legs crossed, arms folded across his chest. His long legs were glistening with sweat and his running shorts were bunched up against his crotch. It gave him a rather comical appearance. Chandy was turning into a fine athlete. He wore no shirt, and his chest and arm muscles bulged for all his wiriness. If it weren't for the ridge of freckles across his nose and the total disarray of his too-long chestnut hair, you'd swear he was years older than his actual sixteen.

"We're getting a bit 'high in the tower', aren't we? Did I detect an edge to your voice just now?" Caleb asked.

Chandy frowned. "I...didn't mean any disrespect. I'm just really getting anxious about this. When do you think I'll be ready?"

Caleb lay back and closed his eyes again. He cradled his head in his two hands held above his head. "You know it's not up to me. It's up to the Keeper. He'll tell us when."

"The Keeper," Chandy snorted. "The old goat. All he ever does is hobble around with that big stick and look like he knows everything. None of the others have to wait for his okay before they can hunt."

"None of the others have been chosen as you have, and I'll thank you to show proper respect for your elders. The Keeper is the one person in the colony that comes close to knowing everything. He keeps the knowledge, originating from "He Who Was Here When We Arrived" and if he has his way, he'll be here when we leave."

Chandy lay silently for a while, watching the mist passing over the valley ridge in the direction of the Great Tower. At last he sighed. "I just want to be like everybody else; that's all," he said.
Caleb sat up, assuming the lotus position in the process, which caused Chandy to do the same.

"Look," the hunter said. "You're special whether you like it or not. It's a great honor to be the Next Keeper, and a great responsibility. Hunting is not to be your purpose in life. It's only a step in your education. "I thought that the Keeper would have set your initiation before this too, but he has his reasons. I'll speak to him about it."

Chandy beamed excitedly. "Really? When? Will you do it tonight?"

Caleb nodded. "Tonight, yes," he said. He stood, carefully brushing the prickly feather grass dust from his own bare chest and turned to look at his reflection in the sheet crystal rock behind them. He was pleased with what he saw. If Chandy was fit, Caleb was exceptional. His long dark hair framed his square-jawed face perfectly. Even in the hazy reflection of the natural rock his deep blue eyes were visible. He was broad of shoulder and small of waist, with legs as long as Chandy's, perfect for running, and his stomach rippled with muscles beneath the skin. Caleb looked a second time, smiling. He was vain about his appearance and he knew it. He didn't even care because, in his estimation, he had cause to be vain. If only he could talk to people the way Chandy did, with unselfconscious ease. For the life of him, he couldn't figure out why he had so much trouble in social situations. He turned away and gave Chandy a malicious grin. "Now let's get down the hill and do some target practice. You're still a little sloppy beyond one hundred yards."

"If I had a real weapon I wouldn't be," Chandy prodded.

"Forget it. Not until you're an initiated hunter. You drink your cup of blood and we'll see what we can do. For the moment you'll use one of the old ones and be satisfied with it. Now get off your ass and on your feet. Let's see how fast you can run down this hill."

The trail meandered back and forth across the steep slope facing the colony. It was a wide, hard-packed path that descended first gently, and then with increasing drop until at the halfway point, runners were virtually falling forward and catching themselves, digging their heels into the earth. As they ran, an occasional crystal bush that had sprung up overnight would catch a leg or an arm, lacerating it painfully, but the pain passed quickly, and the scratches healed with time. For Chandy and Caleb it was as exhilarating as the run up to the escarpment. At the halfway point, where the trail leveled into a wide terrace before starting another precipitous descent, Caleb suddenly came to a halt... On one knee he peered over the terrace, signaling the boy to do the same.

"What?" Chandy said with irritation.

"There's something going on."

"Huh?"

"Look down there," Caleb said, pointing at the colony below.

Chandy looked down and studied the landscape but could not see anything out of the ordinary.

The plain below was no different, a wide flat land with fields and orchards surrounding a large swampy area in the center and lake beyond. To the left were the conical houses of outlanders, many still under construction, where the expanding population had begun a second central core.

The vague outline of a wall was visible on the far side of those new houses. To the right was the colony itself, two concentric rings of wall, an outer one gleaming white in the morning sunlight and the inner one dull and pasty, like chalk that is yet to be smoothed. It all looked the same as usual.

"I don't see anything..."

"Look closely."

Chandy grumbled, "I don't want to succeed the Keeper."

"Tell me what you see," prodded Caleb.

"It's the colony. It?s early morning and people are starting to wake up. There's a cluster of them in the central square, others moving through streets toward their shops. There are the usual guards on the outer wall, two in each post, which means they're changing from the night guard to the morning patrol.... And there's a line of hunters heading down the road toward the far wood.

That's not right."

"And the livestock?"

"What livestock?"

"Where are the pigs and the cattle? Where are the lummox and the Parker geese?"

"I...I don't see any. That's not right either, is it?"

"They should all be leaving to graze about now," said Caleb. "There's something wrong. I think we need to get back. The crowd in the square is growing, in case you haven't noticed."

"Well, actually, that I got."

"Hmm. Okay. That's enough rest. I want to see you beat me this time."

There was a palpable tension in the town when they entered the outer gates but Caleb pushed ahead to the square rather than ask anyone along the way. Chandy started to ask a passerby what was happening, but Caleb pulled him away.

"Not here," said Caleb with a shake of the head. "This far out on the rim we'd only get rumors. We'll find out what's really happening in the square."

Once through the outer gate they entered an area of newer construction where the high cones of personal residents were well-kept and glistened in the sunlight. Their glazed outer coverings gleamed, flawless and multicolored, thanks to the artistry of the builders. Each was a good thirty feet in diameter and rose upward two to three times that distance into the sky. Before each was a retractable staircase that rose to a doorway on the second floor. People were moving about on their way to shops or to one of the canteens that helped feed the thousands who lived here. Caleb loved the bustle of early morning, but today it was different. Those he passed seemed worried, or at least pensive.

When they passed through the inner gates they found Kylie, Chandy's sister, standing by the tailor's shop with a group of other young women. Caleb briefly thought that even in a time of evident crisis, women could still shop. He chided himself for the thought. Kylie wasn't like that and he knew it. She was savvy and intelligent. A beautiful young woman, two years Caleb's junior, she had long red hair and a slender body. The velvety green dress that she wore accentuated her hips and breasts, which she now thrust slightly forward by standing a little straighter. It delighted and confounded Caleb whenever she did this, and he swore that she did it just to watch his idiotic reaction.

"Hi, sis," Chandy said.

Kylie looked at her young brother with disapproval.

"Chandler Crone put your shirt on. You can't walk around in public that way."

Chandy just smiled with his usual charm and shrugged. "We've been running. It's hot out there, even this early. Besides, I want the girls to see what they're missing."

He grinned and winked at Kylie's companions, all two years his senior and therefore quite safe to flirt with.

Kylie glanced up at Caleb and gave him an inviting look. "Is that what your friend's doing as well?"

"'Lo, Kylie," Caleb said. It was all he could get out and he was turning redder by the moment. He pulled his shirt from his belt and slipped it on.

"Are you out to show the girls what they're missing too, Caleb?"

Caleb didn't speak. He broke eye contact and began to back away. Kylie laughed gently and turned back to her friends. He looked one last time to fix her image in his mind and said simply, "We gotta go."

In the central square they found a cluster of elders standing together, surrounding the Master of the Hunt. Caleb and Chandy made their way through the crowd until they stood before the Hunt Master. He was speaking in low, even tones to those around him. When he saw Caleb and Chandy he nodded then continued.

"The Crones and the Dills are searching toward the lake; the Franks and Nordstroms are heading for the forest beyond the paddock. Ari Patel and his sons have gone with Abu Wakombe's pride. They'll need good trackers."

He spoke decisively, as if he had done this hundreds of times, and Caleb looked up at him, admiring his ability to command. He was proud to call this man Father, but he knew better than to show it. Any act of favoritism on his father's part would be seen as weakness and a threat to his authority. Caleb had learned long ago to hold his tongue in public. Still, he wished his father would finish and they could find out what was going on.

He looked down at his son. "Caleb, I have a particular area of search for you and Chandy. Don't go anywhere." Caleb nodded, not sure whether to be pleased or irritated.

When the crowd began to disburse, Jonathan came down from the platform where he had been standing and sat on its edge. He signaled Caleb and Chandy to come closer. "Now listen to me. We've got a problem and my intuition tells me that it's more than it seems to be. Jason Keller left two days ago with his twin sons for their first hunt. They haven't returned. There's no sign of them and all we know is that when his wife awoke this morning, her husband and two youngest sons were not home yet. They were supposed to be one day out and one day back, which would have put them here last night at the latest. The watch didn't see them either. Now it could be

nothing, but until we know for sure, I'm being cautious."
He hesitated for a moment, debating with himself and
then said, "I'm worried that it may be the return of
the plague.?

Chandy took in a quick breath. Caleb grunted.

The Hunt Master continued, "Each clan has been
given an area to search. I'm giving you two an area of
your own." Caleb frowned and nodded.

"I want you two to search toward the Great Tower."

The young hunter's frown deepened. Was his father
trying to protect them in case it was the plague returned?

Jonathan waited for what he had said to sink in.

"Nobody goes near the Great Tower," Chandy finally
said in a very small voice.

"Which is why I want you two to do it now."

Caleb said nothing. He knew his father had his reasons.

"Why?" asked Chandy.

Caleb jerked his head around and glared at his young
companion. One did not question the Hunt Master, but
Jonathan simply smiled.

"He's very much like you, Caleb, isn't he? No wonder
the Keeper chose him."

Chandy reddened but would not break eye contact
with Jonathan.

"I'll answer your insolent question, young man, but don't test my goodwill like that again. This is a very serious situation. Everyone is assuming that the Kellers are to the west along one of the game trails. It's the logical place for them to go. The chances are high that is where they've gone. One of the clans should find them quickly. I'm sending you to the east but I do not expect you to find them. Chandy is still not an initiated hunter. Technically he shouldn't be going at all. He should stay here with the Franks and the Tolls who've been relegated to protect the town with the apprentices.

"I'm using this opportunity to accomplish two things. No one has been toward the Great Tower in a number of years. This is not a good thing if we're to maintain security in this valley. This is not exactly a hospitable land and having no knowledge of what local fauna are living to our east is dangerous. I want to scout it, and this search gives me the excuse I need to do it. If the plague has returned, they could be anywhere. If they're near the Tower, there will be signs of it. Secondly, your insolent young friend here is long overdue for initiation and I'm hoping that sending him out on the search will inspire the Keeper to finally let him have his hunt."

Caleb nodded. Chandy blinked and swallowed hard. He started to speak. Jonathan cut him off. "You have things to do. Go home, both of you. Plan for a three-day-round trip. That's one-and-a half days out and one-and-a-half days back. Don't make it longer. Now go."

Caleb turned and trotted off in the direction of home, Chandy in tow. They didn't speak. If they had each heard the other's thoughts they would have been surprised at how different they were.

CHAPTER 2

It was dark at the complex because of the heavy cloud cover and the lack of reflected light that would have rendered the area quite visible in another time and age, but it had been many years since that time. Nowadays, under the new regimen, all power was shut down at dusk and would not come on again until just before dawn. For the most part, this was of no consequence since there was little that actually took place after the sun set. No industries operated into the night, no malls or clusters of small shops were open to the public and no traffic sped through the streets as it once did, requiring street lights and traffic lights and powered highways to handle the heavy flow of vehicles that they once did. All of that was gone now and it was very dark.

This was all to the liking of the man who now stood on the edge of the great plaza in the center of the complex. As dark as it was he had no need of hiding in the shadows, but he still crouched beside his wheeled sled carrier, listening for any sounds out of the ordinary. He was a strong man, short and stocky but amazingly agile. He had been training himself for this night for years,

controlling himself, harnessing all the nervous
anticipation he held inside, unwilling to have his plans
thwarted at the last moment by of any impatience on
his part.

Eventually satisfied that there was no one about, he
stood and began skirting the edge of the plaza, his carrier
trundling along behind him on muffled wheels. He
moved like a predator against the background of the
buildings, concealing himself as best he could and
sprinting the short distances between structures. When
he had circled nearly half the plaza he stopped before a
rather short structure and felt along the wall for the
telltale raised letters that identified it as his destination.
When he found them, he knew for certain that he had the
right building.

He quickly entered the main doors, carefully guiding
his carrier through the entrance to avoid too much noise.
The inner doors were quickly breached and he was inside.
Around him he could feel the immense size of the space
in which he stood, an enclosed circular atrium more than
eighty feet across and surrounded by a single level of
offices. Feeling his way toward the far side, he reached
out to the nearest door and tried his key. It refused to
open. Moving to the left, he tried the next door some
twenty feet away and found that it, too, would not open.

Reversing his path, he walked past the first door he had tried to the next one to the right. This time the latch cycled easily and the door swung open noiselessly.

"Third time's the charm," he whispered to himself. "Yes sir, I always say that the third time's the charm...or is it the key?"

He chuckled softly to himself as he pulled the carrier through the door and closed it behind him. He crossed the room, stumbling on a single chair some worker had left behind more than twenty years ago and found the twin swinging doors on the opposite wall. He slipped through, set his carrier to one side and put his back to the wall, sliding to the floor and assuming a comfortable half lotus position there.. All he had to do now was to wait for dawn. There was an inexplicable calmness about him, considering the illegal and highly dangerous course he had chosen. So much could go wrong. The odds were high that he'd be caught before he could ever achieve his purpose and if he wasn't, he still ran the risk inherent in using the equipment, now idle for over twenty-three years and untended for all that time. If it did not work properly, he would die before he knew it had happened.

For some reason, none of this bothered him. He was, after all, a very practical sort, and danger was only a concept in his mind. If he died, he died, but if he lived through the next few hours, he would be the most famous man in the culture. He sighed, shifting his position and crossed his now stretched-out legs, folded his arms against his chest and went blissfully to sleep.

Sleeping soundly, his first challenge came. It was just before dawn and there was a dull light beginning to creep in through the glass front walls of the building and on into the outer office. It was just peaking through the small windows in the swinging doors next to him when he heard the sound of footsteps. They were coming his way. With surprising calmness he reached into a pocket on the outside of the carrier and withdrew a needle gun, a small energy weapon preferred by security forces and wealthy citizens alike. He checked the charge, drew his legs up into a lotus position again and placed the weapon in his lap. He waited. Outside, the footsteps halted near the center of the outer room. He could hear the person turn in a small circle, right the chair that the intruder had overturned the night before, and then make another circle. The unseen visitor's feet shuffled as he turned, mimicking the rhythmic hiss of someone performing a soft-shoe routine. The footsteps stopped again and moved closer to the swinging doors.

"I know you're in there," a tense voice called out. "I can see your footprints in the dust and they lead into that room you're in but not out again. You're trapped in a dead end and you might as well come out."

The crouched figure said nothing.

"If you just came to look at the machine, I'll let you go. Just don't touch anything, okay? I'm coming in now. Just relax."

The footsteps resumed, moving swiftly to the doors and then stopping. The crouched figure assumed that he must be looking in through one of the small windows before coming in. From his position beside the door and below, he couldn't be seen. Silently, he picked up the needle gun and waited.

With a sudden burst of noise, the doors swung open and a lone guard, dressed in a military uniform and carrying an energy rifle charged into the room. He stopped just inside the door and dropped to one knee. As he looked around, the crouching figure beside him just watched and smiled. The guard made a full circuit of the room with his eyes and ended staring into the face of the stranger. The stranger smiled and said, "Good morning. Nice day for it, isn't it?" He fired and burned a single tiny hole in the guard's forehead, then swept the weapon's focus along the cranium in an arc. When he stopped, the stunned guard pitched to one side as a single disc of skull and cauterized brain matter fell neatly away.

"Quite nicely done," the stranger said and stood.

Noticing the time, he retrieved the guard's energy rifle and pistol and hurried toward the large cylindrical chamber on the far side of the room, dragging his hand cart with him. He unlatched and opened the heavy metal door and shoved his baggage inside, then turned to a bank of readouts, he waited. Soon the lights in the room came on with a hum and he began punching numbers into a small keyboard on the face of the chamber.

Finally, he slammed the palm of his hand into a large red knob and stepped into the chamber. Just as he pulled the heavy door closed, there was a rush of wind in the room, a vortex that began in the center of the space and spread outward toward the walls. He threw the latch and locked the door, then knelt, huddling with his possessions against the wall. A loud roar penetrated the cylinder, deafening him and pressing against him. He felt as if he were inside a high pressure air tank. Just as suddenly, there was silence. He fell forward and lay lifeless on the floor.

When he awoke it was to a splitting headache and a disorientation that left him befuddled. Moaning and writhing about on the hard deck, he desperately sought to right his world long enough to focus on his surroundings, but initially, it was no use. He was totally disoriented.

Not knowing if he was laying on a floor, a ceiling or a wall, he looked around the chamber. The uniformity of the chamber was no help at all. As his senses began to re-engage, he relaxed, opting to wait for his equilibrium to return naturally, while mentally cataloging all of the sensations and feelings he was experiencing. At length, his mind flowed into a truly waking state and he opened his eyes, squinting at the bright artificial light in the chamber and sat up. He propped himself against a featureless wall. In front of him was the chamber door, exactly as it had been when he first stepped in.

"Damn!" he hissed softly. The transition must not have worked after all. He was right where he had started; he was sure of it. Gingerly, he tested his limbs, moving them slowly at first and then more rapidly until he was sure that everything was intact. He stood and was grateful that his nausea and dizziness was gone. In fact, he felt quite buoyant and perplexed. How long had he been unconscious? Had anyone found the guard's body in the next room? The lights in the chamber were on, so it must be day, but which day? Could he safely steal away and try another time? Unfortunately, the only way to know was to open the hatch and step out. He pressed his ear against the hatch itself and listened, but there was no sound from the other side. Apparently, along with its other characteristics, the chamber was completely soundproof. He stood for some time, weighing his options. Finally sighing, he pulled the pistol from his belt, cycled the lock, and stepped out of the chamber.

He found himself in a small circular room with curving walls that ended in a truncated peak some twelve feet overhead. Four small windows divided the room and between them were several built-in tables and a door opposite the chamber hatch. It looked for all the world like an elevator door. Beyond these features, the room was bare. He crossed to the nearest window and peered out.

What he saw so startled him that nearly fell to his knees. He had done it - Really done it. He was in another world, staring out at a lush green valley surrounded by high cliffs and dominated by a wide crystal clear lake near its center. Below him was a roadway and bridge surmounting a wide stream that fed into the lake and beyond that, into dense forest. Overhead he was startled by the size of the two satellites floating in a cloudless sky. This could only be Two Moons. He had made it after all.

To go east, one must go west, at least that was the old saying that Chandy had learned as a child. The lay of the land and the wide swamp cut off any directly eastern path and it was necessary to skirt the southern edge of the fens before it was possible to move toward the Tower. The other route was to take the meandering river that fed the lake and fens, fighting the current the whole way and double the length of the journey.

There was no contest in this, it would be the fens. Caleb and Chandy picked their way carefully among the tall reeds and rushes, using their walking sticks to prod the ground for soft spots. Their packs were relatively small for a three-day journey, but they wouldn't need much protection from the elements this time of year, and to Chandy's delight, Caleb had handed him one of his own rifles to use on the trip. It was a new model, one with improved power and a larger magazine of deadly glass projectiles. Crispin Toll, the colony's technologist and Caleb's good friend, had even fitted it with improved optical sights for greater accuracy. Three pumps and the weapon were powerful enough to bring down anything short of a ground sloth with a single shot.

They moved silently as Caleb had taught Chandy to do. There was no conversation. From the moment they had left the confines of the orchards, they were officially on the hunt. It was good practice and made good sense in this world. Only half the animals and less than a fourth of the plants were familiar to the colonists. The rest were local flora and fauna, some carbon-based as were humans, others silica-based. Those plants that did not ignore the humans completely were actively engaged in an attempt to eliminate these perceived competitors for food and territory. They were no more than halfway through the fens when they heard the faint hissing sound coming from the swampland to their north.

"Jack darts," whispered Caleb. Chandy simply nodded and reached into the top of his knapsack. Pulling pale straw-colored cloths from their packs they wrapped them around themselves and squatted motionless as the hissing sound became louder. Caleb was surprised at the sudden din. This sounded like a much larger swarm than usual, and when it finally arrived, it passed over them, pelting them as individual pseudo-insects ran into to the camouflaged pair. Chandy was nearly knocked over by the force of the first wave. Caleb braced himself and waited for the second mass to arrive. Around them, jack darts fell to the ground and fluttered about after impacting their tarps. Had the tarps been made of ordinary cloth, they would have both been skewered by hundreds of unseeing members of the swarm until they were shredded. As it was, the woven silica fabric protected them.

As suddenly as it had begun, the pelting ended and the swarm passed on toward the wood. Chandy peeked cautiously from beneath the cloak and looked around. The ground was littered with dead and dying jack darts. He stood, snapping the tarp to remove the last remnant of carcasses and began to fold it. Caleb was already up and doing the same.

"That was one hell of a swarm," Chandy said.

"One hell of a swarm," the hunter replied. "If they'd caught us, you wouldn't be impressing any girls with your muscles any more."

"Aw, Caleb," the boy said grinning. "That was just to piss off my sister."

"And embarrass me?"

"Kylie did that, not me."

"Let's move. I want to be out of these fens by noon."

They were out of the fens before noon, much to their delight, and continued onto the wide sward of feather grass that covered the higher ground. They walked swiftly to take advantage of the relative ease of movement offered by the low groundcover of glassy plants. Caleb made a mental note to gather some before nightfall to cushion their cocoons when they spread them out. As they walked, the caked-on muck of the fens dried and fell away from their boots and pants, leaving no trace behind. It was one of the advantages of walking in native soil, and very different than traversing the fields of terra formed ground to the west of the colony. By late afternoon they were at the thickets that rimmed the deep woods. What maps they studied predicted their journey perfectly so far. They could expect several miles of thickets consisting of both silica and carbon-based flora, but they knew if they stuck to the silica shrubs that they could easily break their way through the brittle branches without much fear of cuts and bruises. As for the carbon-based plants, they would require cutting their way through to avoid the thorns, or choosing a meandering trail among the low brush. A forest of conifers and hardwoods similar to what the teachers said were to be found on Terra, lay beyond that, providing fuel, shelter, and protection from high winds in the blowing season. There was relatively little smaller growth to contend with because of the dense canopy the larger trees created. Most of the fauna, they were told, lived in the high branches. No one knew much about these creatures as they were shy and seldom showed themselves.

Caleb decided to stop early and not try to traverse the scrub before nightfall. They camped on the edge of the sward with their backs to the forest and once the cocoons were spread out with feather grass piled beneath, they erected the domed shelter in case of rain and settled in for a simple meal of bread and cheese. Chandy's mother had packed dried Parker goose flesh and some cappit beans, the former for extra energy and the latter to ease their sore muscles at the end of the day. They elected to save the Parker goose for another day but each avidly downed one of the beans, expecting to be stiff in the morning if they didn't.

Before them, on the opposite side of the valley, the sun was already below the rim and the last rays of yellowish light were rapidly giving way to a deep purple hue as night set in. The two moons were not up yet. One would rise soon, the other several hours later as they parted in their separate orbits. There would be plenty of moonlight tonight. If they stayed awake, they could probably watch the nocturnal animals of Two Moons scurrying about, feeding and hunting on their own. They propped up as darkness set in to watch the show and promptly fell into a deep sleep.

Caleb was up at first light, shaking Chandy out of a particularly absorbing dream involving the Fancher sisters, two delightfully nubile young ladies of about his own age. He was visibly unhappy with being disturbed.

"Get off your ass and into your gear, lazy. We're burning daylight."

"No such," Chandy growled. "Daylight's gonna burn whether I get up or not."

"Yeah, but you're gonna burn if you don't," Caleb chuckled and he kicked the boy gently with his foot. "It's your turn to make breakfast."

"My turn? We just got started. When's your turn?"

"Well it's not today. Get at it."

By the time Chandy had produced morning cakes and Parker goose strips for their breakfast, Caleb was packed and was propped against his knapsack. He ate in silence while Chandy packed his own kit and grabbed some breakfast.

"Okay, let's go." Caleb said.

"Hey! What about my breakfast?"

"Eat it on the way. We need to get through that forest and see what's on the other side."

The boy threw together a sandwich of sorts, slipped the food packs into his own bag and set it, along with the rifle, against the nearest sapling. "We know what's beyond the forest, don't we?"

Caleb said nothing. He was as nervous about approaching the Great Tower as Chandy.

"What do you know of the Great Tower, Chandy?"

The boy shrugged. "What everyone does, I guess. It's a mysterious place where no one is supposed to go.

Terrible things are supposed to happen to anyone who gets too close, but it's supposed to watch over us somehow. There are supposed to be demons there and angels, and we are supposed to respect it and keep our distance. It's said that it's on the other side of these woods."

"Do you believe all that?"

"I don't know. I don't believe in demons or angels, but even the elders speak about the Tower in whispers. No one will discuss it with my friends or me. Even my father won't talk about it much."

"Hmm. Well, I don't know much more than you," Caleb said, "but I'm not expecting demons or angels if we get that far. We're turning back at noon, and with any luck, if you know what I mean, we'll still be in the forest when we do. After all, no one really knows how big the forest is anymore."

"Oh. That's true. Well, that's not so bad then."

"Hmm," mused Caleb. "I do know that even the Keeper speaks of the Tower with reverence. It did save us from the plague, after all. Maybe it will have to do it again."

Chandy shuddered. "Pleasant thought," he said sourly.

They skirted the brush looking for an easy way in, scouting first to the north and then to the south. To the north, they followed the edge of the sward for three or four miles but found only thick masses of carbon-based plants, all prickly with thorns and interwoven to create a solid barrier. To the south, they found a smattering of crystalline bushes but nothing that looked promising. Toward noon they were resigned to turn back and spend the night at their last campsite, then start back home. Both were visibly encouraged by the prospect. It was at the last moment, rounding a jutting mass of tall brush that they discovered that it would not be that easy. Chandy noticed it first. He sniffed the air and looked at Caleb for confirmation. The hunter sniffed as well and picked up the distinct odor of burnt sapwood in the air.

"Campfire?" offered Chandy.

"I think so, but why would anyone be camping here?"

Chandy looked around. "Could it be the Kellers??"

Caleb frowned and shook his head. "I doubt it. We'll see."

They kept moving south, the odor becoming more distinct. Finally, after mounting a small hillock where the brush began to thin, they found the campsite.
Caleb swung his rifle off his shoulder and checked the charge to be sure it was full. Chandy did the same and they each scanned the brush for anything unusual.

"What a mess!" said Chandy.

"Something's had fun here."

The camp was a scattered mass of broken and burned shards. The central campfire was dead but pieces of partially-burned wood was scattered all around. The dome shelter was shredded, only its ribs intact to show where the gores had once been.

"This is a silica cloth dome. It shouldn't be ripped like that," said Chandy. "What could do that?"

Caleb took a step back into the brush and crouched. He signaled for Chandy to do the same.

"Ground sloth, maybe. We need to be careful anyway."

Broken equipment lay everywhere. To one side, the larder bag was ripped open and empty. On the opposite side of the camp, two knapsacks lay in shreds, the contents scattered in heaps nearby.

Chandy looked at the device on the nearest pack. "That's Judah's pack. I recognize the monogram. But where are they?"

"I guess we'd better find out."

They examined the ground closely, using the eyes of a hunter to read the earth. The sward was torn up and stripped of growth right up to the edge of the brush. A great gaping opening in the opposite edge of the thicket led into the vastness of the forest. Caleb nodded in answer to Chandy's raised eyebrows and they stood, crossing the clearing and moving into the gap in the brush. It was a straight path leading directly toward the forest to the east. As wide as two men, it seemed to be cut with the precision of a furrow in a field. Whatever had done this had passed effortlessly through crystal and green brush alike. Eventually there was a sharp turn to the right and they found themselves in a small circular paddock.

"The plague couldn't have done this, could it?" asked Chandy.

"Look around," Caleb said, "but be very careful."

Here, too, the ground was stripped of vegetation. Nothing but claw marks and swirls covered the ground. They made a complete circuit of the clearing and looked at each other.

"Any ideas about these tracks?" Caleb said.

"Me?" said Chandy. "You're the hunter. I'm just an apprentice. Don't you know?"

"I have no idea."

Behind them they heard a grunting sound coming from the direction of the deep wood. Both turned, rifles at the ready. The sound came again from the opposite direction, this time closer. There was a rustling sound in the brush to their left.

"Up that tree!" Caleb cried and made for the closest hardwood. Chandy didn't wait for explanations. He bounded after his mentor and grabbed a low branch on a tree next to Caleb's, then swung himself up onto the limb. He climbed onto two higher branches and dropped his pack in the crook of another limb. He was facing the closest sound, rifle at the ready. A quick glance at Caleb told him that he had done the same.

"Watch the one coming from behind me. I'll take the one coming from behind you," Caleb whispered.

"But what are they?"

As if in answer, a large black mass burst into the clearing. It was nearly four feet at the shoulders and at least ten feet long. Its naked tail swung another six feet behind it, and its large narrow, head thrust into the air, a flat snout sniffing around for intruders. The beast opened its mouth and brandished two sickle-like teeth about eighteen inches long, pointed sharply and rough along the lower edge. Chandy had never seen anything like it. He froze where he sat and promptly evacuated his bowels. Suddenly another appeared directly below him and the odor of Chandy's evacuation attracted him so that he looked up and directly into the boy's eyes. Small red orbs stared up at him with malice.

Chandy heard a crack and knew that Caleb had fired. He saw the skull give way and implode as the glass projectile entered the brain case, shattered and delivered a fatal dose of poison to the beast. It collapsed without a sound and lay still. The spell broken, Chandy aimed at the second beast beneath Caleb and fired. He aimed directly for the center of the cranium, between the eyes, but he was shaking so badly that he couldn't steady the rifle. The projectile struck the beast just behind the shoulder and entered. It staggered but didn't fall. Quickly, he gave his weapon four pumps in rapid succession and fired again. This time, the beast's head virtually exploded. It fell instantly.

Chandy was still shaking. He steadied himself and wrapped the rifle strap around his forearm so that it did not fall. He looked at Caleb whose look of abject determination brought him under control. Trying to speak, he could manage no more than an unintelligible babble. Caleb motioned him to silence. Almost immediately a third beast burst into the clearing and Chandy fired. It fell in a heap next to its headless companion.

"I think that's all," Caleb said, "But we'll stay put for a while to be sure."

Chandy took in a great draft of air and exhaled. "Okay," he said weakly.

They waited for nearly an hour before coming down out of the tree. They examined the carcasses and confirmed that they were dead, then looked at each other and laughed.

"That, Mr. Crone, qualifies as your first kill. I'll testify to it. You're now a full-fledged hunter."

Chandy shook his head and shivered. "If you don't mind, I don't think I want to drink a cup of this blood."

Caleb stared briefly, and then burst into laughter. Chandy joined him. The hunter sat himself beneath the tree where he had fled and looked at the three dead beasts on the ground.

"Chandy, I have three instructions for you."

"Yes?"

First, we need to find a pole to carry one of these things back with us. No one is going to believe this if we don't. Secondly, we need to find if there's anything left of Keller and his two sons. But most importantly and most immediately, will you please clean yourself and change your clothes. I recommend burying those pants!"

Chandy suddenly turned to one side and retched violently. It made no sense. He simply couldn't stop heaving. Caleb rummaged through his pack and threw him his own extra pair of trousers. "Use these," he said. I'll personally buy you another pair when we get home. Whether you know it or not, I think you just saved my life with that third kill."

CHAPTER 3

The journey back to the colony was uncomfortable. They'd been out for nearly a day and a half already and neither of them had taken a bath or washed down. On Two Moons, this was guaranteed to cause discomfort. Even without the blowing winds that would come late in the season, the fine silica silt bombarded them wherever they went, causing a rash that, left untended, resulted in bleeding pustules that left deep scars. Neither of them was very happy about this, but their skin was tough after years in this climate, and it was only now becoming more than an annoyance.

They noticed that the breeze had stiffened a bit, which meant that not only would the silt be a problem, but that larger grains would begin to creep into their shoes. A day or so of that and they'd be crippled until their feet healed. As always, they wore high-top boots of native cloth and long pants that hung down over them and were turned up into wide cuffs. Whenever they stopped for a rest, which was more frequent than usual with the weight of the dead beast slowing them, they would turn out the cuffs and expel mounds of sand. Chandy watched the sky nervously, but Caleb took it in stride. He'd seen it before and knew it was nothing to worry about as long as they were careful.

By that afternoon they were back in the fens, slogging through loose mats of vegetation, both carbon and silica-based, and sinking to their ankles in the muck. The additional weight of the creature slung between them on a pole was considerable. Caleb was wondering if they should have brought it along after all. Perhaps just the head would have done? The creature smelled of corruption and rot, not from its own flesh but from whatever it had ingested prior to being killed.

Even the dried blood on its mouth and shoulders had a repulsive odor about it, yet it was somehow familiar smell, like a memory from somewhere in the distant past. Caleb thought how it smelled of something his mind told him he should be familiar with. Yet he was certain that he'd never seen nor heard of this monstrous creature before.

They skirted the end of the fens as the sun was sinking and decided to keep going. By the time it was dark, the two moons would be up, first Desolation and then Bastion, shedding enough light for them to see way into the night. That and the lights of the outer gates would be all that they needed to navigate.

When at last they found themselves on firm ground, the lowered their load and sat. Chandy rubbed his sore arm muscles while Caleb busied himself emptying the last remnant of sand from his cuffs. He pulled a waterproof cloth from the top of his pack and spread it on the ground, then sat abruptly, leaning back and sighing deeply.

"Heavy load," he offered.

"Very heavy," answered Chandy. He was too winded and too exhausted to say more. They rested for a while, watching the sky turn from blue to lavender and on toward purple. The evening insects were beginning to stir, chattering and hissing in the feather grass, calling to establish territory as they did each night before they took to the hunt. To their left, south toward the swamp, they briefly caught sight of a fen baby, a pesky local carbon base animal that sported a long slender horn on its nose, which now protruded above the grass. The creature had a nervous disposition. Technically, if they encountered it, it could kill them both with its poisonous saliva, but fen babies were such skittish animals that merely speaking would send them scurrying away. Still, they were technically dangerous.

"Time to move on," Caleb said.

"I was afraid you were going to say that. Wouldn't you just like to spend the night here and go into the colony in the morning?"

"Not with that thing stinking up the camp, no. I would not."

Chandy sniffed the air and nearly retched. "I see what you mean. Going in tonight sounds good."

They stood up, hefted the pole on their shoulders, and started off toward the town walls. Caleb thought of his other reason for continuing on tonight. He wanted to bring the beast directly to the Keeper without parading it by half the colony in the process. If he were right about this creature, the Keeper would want its presence kept quiet for awhile.

It was well after mid-evening when they arrived. Caleb stopped before entering the gate long enough to cover their cargo with a ground cloth. As he expected, the watch was asleep and when roused from their dreams grumbled a greeting at the two as they passed.

"Find our missing hunters?" one asked derisively.

"Didn't find them," Caleb said simply. It wasn't a lie, after all. They found no trace of the three beyond their plundered camp. Chandy said nothing, but gave Caleb a quizzical look that soon morphed into one of understanding.

They proceeded directly to the Keeper's house. No one was about at this time of the night, and with the exception of an occasional aroma of cooking for some late meal, there was no sign of life in the town at all. The colony was like that. From years of habit they closed themselves in their houses shortly after the sun went down and generally didn't stir again until dawn. Caleb was thankful for it. He also understood that it might become more than a custom in the future.

The Keeper's home was unlike any other in the city. It had a small unoccupied gatehouse and a courtyard large enough to hold perhaps two dozen people comfortably, with benches built into the ceramic walls. The Keeper called them poyos, though no one knew why. This open air space was often used for consulting with the heads of the clans over matters of importance to the whole colony. These men made up the only form of government that was needed, being a council of advisors who discussed and offered consent by majority rule for any changes that may be deemed necessary.

At the far end of the courtyard was the conical house of the Keeper himself. It was larger than most but otherwise as expected, with the same second floor entrance. In his case, however, rather than a ladder leading to the entrance there was a set of stairs and at the top of this a platform and a short wooden bridge that separated it from the house. Caleb could never remember a time when that bridge was not down. He wondered if it could be raised at all.

They dropped their burden in the center of the courtyard and approached the staircase. Caleb wasn't sure how one hailed the Keeper this time of evening. In his memory, it had never been done. Chandy was visibly nervous, standing as close to the entrance as he could, just in case he needed to retreat. Caleb started up the stairs.

"I thought you'd be back tonight," said a surprisingly deep voice from the shadows where the courtyard met the curve of the house. Chandy and Caleb turned with a start. The Keeper emerged from the darkness and came toward them. He was not a tall man, and being bent over with age as he was, he seemed more an old woman than the keeper of the colony's wisdom and history. He wore loose- fitting pants and pullover shirt of native cloth, and his long white hair was done up in a topknot formed by a ponytail that had been doubled back and tied with a plain straw-colored length of twine. There was a steel dagger at his belt, and he walked with the help of a staff about five feet in length. For all his age, he walked smoothly, almost gracefully, and Caleb suspected that his bent-over posture was for show, not necessity.

"I wasn't sure you'd see us this late," Caleb said.

"My door is always open," the Keeper said simply. "What have you brought me?"

"I'm...not sure," said Caleb. "We found three of these beasts to the east on the edge of the forest separating the valley from the Tower. They attacked us and we killed them. I'm afraid they killed Jason Keller and his sons."

"You saw the bodies?"

"Um, no. We saw their camp and what these things had done to it. There was no sign of the three, but there's not much doubt that they were eaten."

The Keeper looked at the covered mound on the floor of the courtyard and nodded. "Let me see it," he said simply.

Chandy reached down and pulled back the ground cloth. Immediately the odor of the beast filled the air and the hunters turned away. The Keeper merely looked at the body and slowly sniffed the air. He frowned and came closer, bending over the body. For some minutes he examined the corpse, starting with the head and working toward the hindquarters. When he noticed the long tail he inhaled sharply and stood up. He looked again at the head, then at the hunters.

"Now listen to me closely," he said. "You've done exactly what you should have done. We must preserve the head but do not need the rest of the body. I'll send someone for a butcher. Gunderson should do; he can be trusted to keep quiet about this. We need to work quickly and we need to be sure that word does not get out to the colony. Did anyone see you when you came in?"

"Only the watch," Caleb replied, "but the beast was covered. For all they knew we had an immature sloth or a couple of Parker Geese. They saw nothing."

The Keeper nodded thoughtfully. "Good. I can handle this from here. You two can go home, but I want to see you both first thing in the morning. You are not to speak to anyone about this, do you understand?"

"Um, what about my father? As Hunt Master he'll have to know."

"I'll deal with Jonathan Grant in the morning. If he pushes you on it, tell him that you found nothing. Can you do that?"

Caleb hesitated. "He's...my father. I've never lied to him, not even as a child."

The Keeper thought for a moment. "Then tell him I told you to say nothing and that I'll explain in the morning. Bring him with you when you come. Jonathan is a disciplined man. He knows when to not ask questions."

"Thank you," Caleb said honestly. As they turned to go, Caleb had one more thought and turned back. "There's something else, Keeper."

"Well?" the Keeper said with irritation.

"It's about Chandy."

"I assume you are referring to Chandler Crone, my soon-to-be-apprentice?" the Keeper said, looking at the boy. Chandy grimaced, though in the pale light of Bastion, no one knew it but himself.

"Um, yes sir. He killed two of those beasts and saved my life in the process. I know it's not official, but..."

"Consider the first part of his initiation completed. I trust he didn't drink the creature's blood?"

"The Universe save me, no!" blurted Chandy.

The Keeper almost smiled in spite of himself.

"No matter," he said. "Considering the circumstances, we'll do the rituals in the morning. All of the clan chiefs will be here and we can dispense with it in short order. I should warn you, though, Chandler. This is going to be the shortest career as a hunter in the history of the colony. Your studies with me commence as of tomorrow. This particular kill makes that imperative. I'll explain in the morning."

"Y...yes, sir," stammered Chandy.

"Good. Now go, both of you."

They ambled away silently, taking a side street off the square, each deep in their own thoughts. They went immediately to the nearest ablution house and bathed, scrubbing the grit and grime from their bodies and looking for serious rashes and abrasions. Both of them were in surprisingly good shape considering the last forty-eight hours. When they dried and dressed themselves, they returned to the square, and parted, taking separate streets home. They nodded at the separation but neither of them spoke. Breaking the silence of the night seemed somehow profane.

It was nearly half-night when Caleb finally arrived home and he was forced to wait for his father to awaken to his calls and let down the ladder before he could come in. He found his mother preparing a plate of food for him.

"You've not eaten?" she asked unnecessarily and placed the food on the table.

"No, not since this morning. Thanks, Mother."

She smiled and descended to the floor below, more to leave her men to themselves than anything else.

Caleb sat at the table and drank deeply from the mug of hot tea at his place. He looked at the plate of turnips, popple berries and fresh roasted beef. He inhaled the mingling flavors and became aware of just how hungry he was, then settled in and began to eat. As for his father, he sat down beside him, a mug of steaming tea in hand.

"You're home late."

Caleb nodded. "Yes, sir. We didn't get in until mid-evening."

"That was hours ago," his father said. "What have you been doing since then?"

Caleb hesitated. He looked down at his food, then back at his father. "We've been with the Keeper," he said.

"Oh?"

"I'm afraid I can't explain, father. The Keeper gave us instructions. He asked that you not ask me anything tonight and that we all go to see him in the morning. He promises to explain everything then."

Jonathan Grant simply looked at his son, silently digesting this information and considering.

"You found them, didn't you?" he finally said.

Caleb frowned. "I...can't say anything."

His father frowned. "I see," is all he said, and took a long pull on his tea.

"You've bathed?" he said at last.

"Yes, Father."

"No serious wounds or infections?"

"None at all."

"Good. Then I suggest you finish your dinner and get to bed. We'll be up early, won't we?"

He smiled. Caleb nodded, grateful that his father didn't push him any further and spooned the last bit of popple berries into his mouth. As usual, he left everything on the table for his mother to deal with and climbed wearily to the floor above and his bed. In moments, he was asleep.

Chandy met Caleb and his father in the square at first light. The town was already stirring, as usual, heading out for the fields or off to one of the food shops that serviced those who could not or did not cook for themselves. Women were passing through the square on the way to make their daily purchases, each with the traditional conical bag slung across her forearm, ready to accept foodstuffs and other goods as needed. They walked in groups of two or three, chattering like young girls or seriously investigating the available merchandise.

In a small way, Caleb envied the conversational capacity of women. He was reticent to speak, even for a man, and as a result seldom spoke to anyone without a specific reason. He knew it hurt him socially. It was a skill he did not have. He was also hoping to see Kylie, perhaps emerging from a side street with Chandy, but she never appeared. Caleb thought how foolish he was. After all, she was one of the most beautiful young women in the colony. He was just a hunter who couldn't put two words together without stammering. What was it his mother said about what he was feeling? Anxiety? Wasn't that a combination of fear and hope? That was it.

He always had a feeling of anxiety about Kylie, though lately it had been mostly fear and very little hope.

When Chandy entered the square alone and approached them, he said softly, "So be it," and let out a sigh of relief.

"What?" asked his father.

"Nothing, sir," he replied, and hoped his father wouldn't push him on the subject.

As the three of them stood silently before the Keeper's gate, the Keeper appeared at his doorway and made his way carefully down the staircase. He crossed to them rather than waiting for them to come to him, an unusual breach of protocol. He greeted them each in turn informally.

"I am sure you're wondering about all this secrecy, Jonathan?" he said.

The senior Grant gave a terse nod and said nothing.

"I trust you did not question your son too closely?"

"I asked nothing," he said with evident irritation. "I was told that you would explain it all this morning and left it at that. If what he said was true, then I have no reason to seek further information in the night. If it is not true, then I could take care of that at the appropriate time."

"Logical," said the Keeper flatly. "I recommend we go into the house. The clan heads will be here at noon and we have a great deal to do before then."

They mounted the staircase and crossed the bridge. The Keeper ushered them in to the main room. It was much like any other house in the colony, with staircases descending down to the base floor and ascending to the third floor above. Heavy glass windows circled the room, emitting light no matter what time of day or what season it was. The floor was of dark gray stone and the walls were plastered rather than made of the ceramic tile on the outside of the structure. All of this was quite common, but what was not common at all, what was in fact, quite unique about the room, was that there was no circular table in the center. Unlike virtually every other house in the colony whose household activities centered on a large round table, the center of the Keeper's main hall was empty except for a single heavy oak chair and a rectangular side table. On this table was a large book with a binding identical to the dozen or so on the side shelf just inside the door.

Chandy and Caleb scanned the entire room, taking in as much as they could. The Keeper led them down onto the floor below. This room, larger than the one above, was filled with baskets and barrels, boxes and plastic drums, tools, foodstuffs and the largest collection of scrap iron that Chandy and Caleb had ever seen. They both stared at it in amazement. As rare as worked iron was in the colony, any scrap was valuable beyond compare, and to see so much of it in one place amazed them. When the colonists first arrived, of course, they had brought with them a wide array of advanced technology, but over the generations, equipment wore out and expertise was lost until the present, when the only remnant of modern equipment remaining was a smelter and a very limited electrical plant, mainly used for powering the smelter itself. The problem, of course, was the lack of readily available iron ore, which meant their existing supply had to be worked and reworked as needed.

But The Keeper did not afford them much time to wonder. He went immediately to the table in the center of the room and pulled back the ground cloth that was covering the severed head of the beast. Caleb saw his father stiffen, and then compose himself. It was the first time he could remember seeing his father shaken.

"I assume you know what this is,' the Keeper said flatly.

Jonathan Grant stared down at the object on the table and studied it. "That's the biggest one I've ever seen," he said at last.

"Large and different," said the Keeper. "See the snout? Almost like a pig. The tusks are larger too. They must be a foot or more to the tip."

"They've mutated even further," offered Jonathan.

The Keeper nodded with a grunt. "And they're back."

Through all this exchange, Caleb and Chandy stood silently and listened.

"Is anyone going to fill us in?" Caleb asked at last.

Both men glanced at him as if realizing for the first time that the others were there. "I'd have thought you'd have guessed by now, Caleb," his father said.

"'Can't be," said Caleb. "You're telling me that this is the plague returned?"

"We need to recall the hunters. I've already arranged for a meeting of the clan chiefs early this afternoon."

Jonathan offered a brief look of surprise. "Are you sure you want to recall them?"

"Gunderson found human teeth in the belly of this one. Are we missing anyone else?" said the Keeper.

Jonathan Grant shook his head. "No."

"Would someone please tell me what that thing is?"

Now all three turned and looked at a very bewildered Chandy. Caleb chuckled when he saw the young man's look of consternation.

"An inappropriate response at best," Jonathan said, scowling at his son.

"A release of tension, I'm sure," said the Keeper. "I almost laughed myself. Chandler, recite for me the oral history; the one you learned in school.?

Chandy wondered at the rather random request, but cleared his throat and began to recite.

> *"A time came when there were so many,*
> *That room could not be found.*
> *And the people saw their numbers*
> *Were growing without bound."*

> *"The wise ones gathered and discussed,*
> *The nature of their plight.*
> *Deciding that answer was*
> *That some must now take flight."*

> *"And so it was our kinsmen came,*
> *Across the trackless night.*
> *They flew as fast as time itself,*
> *Astride a beam of light.*

> *"And when at last they all had come*
> *To Two Moons and they settled,*
> *They pledged to brave the dangers here,*
> *And show all their true mettle.*

"And each name entered in the roll,
Of heroes in that band,
Is honored in our songs and hearts
As founders of our clans

"Thirty-seven clans in all,
Each family embraced,
By all the other clans who came
Our Lineage is traced.

"The Dills and Crones and Nordstroms came,
The Dairs and Grants and Toomeys
Hmelnetskis and the Gundersons,
And Franks and the Natsumis

"Pacinis stood with Heinemans,
Bonds arm in arm with Barretts,
The Steins and Petros, Peters too,
With Van Zants did declare it.

"Nagels came, and Lis as well,
Coloumbs, Smiths and Moodies,
Joined by Spears and Bullards here,
By Jorgensons and Goody's.

"*Milhouse and Kwan with Flowers came,*
And O'Brians with the Hsus,
Gilbert, Bruce, Wakombe,
And Patels, Morreros too.

"*Thirty-seven clans came here,*
Each bound to all the others,
By hopes of great prosperity,
Working with their brothers.

"*Yet they knew not that with them here,*
They had brought dark plague,
That vexed them when their crops were in,
And smote them arm and leg.

"*Most nobly did they fight the foe,*
Till half their number perished,
But still they fought for those who lived,
Their kinsmen's lives so cherished.

"*And when all hope had seemed to pass,*
When death stood at their gates,
The watchers came from Tower high,
The darkness to abate.

"So when all danger then did pass,
Those left alive did make,
These mighty walls and houses tall,
Beside the shimmering lake.

"So now we prosper, and we grow,
Fulfilling hopes and prayers,
In peace we live and in plenty,
Pass away the years."

"Word for word," noted Jonathan Grant.

"But tell me what it means? Can you do that?" asked the Keeper.

Chandy thought for a moment, uncomfortable with his elders watching him.

"Um, it's a saga to remind us of how we came to be here and why we are the way we are," he said at last.

"Obviously," the Keeper said with mild irritation, "but what does it mean?"

Chandy frowned for moment thinking, then said, "Well, where we came from, the Old World, as I understand it, it was very crowded so people were sent to other worlds, including Two Moons to build colonies. Somehow we brought a plague of rats with us despite all the precautions to avoid unwanted species, and without predators to keep down their number, they grew to such a huge population that they soon ate all the crops in the valley and then began to attack the colonists. They killed nearly half of the four hundred fifty people who came, but were finally destroyed by the Tower and we've been building ever since. Chandy was more uncomfortable than ever. He felt like he was being examined by one of his schoolmasters to decide if he could go on to the next level."

"It's what they told us in school, and what I was told by my friends."

"They told you nothing else?"

"Oh, they told me lots of things. We used to all make up stories about the plague years and the world we came from, but they were just stories. We knew the difference between stories and the truth."

"Hmm," mumbled the Keeper in a low rumble. "Yes. That's what most of our children learn, but there's more.

"Jonathan," he said without looking at the Master of the Hunt, "you need to see to the recall of any searchers still in the field. Caleb, you and Chandy need to stay awhile to hear the rest. Have you eaten this morning?"

Caleb and Chandy shook their heads.

"I'll tell your granddaughter on the way out," Jonathan said, then turned and lumbered up the stairs to the main floor.

CHAPTER 4

At the Keeper's direction, the two hunters removed the head from the round table along with its ground cloth wrapping and wiped down the table. By the time they had finished and settled into heavy oak wood chairs, a petite, lithe young woman was descending the stairs with a tray of steaming tea and three platters of fresh-baked oatcakes served with honey and sausages. Caleb breathed in the aroma of the food, surprised at his own hunger, but Chandy hardly noticed. He was far too busy watching the approach of the graceful server.

"I believe you both know my granddaughter, Jillian." The Keeper said. Caleb nodded but was too busy being hungry to take notice. Chandy simply said, "'Lo, Jillian."

Caleb looked over at the boy and then at Jillian, noting his uncharacteristic reticence. Jillian smiled down at Chandy, but he just stared at his plate and began eating. His face was a very bright red.

"Eat, my boys. We can talk while we fill our stomachs. Jillian, will you join us?"

"I think not," she said somewhat gloomily and turned to go. Caleb watched her cross the room and up the stairs. She was a pretty girl of fifteen, slender with more curves than a girl of her age would be expected to have, and she was incredibly graceful, like one of the dancers who performed at festivals. Her long silky black hair hung down to her mid-back and was trimmed evenly across the ends. The close-fitting blue dress that she wore covered her down to mid-calf, but the material, a shimmering native glassy fiber similar to silk, accentuated her every move. Caleb could see every muscle in her legs when she walked. This was no pampered princess, this one. She was sturdy and she was going to be a very beautiful woman in a few years. He looked back at Chandy who was eating silently, head still bowed toward his plate. Caleb smiled to himself.

The Keeper sat for a moment with furrowed brow, considering, then nodded and said, "Chandy, what I'm going to tell you is more than most colonists know. The whole truth of our being here is not general knowledge, as I think you will come to understand. You are not to repeat anything said here this morning. Do you understand?"

Chandy looked at the Keeper. He nodded earnestly. "Good. Now let's see. The part of the myth about an overcrowded world is true. The Old World were from was once a very fertile and hospitable place where people could prosper easily. Except for a lack of organization and in spite of endless wars fought over territory, progress was made rapidly and the civilization developed at a healthy pace. Basically, we went from savagery to high civilization in less than fifty thousand years."

"Did you say fifty thousand years?" Chandy asked somewhat incredulously. "That's what you call fast development?"

"Very fast, actually. Our development was interrupted by two ice ages, but that's another story for another time. Just hear me out."

"Sorry," the boy said contritely.

"Eventually it became evident that there were soon going to be simply too many people for the planet to support and at this point, the concept of colonization became a viable option."

"So that's when we colonized?"

"Experimentally, yes. We needed to find the best way to carry out a massive migration to other planets. We were originally put here to be observed for no more than three generations to determine the viability of the project. We were not sent here as a colony. We were sent here as an experiment."

Chandy swallowed a last bite of food and looked puzzled. "A what? An experiment?"

"A dozen experimental colonies were set up and ours is one of them. Each was populated by a group of volunteers who were given the necessary technology to cope with their particular environment and enough supplies to establish themselves on a new world. Simply put, the planners wanted to know how 'modern' colonists would handle the problems of primitive living. Not all colonies in history have survived. Indeed, the rule is failure, not success.

We were to be observed for several generations to determine what problems would arise and what solutions could be found to those problems so that future large colonizing efforts could be planned in a way to ensure success."

The Keeper stopped there. He watched both Caleb and Chandy trying to absorb this information. He had effectively replaced their entire paradigm with a new one in one brief soliloquy. It was a great deal to swallow.

"We've gone a lot more than a few generations," said Chandy.

"I'll explain that in time."

"How do they ... observe us?" Caleb asked.

Now the Keeper smiled. "That's the obvious question, isn't it? In two ways. They watch us from the Tower, for one thing. It is an observation platform for those studying human dynamics to gather data on our progress. They are totally isolated from us and have no contact with the colony at all. As far as we colonists are concerned, at least the vast majority of us, it is just a mysterious place that has been declared taboo."

"What about the legend? Doesn't it say that the Tower saved us during the plague?" This question came from Chandy.

"Very good. That's the flaw in their original plan, isn't it? Well, they did save us from the plague. It was an unintended event, an unforeseen circumstance, something that should have been expected in a new venture. They initially decided to let events run their course to see how we handled the unexpected. As I've said, unforeseen circumstances were bound to show themselves on colonial worlds, so why not take advantage of this one and study it? But what they soon found was that this particular plague of rats was a doomsday event. It didn't just challenge the colony; it threatened to shatter it entirely. If that happened, the whole experiment failed and a great deal of time and resources would have been wasted. It was no more than twenty years into the experiment when the population of rats finally reached a critical size and began to threaten the natural balance significantly. The decision was made to wipe out the pests even though it was outside interference, and so they stepped in. Since then, a number of generations have passed and the watchers have not contacted the colony since then."

Chandy nodded thoughtfully. "You said they had two ways to watch us. What was the other one?"

"Ah, now we're down to it. Observation from a distance was fine for determining general changes and development, but to really get at the psychology of the colonists they needed someone to observe from within the colony itself. It's called Participative Observation by those who designed the experiment. They needed a colonist who could report on what was going on inside the colony, someone trained in Social Dynamics Theory. They needed the colonists' perceptions of what was happening."

Chandy sat up a little straighter. "There's a person in the colony that's a watcher?" he whispered, as if someone might hear.

"There is."

"Do you know who it is?"

The Keeper leaned back and smiled easily. "Why, it's me, of course."

They stared at the old man. It was so logical. It made so much sense. He was the keeper of knowledge, the chronicler of the colony and the teacher. He was the one who presided over chieftain's councils but never expressed an opinion of his own. He would have to be a watcher.

"You're a watcher," Chandy said in a whisper, offering more of a question than a statement.

The Keeper nodded.

"But that doesn't make sense. We've been here for ten generations or more. How many watchers have there been?"

The Keeper hesitated momentarily and then offered a weak smile. "Just one," he said. "I've been genetically altered for a much longer life than humans normally experience. You see, they were hoping for continuity over several generations, and that meant a single observer for the entire sixty to eighty years. To accomplish that, my physical systems were genetically altered to ensure I'd be around for that entire time. Don't look so shocked. I assure you that it is not exactly a wonderful experience to outlive everyone and everything that you ever knew. What's worse is that the experiment has apparently been continued for many generations beyond the original design, so I have continued to do my work, passing information to the watchers in the Tower generation after generation. But I'm growing old now, and it is obvious that I may not live out another generation, so someone must be trained to do my job when I'm gone. That's why you're going to take my place."

"Oh. No. I...can't do that. I mean, I don't know how. I'm just a hunter. I'm not a watcher!"

The elder waved the comment aside. "You will be the next Keeper, which is why you will study with me from now on. I can't live forever, you know, and apparently the watchers have added one more little twist to the experiment to see how we manage our little world.. It will be my job to educate you in all of the aspects of social dynamics and cultural structure and for a while, we'll watch together. Then, when I'm gone, you'll be here to continue the work. I've already expressed my intentions to those in the Tower, and their silence is agreement. They would only contact me if they disagreed. So there you have it. Now you know why your education has been longer than the others and why you've become my apprentice."

"I...don't want to," he said bluntly.

"Chandy!" snapped Caleb. "Remember who you're talking to!"

"It's alright, Caleb," the Keeper said gently. "I don't blame him. I didn't want to either, but in the end, I understood the wisdom of it and accepted it. Outside these walls I will continue to be the mysterious old wise man that pontificates and makes pronouncements, who advises and passes judgments in disputes, but when we three are alone together we will all gather for these lessons, I'll be myself, a simple teacher and colleague. Do we understand each other?"

"I still don't want to do it," Chandy said, looking down at the table.

The Keeper looked down at the boy with understanding.. "But you will do it, my boy, because you know you must."

Chandy turned away and stared at his hands, busily entwining his fingers. "Damn," he said softly.

"Just damn."

"Mild compared to what I said, but then, I was a truly free spirit. I was already a full-grown man with the equivalent of a University degree, and I was incredibly rebellious, a quality I like in you, Chandler. You need to be a rebel to do this job."

Caleb cleared his throat and began to speak, but the Keeper cut him off.

"You want to know why you have to attend these sessions as well as Chandler, and I can understand that. It's for the same reason that I taught your father before you. As Master of the Hunt, he's the closest thing the colony has to legal authority and he needed to know the truth.

Since you will succeed him, you need to know it all as well."

"I'm going to what?"

The Keeper gave them an exasperated look. "So he hasn't told you. That sounds like Jonathan. He was never one to give information unless it was absolutely necessary. I don't know when he thought he was going to inform you of all this, but be aware that it was decided more than three years ago. The time has come, and I will announce along with your father that Caleb Grant is to be the next Master of the Hunt, and don't bother to tell me you don't want to. It's not a gift. It's an obligation, a duty. At some point, you've both got to stop playing the Great Hunter and take up your life's work. Now you know what that is."

CHAPTER 5

Morgan Culhane was not antisocial by nature. He was simply a man in search of his freedom. At least that's what he told himself whenever he considered why he had chosen to gather the disaffected among the colony and head out to the far side of the lake to found a second community. None of his two hundred followers were currently of the clan. All of them had chosen to separate from the families both physically through the move outside the walls of the community, and symbolically by changing their family names from clan names to the maiden name of their wives of the first clan heads. Hence Culhane would not be found among the thirty-seven clan titles in the colony. Nor would the names of Rodriguez, Harris, Penianski, Cho, Nguyen, Bond and two-dozen others be found on the roles. All of these extended families had migrated some four years earlier, determined to establish their separate community, free from the control and influence of the Keeper and his ineffective council of chiefs.

In doing so, Culhane had effectively established a new colony with new clans, an irony that was not lost on the man. Independence and freedom were one thing, but operating without the cooperation of one's companions was quite another. Organization was necessary for survival among humans, and this was no less true in the new settlement as in the old. What he hoped to gain beyond a temporary chance at self-determination was beyond even his understanding. He had no doubt that in another four generations the new settlement would be as stilted and steeped in rules and regulations as the old, but in the meantime, he and his children were afforded an opportunity to live their own style of life, following their own principles. He would be satisfied with that.

Morgan was standing on a high platform in the center of what would become the new settlement. Before him were displayed a rough plan for the layout of the town with a grid of four house blocks interspersed with meadows and garden plots, far different from the circular pie design of the colony. The houses were still conical of course, to protect the structures from the intense gales of the windy season, but the general plan would be square, or at least rectangular. It seemed more organized to him that way, and his followers agreed.

He squinted through eyes weakened with age in the direction of the colony, noting with satisfaction the progress of the long straight wall facing outward in that direction. He smiled to himself at the implied message

that lies in starting the wall on that side of the settlement.
Outlanders were announcing their separation and rejection
of all they felt the colony stood for. They were turning
their backs on their former neighbors. The truth was there
for all to see. He pointed toward the wall then looked at
the woman to his right who nodded. "See how it grows,
Olivia? We'll have it finished before winter and then we
can begin on the others. In a year, the new settlement will
be completely enclosed."

"And then we will have achieved our true
independence," the woman said flatly.

"Then we can thumb our noses at the Keeper and his
lackeys, always trying to lure us back into their nightmare."

"Freedom is good," she said automatically.

"Absolute freedom is better," he said in response. He
turned to face the opposite direction toward the new fields
being carved from the forest. Conical houses of every size
were springing up along the margin of those fields,
separated only by a narrow band of feather grass pasture
that would be the far wall of the town within a year.
Protests from the colony had been loud and ineffective over
the issue of clearing the forest. The hunters would just
have to do without these hundred or so acres of game trails.
The outlanders needed the fields more. The land to be
cleared was the minimum needed to feed their population.

As their numbers grew they would need more, but one battle at a time, he thought. He'd deal with the Keeper on that issue when it was time. In the meantime, they had a tight schedule to keep if they were to all be housed before the winds came.

"Have you seen my grandson?" he asked.

"I sent him out with the hunters," Olivia offered. "He should be back in time for preparing the evening meal."

"I need to see him when he returns. Pass the word."

Olivia glared at Morgan sharply, not pleased with his tone of voice. "Pass the word yourself," she said bluntly. Morgan glared back. "You're free to do as you wish, Livy, but if we're going to get this job done, someone's got to be in charge and someone's got to be willing to follow their lead. If it's that important to you, I'm asking you to pass the word."

Olivia softened slightly. "Okay," she said and left the platform.

"Damn independent women," he said under his breath.

"Don't they know someone's gotta be in charge? Damn egos. That's their problem. It's those damn egos. Glad I don't have one."

Morgan Culhane the second, whom most of his contemporaries called Morg, was returning early from the hunt. He and four of his young compatriots had bagged enough game in only a few short hours to feed the settlement for the next week. Combined with the plants gathered as the forest was cleared, they'd have a fine feast tonight. He was pleased with himself, sure that he was as good a hunter as any the colony could boast.

As his group made its way across the newly-cleared fields, those in the midst of planting the root crops for next spring's harvest stopped to watch them pass, impressed with the array of sloth, wild boar, birds and what passed for deer in the valley, all piled onto two travois and a sled, being pulled by the hunters. Morg swelled with further pride when he looked at their expressions. He could not wait to show all this to his grandfather.

They walked by a cluster of half-finished homes on the edge of the fields and down a muddy track that would some day be the main avenue of their new town. Town's people looked up from their work or stopped in their progress to wherever they were going, just to admire the hunters and their catch. It was everything that Morg had dreamt of. He was sure his grandfather would be proud of him for this.

When they reached the temporary kitchen, they dropped their load, women and young girls descending on the kills like locust, quickly and wordlessly skinning the carcasses and cutting them into manageable hunks where they lay, then transferring the pieces to preparation tables to be and readied for the pot. The activity was furious, like a swarm of bees attacking an intruder to the hive, and they seemed to hardly notice the hunters at all. At last, one old woman clapped her hands and grinned, then nodded thanks to them for their efforts. It was Yetti Cane, a woman of great ability and personal strength and the acknowledged mistress of the kitchens. Morg nodded back and silently mouthed, "You're welcome," then turned away as she did the same, scurrying among the tables spread in the open air, directing the others in their butchering process. It was indeed going to be a fine feast tonight.

Stopping at his own tent long enough to wash away the grit and blood of the hunt, he headed for the square to report to Morgan Culhane himself.

"Grandfather!" he called as he mounted the platform.

"I thought you were supposed to be hunting," his grandfather said.

"I was. We had great luck and brought back all we could carry. I've never seen so much game this close to the lake!"

Morgan regarded his grandson, who was beaming with pride. "How close to the lake?" Morgan said.

"No more than two hundred yards into the forest, then everywhere as far as we chose to go. We didn't even bother to kill most of what we saw. There were so many dinners a' walking that we could pick the choicest ones."

"That close," Morgan said, beginning to worry. "That's very unusual."

"It's a sign. It's Two Moons telling us we're doing the right thing!"

"Hmm. Perhaps. Still, I wonder what caused the animals to come this close to people. They usually don't do that."

"Not usually," Morgan agreed, "But they did today. "

"Well, congratulations. I'm proud of you," the patriarch said without emotion.

"Thanks," Morg mumbled, somewhat deflated. His grandfather apparently had other things on his mind. He was staring down at a set of plans for the settlement, but obviously not really seeing them. He was deep in thought. Morg waited.

"I'm glad you're here," his grandfather said at last. "There is a matter that we need to discuss.

I've a project for you and you need to start on it right away."

"All right," the boy said with a bit more enthusiasm.

"I want you to get married."

CHAPTER 6

For the remainder of the morning, the Keeper, Chandy, and Caleb considered their new circumstances and the nature of this new threat. The presence of these predators in their life created tremendous difficulties for their well-ordered colony, from securing their food supply to defending their homes. It was fortunate that the walls of the town were fortified and that at least the outer wall had been well-maintained. Without knowing how many of the beasts they would have to face or how voracious their consumption of food was, they had no way of adequately planning to deal with them. Every imaginable scenario was discussed over the next few hours.

In the coarse of Discussion, Chandy began to understand the importance of the heritage of various families and of who was related to whom through which marriages over the twenty generations between the present time and the time of the plague. More significantly, he began to understand a pattern to these marriages and, why it was that the council of chieftains, with the Keeper's approval, must sanction all marriages. With only thirty-seven families, it was important that no close relatives should wed for fear of creating offspring with detrimental recessive characteristics. It was basically a rule against incest carried a step further, to insure maximum diversity of genetic characteristics. Thus it was prescribed to each generation who was and who was not a suitable mate for those coming of age. The formula was tricky, and when asked, the Keeper promised to explain it to them as soon as was practicable. They did learn, however, that it was instituted after the plague because of the reduction of breeding stock from an original population of nearly five hundred to a population of slightly more than two hundred. Fortunately, no one had ever challenged the necessity or importance of the practice or how it related to those small creatures. It was late now, and Caleb noticed a gnawing feeling of hunger beginning in his stomach. No sooner had his belly begun to rumble in protest than their attention shifted to the sound of feet on the staircase and Jillian stepped into the room. She carried a tray as before, this time heaped with plates of steaming vegetables and fruits. Chandy watched her as she glided across the floor, totally captivated by her grace. She placed the tray on the table, nodded and took a step back silently.

"Ah," said the Keeper. "It must be midday. You think of everything, Jillian."

"The council will be here soon, grandfather, and I know how you are about missing meals. Sometimes I think you need a keeper of your own."

The old man frowned and spread his arms wide and pulled Jillian to him, offering a fatherly hug. Then, looking at his guests, he said, "You see, gentlemen? Even I am under the command of another. She'll make someone a fine companion and a fine mistress someday, don't you think?"

Chandy nodded, turning as red as Jillian. Caleb said, "I couldn't agree more," and glanced at Chandy. The apprentice looked away.

Their host seemed not to notice the inference and simply pulled a plum from the plate, biting off a large chunk of its flesh. "I'm afraid my guests have had a bit of a shock, my dear. They probably aren't too hungry at the moment, but they'll need their strength for what is to come. Eat, my young gentlemen," he said easily. "We'll soon be facing the scowling faces of unhappy chiefs, particularly when they see what you've brought us."

They ate, picking at their food in silence. None too soon, Jillian was back with three small wooden cups of jayberry wine to clear their palates. She removed the trays of half-eaten food and padded away again up the stairs, looking back over her shoulder at the three of them, a scowl of concern on her face.

"Keeper," Chandy said hesitantly, "I have a question. If you've been around for ten generations, how can you have a granddaughter who is so young?"

"More than ten generations, my young friend, but Jillian is my granddaughter by my fourth wife. I was alone for many years before I married Diana, Jillian's grandmother." He drifted for a moment, remembering past times and smiled a tiny smile.

He then stood and said, "I suggest we greet the chiefs. I imagine most of them are in the courtyard by this time. He nodded toward the ground cloth and its contents in the corner. "Bring your trophy, if you will."

Mounting the stairs, they crossed to the entrance, the Keeper going first and the two hunters following. Laying the covered beast head just inside the door, they emerged onto the entrance platform and stood, as instructed, one on each side of the old man and slightly behind him. It was a tableau designed to make a statement. These were the Keeper's men, and there could be no doubt about it. Both Caleb and Chandy were instantly raised in status by merely being there.

Caleb looked down into the courtyard. Arranged on the poyos along the side walls were most of the chiefs. Spaces were left between some of the elders, apparently reserved in some predetermined way for those who had not arrived. Caleb tried to make sense of the seating, seeking some basis for the pattern, but none presented itself easily. The Keeper remained standing with his two young companions in the doorway, looking soberly down at the clan chiefs. The last to enter the courtyard was Caleb's father, who remained standing with his back to the now-closed doors between courtyard and square.

"Are we all assembled?" the Keeper asked formally.

"All here and all in their place," answered Jonathan formally.

The Keeper descended the stairs and took his place at the stone bench at the foot of the staircase. Caleb and Chandy, as they had been instructed, remained standing on the platform above.

"Then I formally declare the council assembled. I believe we have information of interest for us all, some sad, other of immense importance. I call upon Jonathan Grant, Master of the Hunt to inform the chiefs of our discoveries."

Jonathan remained standing at the courtyard doors. "As heads of the families and clan chiefs, you already know that when the first colonists arrived, contraband animals were brought along by one couple in the form of two lab rats. They subsequently escaped into the forest and were never recaptured. Without predators and with such a rich environment, they began to breed, and in a very short time, two became twenty-two, which became hundreds, then thousands and finally millions. The Tower called them the great sickness, and they have been referred to as such ever since."

Chandy looked over at Caleb who remained silently stoic.

"As you know," Jonathan continued, "Jason Keller and his two sons, Judah and Isaac, have been missing and until I called off the search, we had been trying to locate them. They have been found and they are all three dead."

There was a murmur of voices from the assembled chiefs.

"Gentlemen, the plague has returned."

The murmur became uproar. Caleb could smell the sudden fear among the chiefs. They were truly frightened, and they looked about as if trying to find a way to escape from the truth.

Jonathan calmed them. "The Kellers were eaten," he said, and the uproar returned. He waited patiently while the chiefs wore themselves out on outrage and panic. He stood firmly, a rock on the shore of a seething tide of anger. The Keeper rose from his seat and held out his arms to restore order, then turned to Caleb and gave instructions that they could barely hear above the pandemonium below. The two turned and entered the house, returning carrying the head of the great beast.

They brought it down into the courtyard as the chiefs returned to their seats and quieted.

"This time, however, they are different," Jonathan continued. It appears that they are not so numerous, but they have mutated over the years. We have the same threat to contend with, but in a new form."

He nodded toward his son, and Caleb and Chandy dropped their burden in the center of the courtyard, and with a single quick jerk, pulled at the ground cloth, releasing its burden into the dust. The head appeared from beneath the cloth and rolled topsy-turvy across the ground, coming to rest in the midst of the gathered chiefs. They looked down at the beast. Save for a few quick gasps, there was no sound.

"As you can see," Jonathan said, "our friends have become much larger and much more dangerous. We estimate that they weigh between sixty and eighty pounds and stand approximately thirty inches at the shoulder. The reason that we are sure that they are not as numerous is that the valley could not possibly support such a large population of these things and that they are now hunting in packs of two or three. At least that is the group size my son and Chandler Crone encountered in the forest near the Tower. From their account, the beasts are fast, intelligent, vicious, and can, in a rudimentary sense, cooperate in the hunt. It was by the grace of the Universe and quick thinking that the two did not fall victim themselves. It is because of their courage and demonstrated prowess that we now announce the elevation of these two hunters, Caleb Grant to apprenticeship as the next Master of the Hunt and Chandler Crone to initiated hunter and my apprentice."

Jonathan stepped forward carrying an ornate cup. Where it came from, Caleb couldn't guess. He handed it to Chandy who looked down at it, noting the dark red liquid inside.

"Don't worry," Jonathan whispered. "It's blood from a Parker Goose. I slaughtered the bird this morning."

Chandy took the cup holding it with both hands and after raising it above his head as if in sacrifice drank it down. A deep rumbling chant filled the air as the clan chiefs stamped their feet on the ground and huffed loudly.

When he had drained the cup there was again silence. Everyone seemed stunned by the revelation of the return of the plague. Caleb and Chandy were closest to the head of anyone in the courtyard, now truly decomposing in the midday heat. The stench was stifling. The hot wind seeping over the walls did little to abate their rising nausea. The head lay sideways on the ground, its great maw opened in a fiendish smile, the tusks glistening white in the sunlight. Caleb wanted to disappear into the streets, to lose himself among the people and pretend that none of this was happening. "Hunt and kill these tuskers now!" shouted one chief, ignoring any notice of the two hunters' new status.

"We do not have enough hunters for that!" called another.

"What about the crops? What do we do this winter?" asked a third.

The Keeper nodded to Jonathan and he called for silence. "As your advisor, I counsel caution and planning, but first things first. This is not a discussion for any but those gathered here. First we plan, and then we act. Are we in agreement?"

CHAPTER 7

Young Morg simmered at the thought of his grandfather's pronouncement. 'Get married', he had said. Just think about it and get used to the idea, he had told the boy. He couldn't imagine such a thing. He was only sixteen, for Universe's sake and didn't need to be thinking about things like that for a long time. There was the new colony to develop and organize, and he saw himself as his grandfather's successor someday, a dream that would absorb all his attention from now on. Besides, he was having much too much fun with his new found freedom and newfound celebrity to think of settling down with only one girl. It was unthinkable.

"I want you to get married," Morgan had said.

"What? Why?"

"It's necessary."

"I don't ... follow," he had said.

Morgan had looked at him sympathetically, which the boy found all the more irritating and had given him an insincere smile.

"Listen to me, Morg," he had said, "The town needs stability and we need to keep good relations with the colony if we're going to survive. That means forging alliances with clan chiefs and developing family ties free of that meddling Keeper and his rules. You do see that, don't you?"

He had to admit that he did. "But why me?" he had said.

"You're my grandson, and it's expected that as leaders, the members of my family are going to do the things we expect of others. I can't ask anyone else to marry for the sake of alliances if my own family isn't willing to."

"But who do you want me to marry?" he had asked.

His grandfather had frowned, shaken his head and said, "I'm not sure yet. I have some ideas, but I don't want to discuss that part now. Just get used to the idea. It's your duty."

"My duty," Morg mumbled as he worked with the tilers.

"You say something'?" asked the young man working beside him.

"Huh? Oh, nothing." Morg said, resenting the intrusion.

They were pulling together, sliding one of the long curved triangular sections that would soon be the glazed exterior covering of a conical house. Now dried and fired, it had been coated with the slip that would become the outside surface and had to be carefully maneuvered into the makeshift kiln on the edge of the tiling yard. It was hard work, but he didn't mind. One of the positives of being an outlander is that you were allowed to do virtually

any job that you were good at. He was a hunter and
learning to be a tiler, as well as helping with the furniture
making and construction of the outer walls. There was
never a lack of things to be done in the new town, and he
knew the more he understood about life here, the better
leader he would someday be. His father had told him at a
very early age that you should never ask another person to
do something you're not willing and able to do yourself.
Morg had taken the suggestion to heart. When the time
came, every outlander could call him colleague and brother.

They finally pulled the sled holding the section into the
huge brick kiln and carefully moved it laterally from the
sled onto raised braces with dozens of other identical
sections. When fired, the pieces would no longer be so
delicate and could be hauled more easily to a building site
where they would be fitted and mortared into place to
form, in this case, the highest course of exterior sections.
That was a job he had yet to do. Muscling ten-foot long
needles of tile into position twenty feet in the air was a job
for experienced tilers and glaziers. For the moment he was
content to work up a good sweat and exercise the muscles.
If nothing else, it kept him in shape.

Morg enjoyed the work immensely. Tiling was an art,
one that could only be done by the highly trained. He was
fortunate to have been allowed to learn the process.
Beside forming and firing the raw pottery, he had learned

the mixing of the mortar, a combination of sand, and river gravel. He knew how to balance that with the burned shells of mollusks found in the shallows and along the banks of the narrow river feeding the lake. Having participated in all of it, including the burning of the shells, which broke down into a fine powder, Morg had a clear understanding of all the processes necessary, if not the expertise yet. The master tiler had explained that the white powder made from the shells was the crucial ingredient in the mortar. He called it lime, which confused Morg, as he could find no logical connection between the white caustic powder and the sour fruits of the trees by the same name in the colony's orchards. When asked, the master tiler merely shrugged his shoulders. "That's just what they call it," he said and left it at that.

It was when they were returning to the rough kiln with the sled that he spotted Olivia headed in his direction. She was in a hurry, as usual, she was irritated, as usual, and she was looking for him, which was not usual at all. Morg felt his stomach begin to churn. Of all the elders in the camp, this was the one person that he feared, and he had no idea why. One thing he was sure of, if Olivia was looking for him, he probably wasn't going to like the resulting experience.

He watched her as she made her way among the flotsam and discarded shards of the boneyard, as the dumping ground for broken ceramics was called. As she moved, her long hair flapped in the breeze, flailing at the air in clumps, like whips randomly swung in arcs. Her white overshirt was open to the waist, revealing a tight-fitting linen shirt beneath, and was tied with a wide leather sash fitted into a huge double knot to one side. Her legs were covered with tight-fitting white trousers of local weave, more protective in the fields of feather grass and fragile bushes that could cut and slice when brushed against. On her feet were thick-soled black boots with high sides, wrapped in a thin white cord.

Her gait was more that of a man than of a woman, which everyone noticed and on which no one commented. This was a formidable woman, and others either came to some sort of accommodation with her or steered clear of her altogether. So far, Morg was unwilling to do the first, and unable to do the second. He waited to see what misery she was going to throw at him now.

Olivia walked directly up to him and stood in his path. Morg stopped and faced her. "You're needed at the butchering tables," she said flatly.
Morg gave her a sour look.

"I've work to do here," he replied, trying unsuccessfully to sound firm.

"You've got work everywhere, Morgan, and right now, the most pressing is at the butchering tables. Now get over to the kitchens and talk to Yetti Crane."

"What the hell does she want?" he asked.

Olivia glared at him, her eyes burning. "I'll take that from your grandfather, Morgan Culhane, but not from you. How the hell should I know what she wants? She needs you and she said it's important. I'm here to see that you go. Now move!"

He dropped the sled rope and walked away, purposely turning his back on the woman. Moving around the bone pile rather than retracing her steps, he made his way toward the kitchens as he felt her eyes boring into the back of his head. Someday, he thought, I'm going to have to kill that bitch, for the sake of the town if nothing else. The thought gave him a sense of pleasure and a little relief from the anger he was feeling. He began to fantasize about how he would go about it, and of how to maximize her pain in the process. He actually grinned, pleased with his own creativity. For him, there was no shortage of scenarios as to how to make Olivia's dying moments most uncomfortable.

At the butchering tables, Yetti Crane was busily directing her swarm of women while cleaving a large haunch from the ground sloth they had brought her that

morning. She looked up and noticed him coming, then
returned to her work, still barking orders and not wasting
breath on acknowledging the boy from a distance. Morg
liked Yetti. She was like everyone's grandmother, plump
and round, somewhat squat with graying hair pulled back
in a tight bun and muscular yet flabby arms that fluttered
each time she swung the cleaver into the haunch. Morg
had always liked the woman who was practically a parent to
him. Since his parents died, she had taken an interest in
him and seemed to sense when he needed comforting after
a session with his grandfather...or when he needed
someone to light a fire under him. Somehow, he had the
feeling that this was going to be a case of the latter.

Several of the young women looked up at him as he
passed and he considered for the first time if any of them
would make a suitable mate. They were all fair and several
downright beautiful, but he was still not interested in
romance. There was no promiscuity in either the colony
or among the outsiders, at least none that was admitted
openly. The taboo against sexual encounters among
unmarried young people was too strong and the
community too tight for that. Beyond the possibility of a
tryst, he had little interest in the opposite sex. He put the
thought from his mind.

"About time you showed up," she said with mock irritation.

"I was working at the kilns. I came as soon as Olivia told me."

"Took the long way around, no doubt."

Morg chose to ignore the remark. "Did you want to see me, Yetti? They really need me for the glazing. We've got a whole top section ready to go and I haven't seen it done yet."

"They'll do fine without you," she said. "I have other duties for you, some you're more temperamentally suited for." Morg's eyes narrowed. He began to suspect that Yetti had been talking to his father. Was this stage two of the marriage campaign?

"I don't want to get married," he said sharply.

Yetti looked at him, confused if not stunned. "Um, that's nice," she said, recovering. "I really don't need a husband, you know, but thanks for
thinking of it. I was just going to send you out hunting again in the morning. From what you said, there's lots of game out there right now."

"Oh. Well, yes. We can do that, but why? We brought in enough to feed the whole town for several days."

"It's not today or tomorrow I'm concerned about. It's the coming windy season and the winter to follow. We'll need to finish drying and pickling if we're going to have any meat this winter."

Morg's stomach gave a lurch. The thought of the tough, dried meat made him nauseous and had since his bout some years ago with jack dart eggs in the dried flesh of a lummox. He'd been sick for days. Still, he understood that, until there were crops to be harvested, which couldn't happen before the spring thaws, they were short of provisions. Personally, he intended to stick to vegetables and roots gathered in the forest. He swallowed, and then nodded.

"How much do you need?"

"If you can match today's hunt three or four times in the next week or so, we'll be fine."

Morg smiled to himself. He loved the hunt. Being out for the next week or so hunting, he could avoid Olivia's bile and his grandfather's nagging. He warmed to the idea of organizing and executing the hunt. It was the closest thing to being a Hunt Master he could imagine, and that appealed to him greatly. "Consider it done," he said.

He headed back to the kilns, determined to see the firing and arrived just in time to see the now-closed chamber being ignited. Huge fagots of wood from the cleared fields and piles of charcoal had been placed in the kiln with the sections until they covered them to the ceiling. Now from a series of openings at the base of the structure, fires were being lit by torch. Soon, the entire interior was in conflagration, smoke bellowing from the hole in the center of the roof, and so much wind being sucked in through the base holes that it could be heard whistling. Morg was so near to the kiln that he could feel the breeze stirred up by the rising heat inside. He stepped back a few paces out of the heat and stood beside the master tiler, grinning.

"You almost missed it," the tiler said.

"I did miss loading the fuel, but it's a minor point."

The tiler looked down at them and shook his head. "When are you going to learn that there are no insignificant steps in this process? If the fire's not laid properly, the firing will go badly and we could lose some of the sections. You should have been here."

"You're right, of course, which brings up something else. I'll be hunting for the next week, perhaps more. The camp needs meat to dry for the winter."

"So? You'll take half my apprentices with you, I suppose? How are you people ever going to learn if you keep leaving for other jobs?"

"They'll be back," Morg said, pointedly not including himself in the statement. Someday he'd be back as well, but who knew when? There was already so much to learn, so much to absorb. He turned and headed for his grandfather's tents to prepare for the hunt.

CHAPTER 8

Once outside the courtyard, Caleb and Chandy looked at each other, each at a loss as to how they should proceed. After the council of chiefs, they had been sent on their way with a promise of further instructions later. For the moment, they walked through the square and down a wide avenue that led to a section of the town devoted to shops. It was an unconscious act, void of volitional decision. They were wandering and nothing more.

For some time, neither of them spoke, each mired in their own thoughts. Caleb began to notice those around them as they walked. People moved through the streets in twos or threes or alone, busily going about their daily business, totally unaware of the danger that was gathering outside the walls. Around him he heard the sounds of tradesmen, the clanging, clunking, rasping and scraping of people producing goods to sell. It mixed with the sounds of voices murmuring in conversation and the melodies of street musicians, hoping someone would stop to listen to their tunes and favor them with some small coin. Down one small alley, he heard the voice of an infant crying out to be fed and a mother soothingly singing lullabies to the child.

The air was alive with the smell of cooking and of animals and of people, some perfumed, others sweaty, emitting the pungent aroma of last night's dinner through their skin. It was the sounds and the smells of the town and he noticed it as never before. It was simply part of his world, but today it was more alive and more beautiful to him than ever. What would these people think if they knew the truth? What would that young mother do to save her child if the beasts entered the city? How would they protect themselves? Most unexpected of all, and most disturbing to him, was Caleb's almost elated feeling of being alive, more alive than he had felt in years, because of the sudden shift in his whole world brought on by that creature whose head lay in the courtyard of the Keeper's house. He felt almost guilty at the adrenaline rush the prospect of doing battle with these horrors brought to him.

"Can...we talk about this between ourselves?" Chandy asked, breaking the silence. .

"Not here. I don't see how they can expect us to just forget we heard it, but talking about it in a public place is too risky. What if someone overheard? There'd be panic everywhere."

Chandy frowned. "If they believed it at all. Do we just pretend nothing happened?"

Caleb smirked. "Maybe you can, but I'm not that good an actor. I think maybe we'll just tell anyone who asks that it was private business between the Keeper and ourselves and that we can't discuss it."

"You don't think that will start rumors too?"

Now Caleb smiled. "I'm sure it will, but they'll never guess the truth. If they have to have a story, we can make it seem that we were brought to task over something we did."

Chandy agreed, nodding. "I can see that.

"Good. Well, my friend, you wanted an initiation. How has it been so far?"

Chandy frowned. "Not what I expected," he said solemnly.

When they finally noticed their surroundings they found themselves in a street of small shops catering to the frivolous goods of the population, selling everything from clothing and artwork to toys and household trinkets. Neither of them was particularly familiar with this quarter since neither of them was given to such shopping. As men they were in the minority here, which did not particularly bother them, and they studied the behavior of groups of women and young girls, picking over dresses and slippers, jewelry, and what Chandy's father would call 'fancies', those small creations of color and light that often decorated the main hall of many of the families. They were surprised at the industry and serious consideration that the shoppers gave to their search.

"Why do they do that?" Chandy asked at last.

"Do what?"

"Worry over such nonsense. I mean, how different is one slipper from another?"

Caleb shrugged. "My father says it has to do with genetics. He said it's something about hunting versus gathering in early humans. I don't know. It seems to me that if you want to buy something, you just go to where it is, buy it, and then take it with you. The ladies seem to actually enjoy the process of picking over everything until they find what strikes them."

"Well, it seems pretty silly to me," the boy said.

Their attention was drawn by a familiar laugh at a shop behind them and to the left. They turned to see Kylie with her two constant girlfriends smiling and discussing a brilliant white diaphanous scarf of feather grass, delicately embroidered with emerald and red mineral threads. Caleb had to admit that it was quite beautiful, but he was more interested in watching Kylie. Her eyes actually sparkled when she smiled. He could never get over that, and truth be known, he had no desire to. Caleb had long ago decided that this was the most beautiful woman he'd ever known, but today she seemed more beautiful than ever. There was a casual ease in the way she carried herself, an unconscious grace that was so natural he wasn't even sure if she realized how enticing it was. Her long red hair fell loosely over her shoulders and cascaded down her back in relaxed curls. Against the brilliant yellow of her dress, she looked like springtime itself. Kylie always looked extraordinary but it still took his breath away when he saw her. Her conical sometimes-hat-and-most-of-the- time-bag was hooked around her left arm and it swung against her hips as she spread a scarf out and held it up to look at it. As it brushed against her, he watched it, mesmerized.

"It's Kylie," Chandy said unnecessarily.

"I noticed."

"So why is it you have such a hard time talking to girls?" Chandy blurted out.

"What?"

"Oh, come on, Caleb. You know what I mean."

The hunter could feel himself turning crimson as he always did when the subject came up."I'm...just not much good with girls," he said weakly. "I mean, I know just what to do on a hunt, or when I'm with my buddies, but women are different. They confuse me."

Chandy smiled "The great hunter is afraid of women?" he teased.

"Stop it, Chandy. Don't joke. It's a problem I have. I notice you weren't exactly gabby with Jillian today."

Chandy's expression changed. "That's different. That's not women in general. It's just Jillian that does that to me."

"So with you, it's just the one and with me it's all of them."

"Yeah, okay, but you need to get over it."

"Do I?"

Chandy leaned closer and lowered his voice. "How do you ever expect to win Kylie's heart if you won't talk to her?"

"I...um... that's not..."

"Oh, stop it. You love her and everybody, including Kylie knows it. She won't wait forever, you know."

Caleb felt helpless. A sixteen-year-old boy was giving him advice about women, which he had to admit he needed. He hated it. To make matters worse, Kylie turned and spotted them, smiling invitingly at Caleb and not being the least reserved about it. If he didn't know better, he'd think she'd heard them talking. Chandy just said she knew he loved her? Had he heard that?

Chandy waved. "Here's your chance. We're going over there and you're going to actually carry on a conversation." Before he could protest, the boy was dragging him toward the three young women and chattering a constant stream of jokes and compliments as he did so.

"Buying out the store?" Chandy said.

"Just looking, really. What brings you two down this street?"

"We're just wandering," Caleb said. He couldn't believe he was actually speaking.

"We were talking about the hunt and got lost in the conversation," Chandy added quickly.

"How was the hunt?"

"Um, challenging," Chandy said.

"He's very good at it. He had his first kill yesterday,? Caleb offered.

"You do love to hunt, don't you, Caleb?"

He refused to look away. She wasn't teasing him this time. She seemed genuinely interested.

"Yeah, actually. It's pretty much the same thing you ladies are doing now, but we have something specific we're after."

Kylie's friends looked insulted, but Kylie just smiled and held his gaze. "Actually," she said, "I think you're right. We just hunt different things with different purposes, don't we?"

"Yes, I suppose you're right."

"It sounds to me, Mr. Grant, that we have more in common than meets the eye, wouldn't you say?"

"I would like to think so," he said and smiled slightly.

Her eyes laughed to match her upturned mouth. "I think we should discuss this further. Chandy, bring your friend here to dinner tonight. I'll prepare something special."

"Oh, I wouldn't want you to go to any trouble..."

"He'll be there," Chandy interrupted. "My sister needs the practice anyway."

Both of them looked at Chandy, Kylie with some mild irritation. Then they looked back at each other and laughed.

Caleb said, "I would be pleased to come."

"Good," she said. "You know our house, of course?"

He nodded. Kylie gave a short curtsy, placed the scarf back on the counter and left with her two friends, who were giggling uncontrollably.

Chandy put his hand on Caleb's shoulder. "Now that wasn't so hard, was it?"

"Don't push it, Chandler," the hunter growled. "Now you owe me a run, since we didn't get a chance to train this morning. Up the hill and back, please, and take a rifle, just in case."

"Aw, Caleb..."

"Now!"

Chandy turned and trotted off in the direction of his house. Caleb watched him go, then turned back to the counter and picked up the shimmering scarf with the green and red inlay.

"How much is this?" he asked the shopkeeper, and reached into his pocket.

CHAPTER 9

Chandy's father, Donald, was not an easy man to know, and most people felt that was just fine with them. A sullen, reclusive man, he always gave the impression that he was surrounded by darkness and shadow, even on the brightest of days. Caleb had met him formally some five years ago, when he began to tutor Chandy in the arts of the hunt, but he had known about him from gossip and derisive comments among the adults from early childhood. Caleb often wondered how such a morose figure could have fathered such bright, intelligent and energetic children. He wondered if they had taken on their positive roles as a simple counterpoint to the life they must be living at home.

There had been a mother, of course, and another sister who would have been two years younger than Chandy, but they were both dead and had been for nearly ten years. Jonathan Grant always said that was when Donald Crone began to withdraw from his neighbors and friends. According to Caleb's father, he had once been as buoyant and in love with life as his children. Kylie had apparently taken over the motherly duties quickly after the deaths of her mother and younger sister, and that at a rather tender age. It amazed Caleb that she was able to maintain her natural optimism in the face of all that pressure.

He thought of these things again on his way to the Crones' house that evening, trying not to focus on his seriously-mixed feelings about what was coming. On the one hand, there was the opportunity to spend time with Kylie, a prospect to be devoutly desired and one that she was apparently in favor of. On the other hand, there was the prospect of time spent with her father.

In all the years he had been working with Chandy, the father had spoken to him no more than two dozen times, and then in short, direct questions or statements regarding his son's prospects. He didn't seem to care a bit about Caleb as a person, only as a means to his son's success. He seemed somewhat indifferent to that as well.

As a result of all this, Caleb made slow progress through the streets and was in no immediate hurry to arrive at the Grants. If he took his time, he might arrive just before the meal, which would cut back on the awkward process of trying to carry on a conversation with his host. He ambled through the streets in the twilight, the carefully packaged scarf under his left arm. Around him the few people who were still out were scurrying home before dark, either determinedly after a hard day's work, or nervously, hoping to arrive before the sun went down and it became more difficult to see in the dark avenues.

Caleb didn't worry about this. He knew that both of the moons would be high tonight and that they were in close proximity so that their combined brilliance would offer plenty of light for the journey home. He tried to remember which of the two moons would be leading and found he simply wasn't sure. For a hunter, this was a serious lapse. The positions and timing of the moons dictated much of what could be expected in the night, particularly this close to the windy season. It was only about eight weeks away, and the jack darts would soon begin to swarm. They loved to ride the denser night air. Being unprepared for an encounter with the small fliers could mean a hunter's death, as the jack darts blindly flew into any obstruction along their way, including a human body.

His mood did change as he neared his destination, the trepidation vanishing in the anticipation of seeing Kylie. Perhaps Chandy had been right. Perhaps she did know that he was totally enchanted by her and deeply in love. If that was true and she had invited him for dinner, wasn't that a good sign? It pleased him to think so, and the way she could put him at ease as she had done that afternoon encouraged him. She was, after all, easy to talk to. In the face of all the danger and uncertainties he encountered on the hunt, the fact that he was completely cowed by this gentle young woman seemed more incongruous than ever. He relaxed a bit as he made the final turn into their street and climbed the steps to the Crones' house entrance.

Before he could announce himself, Chandy swung open the door.

"Almost on time," he said, grinning.

"Hi, Chandy."

"Hi yourself. 'Have trouble finding your way?"

Caleb frowned, but it was playful. "Is this the way it's going to be all evening?"

"Nope. 'Just wanted to get in a few digs while I still had time to talk to you."

"Oh?"

"Oh yes. Once Kylie starts in, I won't get a word in all night."

"Chandler Crone, you stop that!" called Kylie from the interior. "Come in, Caleb, and don't pay any attention to that pig-mold that masquerades as my brother."

Chandy stood aside and Caleb entered. He'd been here hundreds of times before, but having never really paid much attention, he took the time to really look around. It was a standard arrangement for a colony home. The curved stairway ran down and up along the wall on the far side of the room, directly opposite the doorway. To the left was a large enclosed bed for guests and for bundling during the cold winter season. The framing of the bed was native wood, not expensive, but dense and sturdy, with delicate carvings at the four corners of the crown and interior blankets, almost tapestries, hung on the walls. The doors, now pulled closed, were louvered, an unusual feature, and Caleb decided it was for control of circulation. If this was a very tight house, the heat rising from the floor below could become excessive, even in winter.

In the center of the room was a heavy wooden table large enough to seat six, though only two chairs and two benches flanked its circumference at the moment. It was plain and of dark wood, but in the center of the table was an arrangement of Spanglar Glass, a native plant that grew, not from seed but from a single crystal shard with a memory for form. Usually, Spanglars were chaotic, growing overnight into masses of sharp cutting limbs and prismatic leaves, but in the hands of an artisan, they could be trained to grow into beautiful displays that reflected light in all its hues, whimsically or dramatically, fantastically or tightly-ordered, at the behest of the grower. The fantastic display of shifting colors reflected by the delicate plates of this specimen bespoke an artisan of high skill. It was breathtaking.

To the right, opposite the enclosed bed, was a large settle, a bench with a high back, and it faced the room's only window. Made of thick, ripple glass, it was better at emitting light than at offering a true image of the outside, and it was flanked by double shutters. Normally, only one leaf of each shutter was folded back, giving the impression that the window was smaller than its actual size, but for this evening, they were double folded, allowing a flood of twilight to enter.

Bastion and then Desolation were both just rising over the far rim of the valley, and their light flooded through the window like a beacon. It was the first time Caleb had ever witnessed the effect and he began to understand the size and the positioning of the window.

"Beautiful, isn't it?" said Kylie.

He turned and saw her just emerging from the bottom floor, a circular tray of serving bowls and plates in her hands. She was, of course, stunning.

"Yes, it is. I've never seen anything quite like it," he answered, crossing to help her with her burden. She shooed him away.

"Go sit. You're a guest. I'm a big girl, you know. I can manage."

He retreated to the center of the room and sat at the large table there. He wondered if he had just committed some social error by offering to help.

Kylie set the tray on the table and began distributing the load. "My father built the window when he first became head of the family. His father had always had a very small window. He said it kept out the sickness better, which doesn't make sense to me, but my father enlarged it and had the large pane made especially for the opening. I don't think there's another like it in the whole colony."

"I don't think so either. I've never seen anything like it."

She sat beside him, moving her chair close to his so that they could both look toward the window. "I've always loved that view. Except for the winter, I can sit there for hours and look out at the sky or down into the streets and watch the people. It's like spying on them. I see them, but they don't see me. Is that terribly wicked of me, do you think?" She turned and caught his eyes with her own and he was hopelessly ensnared and he knew it.

"I think it's incredible. I do that sometimes from the hills where Chandy and I run. From up there, you can see the whole valley. When I was a kid I used to go there and look down, watching all the people in the fields and on the lake, and those in the town, moving around like so many small insects. I think it's the energy that attracts me."

"Yes," she said naturally. "I can see that! Caleb, would you take me sometime?"

They were both startled by the comment. It was forward beyond belief, and they had only just begun to talk. "If you like," he stammered at last.

Kylie broke eye contact, apparently embarrassed.

"So you watch from the window. Is that why the settle is there?"

"No," she said. "It's there for my father. He placed it in that spot the day my mother died and no one is allowed to move it. He sits there often as well, just staring out at nothing."

"I'm sorry. I'm sorry for his loss and for yours and Chandy's. It must have been hard for you, taking on her duties."

Kylie nodded. "Hard at first, but I enjoy it." She smiled. "You notice it didn't slow me down any, now did it?" She looked down at the package Caleb still held in his lap.

"Is that for me?" she asked.

"Um, yes," he stammered and handed it to her.

She took it from him and opened it carefully, and when she saw the scarf, her eyes grew wide. She uttered a muffled 'oh!' and stood, wrapping it around her shoulders. She twirled around in a circle, admiring how the scarf's tails fluttered as she turned, then looked back at Caleb, grinning.

He laughed. He couldn't help it. The woman was so natural and unassuming that she was like a small innocent child. Whenever she spoke, flowers filled the air. When she moved, it was like the wind in feather grass.

"So when do we eat?" Chandy interrupted, coming down from the floor above.

"When your father comes down,"

"Good. He's on his way."

Kylie carefully folded the scarf and replaced the wrapping, her silent look offering thanks to Caleb, then she was up and away, heading for the stairs and kitchen below.

"Cups, Jug, spoons," she called over her shoulder, and Chandy busied himself at a cupboard beside the door.

Donald Crone descended the stairs. Caleb watched him and wondered what kind of reception he was going to receive. He tried to look at the man with fresh eyes, taking him in completely. This was a huge man, muscular and broad of shoulder from his work at the kiln. He reminded Caleb of one of those heroes from the Old World tales, like a John Henry, or an Arnold Schwarzenegger. He wore simple, well-made clothes, light-colored slacks of lummox wool, and a woolen shirt that was well tailored and sported four large wooden buttons. They bore the same carved faces as the four corners of the boxed bed. His shoes were workman's shoes but were spotless and this surprised Caleb since Donald Crone worked the fields as well as the tiling yards during the day. To his surprise, the master of the house looked him directly in the eye cheerfully. "I see our guest has arrived," he said.

"Good evening," Caleb said formally. "I'm glad to see you, Mr. Crone."

"Call me Donald, Caleb. After all this time, formality seems a bit silly, don't you think? You've been coming here for more than five years."

"Donald then."

"Good. Now where's that daughter of mine?" he asked, crossing to the table. He noticed the positioning of Kylie's chair close to Caleb's and moved it, saying nothing.

"I'm right here, Father, and if you'll be a bit more patient, we just might eat."

Donald Crone offered Kylie a gentle smile that widened to a grin when she brought the final platter, which held a fine young Parker goose. It seemed cooked to perfection, with a crisp, dark crust and assorted vegetables surrounding it.

"I'm glad you're here, Caleb. We don't often eat this well. My stomach thanks you for coming." He laughed heartily.

Caleb laughed as well, wondering what had become of the sullen Donald Crone he was used to. He was not at all like he had been on other visits. If he was just putting on an act for company, he was doing a very good job of it. Chandy slid easily into his chair on Caleb's right and Kylie into the chair on his left. She offered a moment of thanks to the Universe for the food they were about to eat, then she began filling bowls with a broth that smelled of savory spices and wild grasses. Caleb's appetite soared.

"Now be careful of the soup," she said, like a mother addressing a child. Caleb wasn't sure to whom she was actually speaking, but at this point, if it was an attempt to mother him, he really didn't care.

"It looks delicious," he said.

"Of course it is, but it's very hot, and it only reaches its full potential when eaten with the goose. The flavors reinforce one another, you know. The combination is totally different than each one separately. You'll see what I mean."

"Yes, ma'am," he said.

Her father laughed loudly. "You watch out for her, boy. She rules this house with an iron hand, and if you let her, she'll rule you the same way!"

Kylie kept her composure. When she had finished serving the soup, her father proceeded to cut the goose, which was succulent, tender to the point of falling off the bone, and not at all greasy. Handing Caleb a plate of meat and vegetables, he said, "Eat." They all did so.

The meal was filled with small talk about the colony and the preparations for the windy season. Working the fields as he did, Donald Crone was a wealth of information about how the crop was this year and what was being harvested when for best storage. He spoke easily, as if he had guests at his table all the time, and try as he may, Caleb could not detect any deceit in him. This man was as different from what he had expected as he could possibly be. They spoke of hunting and of Chandy's prowess at tracking and with the rifle. They spoke of the coming winter and who would need help with their houses if they were going to survive the intense cold. Donald Crone slid easily from subject to subject, subtly omitting certain topics, such as all reference to his wife and other daughter, or the recent missing Kellers. Somehow he seemed to intuit that the latter was a taboo subject, and subtly informed the young hunter that any mention of his missing family was taboo as well.

When at last they had finished the meal, Donald walked to the cupboard by the door and returned with four small glass cups and a ceramic jug. Caleb could tell from the workmanship and the decorations that it was from the Old World, a rare possession for any colonist. The huge hands manipulated the jug carefully, pouring no more than an inch of its content into each glass mug and placing them in front of the four of them.

"This is called cognac. My ancestors brought it with them from the Old World." He said. "It's very heady stuff, so sip it slowly. The jug is tapped perhaps a half dozen times in a Crone's lifetime, but somehow, I feel an urgency to share it here and now. I hope you don't mind."

"No, sir. I'm honored," said Caleb. He took the small glass and sipped the deep amber liquid, letting it roll over his tongue as he would a suspicious water source in the forest. It burned his tongue and the sides of his mouth, but once swallowed, the flavor and aroma lingered as nothing he had ever tasted. It was delightful.

"I see you like it," said his host.

"It's incredible. I've never tasted its like."

Donald Crone leaned back and sipped from his cup. "That's good. Most people need to develop a taste for it. You seem to have found its perfection on the first try."

"I can't imagine someone not liking it," Caleb said.

"Well I can," grumbled Chandy, passing his glass to his father. "It burns in the mouth, it burns in the throat, and it burns in the stomach. Yuck!"

His father simply leaned back and said "Opinions differ."

While Chandy and Kylie cleared away the table, Donald brought Caleb to sit on the settle with him before the great window. Bastion and Desolation were high in the sky now, beyond the view of the window, but the brighter stars were clearly visible, forming patterns within patterns across the sky. Caleb wondered why he had never noticed the display in quite this way before. Perhaps it was the subtle distortion of the ripple glass that caused the effect.

"You're familiar with the stars?" Donald asked after a pause.

"Every hunter is," Caleb said.

"Not like this, I imagine."

"No, never like this. Here they're not guides, they're just beautiful."

"Yes. Someone else used to say that."

His host fell silent, looking up at the stars. Caleb was very uncomfortable. He was not certain that he liked being this close to the man, though there was plenty of space on the settle between them. It simply felt intimate, as if two friends were sharing themselves, and he was not used to that with anyone. A hunter's life was too solitary for developing those kinds of friendships, except, of course, for Chandy, who was more brother than apprentice.

Suddenly, Donald stood and smoothed the folds of his trousers. "You should be sitting here with Kylie," he said somewhat sadly, and walked away.

Caleb sat there on the settle, thinking. His host was more enigmatic in his mind than ever, a study in opposites that Caleb was not sure he had the ability to unravel. It disturbed him greatly and brought back the anxiety he'd felt before he'd come here. He was not used to being so off-balance and started to stand, feeling foolish seated alone on the settle, but before he could move, Kylie appeared and sat beside him. Her smile faded into a quizzical expression when she looked at him.

"You don't look happy," she said.

"Well don't try to sneak up on the subject, lady."

"Sorry. Father says I'm too blunt. I guess it's because I never really had a mother to teach me any other way."

"It's okay. Actually, I like it."

She looked surprised. "You do?"

"Yes, I do. I'd rather have honesty any time."

"Not unlike yourself, my friend, though in your case, you just can't hide the truth very well when you try."

"Really?"

"Really."

"For instance?"

"For instance your repeated attempts to deny you're interested in me."

Caleb actually slid away from her on the seat. She was no more surprised at this than he. He had to admit that she was right, of course, but to just come out and say it?

"Well, okay. I'm...just not very good with girls."

"I'm glad."

This was becoming more confusing than ever. He declared that he'd never understand women and that he might just as well quit trying.

"I don't understand."

"Well, suppose you were more like Chandy. I believe that boy could charm the calves away from a lummox. If you were like him, you'd have a string of women following you around, and by now, one of them would have snared you."

"You make it sound like a game, or a hunt."

She looked at him with those deep eyes of hers and shook her head. "It is kind of a game, I guess. I've just gotten tired of waiting for you to take the bait. Now do you want to kiss me or not?"

"Wh...what? Uh, uh..."

Kylie pulled him to her and slipped her hand around his neck, then leaned forward and kissed him deeply. Not being able to describe what he was feeling, he finally had everything he'd ever wanted at this moment in time, and he didn't know what to do with it. Finally she pulled away, leaving him open-mouthed and stunned.

"Now was that so terrible?" she asked.

"Uh-huh"

"What?"

"Um, no. At least, I don't think so. Maybe we should try it again."

Before he left for the night, Caleb had promised to go jayberry picking with her tomorrow. He had never been jayberry picking, though he wasn't sure why. It was a seasonal milestone for everyone in the colony, marking the end of the warm summer and the coming of the wind. It was also an activity often used to signal an understanding between lovers, since normally one only did it with one's family. The small, amber-colored fruits of the jayberry bush were succulent and filled with a sweet juice delightful beyond description, and they only came into their own for a short four-day period just before the winds begin. Within a week, the bush would be dripping their then-withered berries, ready for the strong winds to lift and scatter them so that they could lie dormant through the winter and begin the building of new plants in the spring. Fortunately, the plant was prolific, producing thousands of berries that covered an individual bush like a beaded blanket. The jack darts loved them, as did most of the local fauna, and the cattle and sheep ate them as well. As for the colonists, they would gather them by the sack full, turning them into wine and reducing them to a thick sweetener for cooking. It was the colony's chief source of sugar. For Caleb, that sweetness now took on a new meaning. Tomorrow would be a wondrous day.

CHAPTER 10

C aleb walked briskly through the night air.
Bastion and Desolation were low on the horizon
now, though Desolation lagged behind enough to
provide good light and cast long shadows over the town.
He could see small creatures of the night making their way
on some nocturnal hunt for grubs and local insects, and
allowed his mind to play with the shadow shapes of
buildings and flotsam propped up against this wall or that.
He thought of tomorrow's picking, and of the festive
atmosphere that always accompanied it.

Anyone who was not otherwise engaged would be out and
about in the glades near the forest's edge, women babbling
on as they picked, men purposefully and systematically
stripping bush after bush, while children skittered about
gathering berries from the lower limbs and eating as many
as they bagged. Young people would be there as well, of
course, the married and the unmarried, sneaking off into
the woods for a bit of privacy in the midst of the chaos
and laughter to steal a kiss or a few moments to
themselves, and tomorrow, he would be among them.
How magical, he thought, and how sad he'd never taken

the time to involve himself before, at least, not since he was a child.

As he neared the central square he saw yet another shadow skulking along the edge of the avenue to his left, but something didn't seem right about it. It moved too slowly and it was too large to be any of the local creatures he was used to encountering in the night. It disappeared as quickly as it had appeared, and the accompanying scuffle of its passing ceased almost immediately.

Without thinking, he tensed and reached for his knife, which, of course was not at his side. He looked around for something to defend himself with if necessary, but there was nothing. Feeling foolish about slipping into hunter's mode in the middle of the town and in the middle of the night, something told him it was a good idea. Moving slowly to the side of the building on his right and he blended into the shadows.

Desolation slipped further to the horizon, appearing between two buildings behind him and casting a long bright beacon of light on the square. He peered sharply, diverting his eyes slightly to avoid losing all of his night vision in the brighter light of the moon. Again he caught a movement of something shifting back into shadow opposite him. It seemed to be squeezing itself under one of the stone benches along the outside of the Keeper's

compound wall. Caleb crouched, sure that he was still
hidden in shadow himself. He waited.

For some time, nothing happened. Then as suddenly as
it had appeared, Desolation disappeared beyond another
building and the square was left in near darkness. At the
same moment, Caleb felt more than heard a stirring in the
direction of the stone bench. A dark figure rose from the
space beneath the slab and stood. It was man-like and
nearly five feet in height.

"Who's there!" he challenged sharply.

The figure turned towards him, and then darted off
in the direction of the main gate. Caleb followed at the
run, keeping the fleeing figure in sight as they passed
through narrow streets and out onto open avenues.
Always the figure was in the shadows, or appearing only
briefly in the light of a torch or lantern hung in a doorway.
Caleb could never quite make out who or what it was, but
it ran swiftly and economically, not wasting energy or
motion in its flight. He could hardly keep up with it and
he was sure that, except for Chandy, no one could overtake
it, whatever it was.

At last, it disappeared around a corner to one side of
the main gate and silently disappeared. Caleb rounded the
corner cautiously and came to a halt. He was in a blind
alley. On either side of him were blank walls, free of
doorways or windows, and at the end of the alley was only

the inner wall that surrounded the inner ward of the town. When he looked up, he spotted the figure on the top of the wall, some ten feet above him. It paused momentarily and looked back at him, crouched as it was on the edge of the wall, its wide shoulders and thick torso twisted halfway between its pursuer and its freedom. Then it leaped and disappeared.

Caleb burst through the inner wall gate but knew even before he looked that he would see nothing. Whomever or whatever it had been, the apparition was gone. Standing there, panting, trying to catch his breath, he had chased the figure for more than ten blocks, neither of them letting up the pace, and he was spent. If that was a man he'd seen disappearing into the night, he didn't want to meet him in anger and definitely not in the night again. He returned to the spot on the inner wall where the shadow had leapt and gauged the height to be a good twelve feet. How could anyone do that?

As he turned, his foot bumped an object on the ground and he knelt to pick it up. It was a small leather pouch. He shook it and heard a strange clacking sound. Opening it, he moved back into the light near the gate and poured the contents into his hand. The pouch was filled with Spanglar crystals, but not like any he had ever seen. They were larger than normal, and nearly smooth with no more than three or four protruding spikes on any one of them. Caleb examined them for a moment, and then slipped them back into the pouch carefully and looped it under his belt. He made a mental note to give them to Kylie. With her expertise with Spanglar, perhaps she would know what they were. Caleb made his way home, trying to decipher the enigma of the night creature and his strange cargo of crystals. He knew every type of animal in the valley, both native and from the Old World, and this fit none of it. He searched his memory for tales told around open fires and in the homes of older hunters and nothing even remotely resembling this creature came to mind. He considered the tuskers that he and Chandy had killed in the clearing near the Tower and not even that abomination fit the image he'd followed tonight. Just what the town needed, another mystery to deal with. What could it have been?

At home he secured the doorway, something he'd never bothered to do before, and slipped quickly into his bed and instantly fell asleep. His sleep was filled with dreams, and his dreams filled with images of fantastic creatures that appeared and disappeared at will, wreaking havoc among the colonists and eating the dead. They accosted him from every side, sporting faces as unimaginably ugly as his mind could conceive, ranging from featureless masses of loose flesh to angular heaps of bony plates that shone pale in the light of the two moons; naked or covered in fur, scaly as fish or robed like elders; attacking his family, kidnapping his woman and devouring his friends. They tormented him throughout the night, leaving him exhausted in the morning, trapped in the twisted heap of bedding on his pallet. Awaking in a cold sweat, Caleb was panting from the last vicious attack of unseen demons. Without thinking about it, he was up and washed in minutes and left. It was early. No one was about yet except for the night watch and a few early risers beginning their day. Smiling and greeting him as he passed, they were unaware of the horrors that invaded their peace by night, or lurked in the forests, ready to kill and maim. Caleb felt burdened and badly in need of counsel. He had to see the Keeper.

CHAPTER 11

There was the usual enthusiasm at the thought of a hunt among Morg's companions. Any opportunity to escape the drudgery that accompanies the building of a settlement was an opportunity worth taking. That, coupled with the fact that they were indulging their favorite sport, was all the motivation needed. More than a dozen young men enthusiastically made their way to the edge of the wood just before dawn. The sounds of the night had long given way to the sounds of an awakening wood, first erupting into the cacophony of creatures re-establishing territories after a night of sleep, then to the howls and cries of other fauna, large and small, calling to mates and potential mates in a last ditch effort to establish themselves before the coming winds.

Everything on Two Moons centered in the seasons. Understanding them was essential to the sowing and harvesting of crops, but beyond that, the seasons were so violent and so different in their sudden arrival and departure, that a miscalculation could easily lead to disaster. The local creatures had long since adjusted to these conditions and were hard-wired genetically to cope with it. Colonists either learned it quickly or perished. So it was with this season. The gathering of food and the establishment of homes were the main priorities for the separatists. If they couldn't feed and house themselves for the next five months, they would die. It was as simple as that. Winter crops were being planted to ensure that there would be food in the spring, and nearly everyone was busily going about the process of building the conical houses that could withstand the winds and the winter ice. For the separatists, that meant smaller, more compact housing for this first year since the building of full-size structures was beyond their timeline. For Morg and his compatriots, it meant that they could hunt to their heart's content and still serve the village's survival.

Morg and his two friends, Alan Priest and Paul Creole, had worked out the plan early last evening. They were now ready to begin. It was a simple and straightforward plan, considering the wealth of game that had presented itself to them recently, designed for maximum efficiency and maximum yield. Working their way into the forest in two groups about a half a mile apart, penetrating to a depth of perhaps two miles, they would then start back toward the village, driving the animals before them. A third group, who would be waiting near the edge of the wood, would be in place to kill the game as it approached, and those hunters following would join in the slaughter. With luck, they could bag at least an animal apiece by noon, and if they were large enough, only four or five animals would constitute a successful hunt. As for Morgan, his personal target was the elusive Old World bird that had come with the original colonists but which had escaped into the wood. They were called turkeys. According to the Keeper, they were the most efficient animals for turning vegetable matter into protein for human consumption, and it gave them great versatility in terms of what to eat and how to live. This versatility would explain why they had not bothered to develop major mutations in the new environment, other than a renewed ability to fly, something they had been unable to do in their domesticated form. Not even predators were a worry to them since once they had escaped into the wild. They were the most elusive animals to hunt. One seldom saw one, much less scored a kill, and when they were brought in, it was reason for much rejoicing among those able to have a share of its flesh. With luck, Morgan thought, he'd bag one today and present it to his grandfather.

Three groups of four hunters were quickly organized and the two penetrating columns entered the forest. The third busied itself with establishing blinds about a quarter of a mile in from the fields. Any closer and the animals would likely shy to one side of the trap or the other. The two groups worked their way into the forest silently, moving slowly and keeping to the shadows. Open glades were skirted, water courses crossed downstream from their hunting area or leaped across at the narrows to avoid their scent being carried downstream toward their prey.

As they went, they took note of obvious bedding spots for ruminants, which usually returned to the same area each night if there was no danger. These locations would become important targets for the next day when the hunters broke up into smaller two-or-three-person parties. Morg noted everything, constantly cataloging likely hunting fields and escape routes for both the animals and him. There were, after all, still dangerous animals out here if one was not careful. There were feral pigs and the native frumius to contend with, all claws and teeth. Even the lemaceous ground sloth could kill with a clean swipe of his clawed hands if disturbed.

By the time the sun was high overhead the two groups were ready. Morgan put his whistle to his mouth and gave a loud call. Another immediately answered from his right. The other group was closer than he would have preferred, but nothing could be done about that now. He followed up with two loud blasts on his whistle, was answered with two toots in return, and they all spread out, starting back toward the camp and all shouting or blowing their whistles.

Almost immediately animals broke cover in front of them. They were mostly smaller herbivores, though a family of three white-fang skip cats darted in front of them, cutting across their path and disappearing into a thicket of crystalline brush. The hunters ignored them. At a distance of perhaps one hundred yards they spotted a group of deer bounding through low brush and out into a glade, that they traversed in short order, then disappearing into the wood beyond. Morg smiled. They were headed directly into the path of the waiting ambush. If we get those four alone it will be a good days hunt.
Cries erupted from the right and the cry of a ground sloth apparently in the last throes of death.

The other group had made a kill. It would be a long haul back to camp from here, but that much meat made it worth it. In his mind's eye he could see Paul's group arguing over which two of them were going to remain behind to dress and carry the sloth and which two were going to continue driving game before them. Knowing Paul, he'd settle any arguments quickly.

They continued on, hearing splashes from the creek as they approached. The animals were close now and beginning to bunch up. In another half mile or so, they'd be at the sight of the ambush and the killing would begin in earnest.

"Safeties off," he said, and began blowing his whistle again. They were all blowing more insistently now. The game was on and their blood was up. There would be a great slaughter and he could feel it. They pressed forward at as fast a pace as the terrain would allow.

Ahead they heard the shouts of the third group of hunters as they began the harvest. Two of Morg's group broke into a run, and though it was against his judgment, he and his third companion joined them. Soon they were running among tall trees free of underbrush and making good time. Paul and a companion came into view to their right and lined up with them, pressing forward. They could see bushes swaying no more than fifty yards ahead as terrified animals ran before them. A single shot ran out as Paul dropped a deer. He whooped and kept running. There would be time later to come back for the carcass. For now, the important thing was to keep these animals on the run.

The cries of animals rang out just ahead of them through the trees. They were very near. The six remaining runners crouched and moved off to the left and right to avoid being shot by their own companions. They'd have the animals in a crossfire as soon as they passed this final cover of trees, and the hunt would turn to butchery. Morg was panting now, more from the excitement than from the running, and as he broke cover, he found himself in a small field with perhaps thirty animals milling about while another ten lay still on the ground. He was astounded. Never had he heard of such a hunt in all the history of the colony. This one would be spoken of for years to come. Systematically, they chose the healthiest and largest animals from among those in the field. Small animals were allowed to escape, animals that normally a hunter would have bagged for his family's evening meal. The larger ones who were obviously old or too young to be taken were allowed to escape as well.

In the end, they downed another eight, including the three remaining deer that they had seen earlier. By the time it was over, some eighteen large game animals lay dead, awaiting cleaning. Seven deer and four ground sloth topped the list, along with three geese that never had the opportunity to take flight and a feral pig, his tusks glistening in the late morning light. The hunters were all stunned. They stood silently, panting, grunting and looking over the killing field. Several laughed maniacally.

Morg broke himself free of his hysteria and took a critical look around. "All right," he shouted, "That's it. Let's start dressing these animals down. Clint, go back to the village and see if you can get some people out here to help us. We'll never get all this meat back by ourselves.

While you're there, tell Yetti what's happened. She'll need to get ready."

Morg smiled internally. Just listen to him. He was barking orders like a true leader. He knew what he was talking about, and no one was arguing the case. He had come of age this morning and was going to make a good leader some day. As an afterthought he looked over at Paul.

"Paul, how far back are those other two and what did they bag? It sounded like a ground sloth."

"Just a boar, Morg, but a really big one."

"Do they need help?"

"I don't think so. They should be up with us about the time we finish butchering here."

Morg nodded, pulled the sheath knife from his belt and pinched the belly fur of the nearest deer, making a perfect incision and slitting the hide up toward the neck. He wished he could string the animal up so that the entrails would simply fall out when severed, but in this field, what he was doing would have to do. He licked the edge of the knife after he'd finished the first cut, then slit the skin in the opposite direction, avoiding and tying off the anus. In moments, the deer had been gutted.

Nearly half an hour passed before the villagers arrived to help with the transport of the carcasses. By that time they had all been gutted and cleaned and the two hunters claiming their first kill had each drunk a cup of their trophy's blood. It was a good day and an incredibly good hunt. Morgan looked around in satisfaction as the animals were tied onto poles and hefted on the shoulders of hunters and villagers alike, ready for transport. At length, he looked over toward the deep wood.

"Paul," he called. "Where are your hunters? They're still out there."

Paul looked up from tying the legs of the last deer to a long pole. He peered toward the wood.

"They should be back by now," he said.

"Who are they?"

"McCallum and VanHoorse"

Morg thought for a moment. They were both experienced hunters and there was nothing to worry about. On the other hand, they should be here by now. If they'd killed a boar, were there others? They could be dangerous.

"Can you handle things here?" he asked.

"If you're going after them, I'm coming. Alan can take over here."

Morg nodded and they gathered their rifles. Paul picked up a twenty-foot length of rope in case it was needed for the carcass and they reentered the forest.

"I think it was right about here," Paul said fifteen minutes into the hike. "I think they were over there in a clearing."

The two of them brought their rifles to the ready and released the safeties, checking the charge to be sure there was enough pressure in the cylinder to do the job, the veered off in the direction that Paul had indicated. They made their way through a small thicket of crystalline bushes and through a small cluster of tall, thin trees to the clearing. No one was about.

"Already gone," Morg said.

"No tracks," Paul noted and looked around more carefully. The only evidence of anyone having been there was a bloodstained depression in the feather grass and two thin trails leading off toward the deep wood.

"I don't like it," Morg said at last.

"So what do we do?"

"Follow those trails?" asked Morg.

Paul nodded. They headed for the deep wood, carefully picking their way through the underbrush and doing their best to avoid the clear, sparkling fronds of Spangler brush as they did so. Enough encounters with the fragile silica structures and even their protective clothing could give way, leaving nasty hairline cuts on their arms and legs. They moved silently, scanning left and right and trying to get some sense of the destination of the meandering cuts through the forest. Periodically they came across another bloodstain, usually small and spread against some green foliage or the scales of a tree.

Half a mile further in, they found themselves on the edge of another clearing, looking at the horror of what had taken place here. The half-eaten carcass of the boar lay more or less in the center of the grassy space and near it, the upper torso of VanHoorse. There was no sign of McCallum.

"Dear Universe," Paul said in a whisper, and turned aside to retch. Morg on the other hand, was surprised to find his blood up. He was ready for a fight now. Whoever or whatever had done this was going to die. He brought his rifle to his shoulder and aimed into the brush, sweeping left and right, looking for some target. He could see nothing.

"They're gone," said a voice from above him. He whipped his weapon around and pointed it in the direction of the sound. On a limb above his head sat George McCallum, his right arm a mass of bloodstains and torn flesh, his left clutching his rifle. He looked down at Morgan with dull, half-opened eyes.

"Don't do that!" Morg said uselessly. "I could have shot you!"

McCallum smiled weakly. "I'll remember that if I'm ever in this situation again. Could I get some help here?"

Between the two of them they were able to ease George McCallum out of the tree and propped him up against its trunk. He smelled of blood, sweat and something vaguely soporific. While Paul inspected his arm, Morg scanned the trees for any movement. There was none.

"What the hell happened here?" Paul asked at last.

"I'm...not sure. We were attacked. We'd just finished gutting the boar when something came at us out of the forest. There were two of them. One grabbed the boar and the other grabbed Richard. They were so fast that I didn't even have time to reach for my rifle. They simply picked them both up and ran into the trees. Richard was screaming bloody awful and then stopped. I couldn't have stood there more than a minute and then followed on the run."

"And they led you here?"

McCallum nodded. "I caught up with them here. I was making so much noise that they had to hear me. I don't even think they cared. When I broke cover, they looked around and the nearest one lunged for me."

Paul nodded at the arm. "Is that when this happened?"

McCallum nodded. He refused to look at his ruined arm. "It missed the bone, which probably saved my life. It just took a chunk of flesh and ripped it out. I don't even know how I got up in the tree. Just instinct, I guess. Anyway, by the time I got up here, the one that attacked me was on the way up the trunk after me and I just pointed the rifle and fired. Its head exploded."

Morg and Paul looked around.

"Don't bother. There's no body. A third one showed up and grabbed the body. It was eating the one I killed when I heard you coming. I suppose they decided that they'd had enough and the two of them dragged the third one off in that direction." He nodded in the direction that the trail of broken brush indicated.

"Great Universe, George! What were they?" cried Paul.

"I don't know. They're not like anything I've ever seen. They're about twice the size of the boar and have a tail as long as their bodies. I just sat here, watching them eat and wanting to do something, but I was out of caps. I was trying to figure out if they were going to come after me once they finished everything else when you two showed up. They just took off."

Morgan looked at the half-eaten bodies. "We've got to get out of here. They could come back any time."

"I was thinking the same thing," Paul added. "No wonder the game is bunching up close to the settlement. They must be trying to get away from those things."

"I'm going to lose my arm, aren't I?" asked George McCallum.

They looked at him. "I'm pretty sure of it," Morg said.

George McCallum smiled weakly. "Not so bad," he said. "I'm left-handed anyway."

"You'll need to be taken to the town. There's no one in the village that can deal with this. They need to know about what happened here, too."

Paul shook his head. "Your grandfather's not going to like that, Morg. You know how he feels about the colony."

"Can't be helped. I'll deal with my grandfather. George's going to lose his arm as it is. We don't want him to lose his life too."

They gathered him up between the two of them. They took turns carrying him over their shoulders, one carrying while the other kept watch. George's arm swung uselessly as they moved, which kept most of the smaller insects from nesting in the open wound, and they stopped several times to loosen the tourniquet just enough to save as much of the arm as possible. What concerned them more was the rapid deterioration of the wound itself. It was already beginning to smell of corruption. Whatever had made that cut must have had a terribly foul mouth. None of them could remember anything rotting that quickly. Blessedly, within half a mile, George McCallum had gone unconscious, either from shock or from loss of blood.

As usual, Morgan Culhane was busily poring over the plans for the new village, checking the progress that he could see from his vantage point on the platform and comparing it with what must be done before the winds came. Time was getting short, and thought they had made good progress since coming here, he was beginning to wonder if perhaps they had not been too optimistic about what could be accomplished in one short summer. True, once the houses were up they could continue working indoors, even in the midst of the howling winds, but after that there would be the long four months of winter, with bitterly cold temperatures and the isolation, with only a few hours each day when they dare emerge from their homes to gather fuel and proceed with necessary chores. If they did not gather in enough supplies in time, the entire enterprise was in danger.

It was close to noon and the sun had been up for almost eight hours. Most of the people were taking rest and food after the long morning. Other than cooking fires and the gathering of the villagers at the tables, Morgan expected little movement in the village. It was a warm day, though the heat was not particularly oppressive. Another eight hours lay before them before the day ended, and he had insisted on at least a two-hour rest at midday. He was sure that if he'd not forced the issue that many of these people would have worked until they dropped, and it was for this reason that the scurry of activity to the west at the edge of the fields concerned him.

"Olivia," he said pointing at the knot of villagers in the distance, "What's the commotion there? I can't make it out."

Olivia looked up from her own work, designing the irrigation system that would be needed in the spring. "What's the problem, old man? Your eyes failing you?"

She stood and shaded her eyes from the overhead sun, peering squint eyed at the group.

"It's your grandson, I think, back from the hunt. He's with a group of field workers and they seem to be carrying something."

"A prize kill, no doubt," Morgan, said, returning to his charts.

"I don't think so. It looks like a man."

Morgan swung around and looked more closely. He could see more clearly now that they were indeed carrying a hunter, two field workers on each side of him, and they were hurrying toward Yetti's butchering tables and the medical tent next to it.

Morgan left the platform, Olivia having already broken into a trot, moving toward the tents. They made their way quickly, arriving at what served as the hospital area at about the same time as those carrying the unfortunate hunter. Yetti was already there along with three others, all older women known for their healing skills. As they converged, Yetti began barking orders.

"Put him on the table here. We'll need hot water and bandages, and some gut and needle. Heat an iron as well. We'll have to cauterize that wound."

Morgan could clearly see the ruined arm dangling limply as they hefted George McCallum onto the table. It pained him to see the poor boy, ashen and contorted in pain. He knew his father well and remembered their bitter parting when George decided to go with the separatists to found the new village. George's father had made Morgan swear to look after his son. At the moment, he didn't seem to have done a very good job of it.

Yetti examined the arm, shaking her head and making guttural sounds of distress. She peeled back his eyelids, felt his pulse and set the back of her hand across his forehead.

"How long ago did this happen?" she asked.

"About an hour," Morg said.

Yetti looked at him in shock. "And he's already this deep into infection?"

Morg nodded.

"The arm comes off," she said flatly, looking at the other healers. "There's no time for anything else, and if that infection spreads, he'll be dead in a few hours. Olivia, get these people out of here. We don't need an audience. Morgan, take your grandson somewhere and find out what happened."

The other women nodded agreement and began to prepare for the procedure. If it hadn't been for the circumstances, Morg would have been amused at the way Yetti ordered the leaders around and at the way they obeyed without comment. Olivia immediately began herding the onlookers away, sending them back to their tasks or rest.

Morgan signaled his grandson to follow him back to the platform. Morg followed without comment. When they arrived, Morgan sat him down and poured him a mug of brandied tea. He insisted Morg drink it all. "It'll settle you down a bit, boy. Now tell me what happened."

Morg explained all that had happened, how they had found the two hunters in the glen and how some unknown predator took VanHoorse. There was one dead and another might die and all in a morning. This was not a good situation.

"And you didn't see the creature that did it?"

"Just George, and I've told you all that he told me."

"Not good," Morgan said flatly, "Not good at all."

He was about to question his grandson further about the hunt and the accident when Olivia mounted the platform looking grave.

"Yetti says that if we don't get him back to the colony, he'll die. She's removed the arm and cauterized it, but he needs herbs we don't have here. He'll have to be taken back."

"Back to the colony," Morgan said sadly. "We all know what that means."

Olivia shook her head. "It can't be helped. If you're thinking this looks like an admission of failure on our part, then so be it. That boy's life is more important than your asinine pride, old man!"

Morg waited for the explosion of his grandfather's infamous temper, but it never came. He stood calmly, a slight smile crossing his face and he looked directly at Morg.

"It occurs to me that we may be able to work this to our advantage. Morg, you are going to lead the party that carries George back to the colony. Now don't look so shocked. It's not a foreign land, you know. You grew up there for most of your life. I want you to lead the party, and when you've delivered George to the healers, I have further instructions for you. Are you fresh enough to leave right away? I assume it's important that we take him right away?"

"The sooner the better," Olivia noted.

"I'm fresh enough. Besides, it'll take most of the day for the butchering and I don't want to waste my time on that."

"Good," Morgan said with finality. "Then come to my tent and I'll give you instructions. Olivia, would you please see to it that George is ready for the trip and that we have some litter bearers?"

"Done," she said without a hint of irritation. Rail as she might about having to take orders, when a job needed doing, she would still see to it.

It was a confused and anxious Morg who left an hour later, making his way to the east, toward the lake and the old colony beyond.

CHAPTER 12

T he past four days had been like high holidays back home. He could hardly believe his good fortune or the sights that he'd experienced since arriving on this new world. To think that they all said the colonies were a lost cause and that travel to the stars was impractical. Impractical indeed. He was here, wasn't he? He was here and he was doing quite well. After the initial shock of actually succeeding in his bizarre scheme subsided, he had gone about the business setting up housekeeping in his hidden chamber at the entrance to the transport machine, arranging his supplies meticulously and quartering the room into living, cooking, working and recreational space, much as was his habit on Earth.

Once that was done, he had begun his observations. Heavy optical binoculars were used for observing the colonists at work, which was not his favorite technique, but the power drain and size of more sophisticated equipment had ruled out their use from the beginning. Actually, he enjoyed the almost conspiratorial feeling of spying offered by the heavy instrument, scanning the scene in the distance until he decided to fix on some individual or group of individuals and study them more closely. To his surprise, they seemed quite organized and extremely industrious in a manner similar to an agricultural community of the mid-to-late nineteenth century, C.E. Of course there were some signs of sophistication, including occasional solar powered spotlights in the larger town, but most of the activity was of a more primitive nature, employing hand tools, beasts of burden, and handicrafts rather than industry. The one exception was a single installation near the smelter that apparently re-purposed iron and steel, fashioning it into various weapons and implements. He made a mental note to check on the list of modern equipment that had arrived with the original settlers centuries before. Of course, the observers would have such a list, but that particular source of information was quite out of the question. In spite of these apparent technological shortcomings, the colony appeared quite prosperous.

He had also busied himself with observations of the local fauna and flora, following their movements and recording their behavior patterns and as much of their life processes as he could. After only a few days he was beginning to separate the herbivores from the predators and the carbon life feeders from the more delicate silica feeders. There were shadowy creatures in the stream near the bridge that still baffled him as did the tangles and thickets of sparkling crystalline plant-like structures on the edge of the wood, but all in all, he felt he was making real progress.

In the back of his mind, he began to formulate how best to undertake closer observations if possible. Though he was not yet fully aware of it, he was beginning to formulate other more permanent plans for himself in this world, plans that went far beyond the simple study of an isolated society on another world.

He wrote in his journal:

Day four: I've not ventured out of my observation site yet, contenting myself with viewing the subject populations at a distance. From here, I have observed little but what I would expect from a settlement bereft of modern equipment as it attempts to survive in a primitive environment. The colony seems to have fared rather well under the circumstances. They appear to be an industrious and well-organized people who have adapted to the conditions here in only a limited number of generations. Evidence of a second settlement on the far side of the lake speaks well of their breeding practices and the accompanying need for expansion. Apparently, profundity is not an issue, either in the humans or in the animals. I have observed both agriculture and hunting taking place, though from here it is difficult to be sure of the methods and types of foodstuffs that they rely on. Several of what appear to be domestic herd animals are baffling to me, presumably of local origin. I do know that they bake bread, that the power plant and smelter are capable of limited output, and that they appear to have no advanced means of communications. I have been careful to avoid detection by either the colonists or other observers and this necessity has hindered my research mightily. In the last few days I have noted an increase in activity, however, that I find puzzling. There is a great deal of building taking place in the second town, as if they have stepped up their construction efforts for some reason. This may be a seasonal consideration. Additionally, I have noted a number of the inhabitants of the larger and older town preparing for some type of activity at the edge of the wood to the east (as I reckon the local geography to be) of the lake. Whether it is agricultural, religious or cultural I cannot tell. I plan to venture closer tomorrow morning to see what I can discover.

When Caleb arrived at the Keeper's compound, he found Chandy dozing on a poyo outside the enclosure. The town was coming to life now, but still there was no one else in the plaza, and as Caleb crossed, his footsteps echoed more loudly than he would have liked. He was busy thinking about the last night's encounter and was not paying attention to any thoughts of hunter's stealth. As a result, he was more than thirty feet from Chandy when the sound of his footfalls awoke the nodding boy.

"That's no way for a hunter to walk," Chandy offered not even bothering to open his eyes.

Caleb ignored the comment.

"What are you doing here so early, Chandy?"

Chandy looked up and smiled faintly. Stretching out his legs in front of him, he nearly slid off the hard stone bench and stretched out his arms. He made a growling sound that signaled the pleasure of the stretch and then sat up. "The Keeper said I was to take his granddaughter to the jayberry picking today.

Caleb looked at him carefully, trying to decide if he were joking or telling the truth. For his part, Chandy broke into a wide grin.

"You're serious," Caleb said.

"Absolutely," Chandy said with a great deal of self-satisfaction. "Its rough duty, you know, but it has to be done."

"How the hell did you maneuver that one?"

"Darned if I know, Caleb. He just told me to do it. The stupid thing is that I almost protested."

Caleb smiled and nodded. "Sounds to me like our Keeper is trying to do a little maneuvering of his own."

Chandy continued to grin. "I hope so, I do. And that's all good, but what are you doing here this time of the morning? I would have thought you'd be at my house looking for my sister."

"Hmm. That's later, which reminds me. The fact that you're taking Jillian to the jayberry picking doesn't explain why you're here now".

"Oh. That. Well, the Keeper asked me to come by early this morning and talk about the plans for the colony. I don't know what that means, but that's what he said. I'm not sure what I could say that would be useful, but the Keeper says jump and I ask in what direction. Now how about you? Why are you here?"

"Well," Caleb hesitated, "Right now I need to talk to the Keeper about something else."

Chandy's expression deepened. "What's up?"

Caleb told him about the encounter with the apparition the night before. He explained that it bothered him enough to want to discuss it with the Keeper, but failed to mention that he was also curious about Chandy's father and his changing nature. That was hardly the kind of thing he wanted to discuss with his young apprentice. When he finished, Chandy became quite excited. Once he understood that this was not one of the beasts, he smelled mystery and adventure, and he had hundreds of questions about what the shadowy figure in the night was like.

"How big was he? How much do you think he weighed? How fast did he run? Did he really jump to the top of the wall? Why didn't anyone else see him? You say he made no noise?" The questions poured out of him like a river, exciting his imagination. Caleb saw a gleam of hunter's anticipation in the boy's eyes. It was a pity that he wouldn't have time to become the hunter he could be. In time, he'd be the best the colony ever had, but his path led him elsewhere. Caleb felt a twinge of sadness about that, wondering if perhaps the separatists weren't right in choosing their own destiny in spite of the order offered here. That such thoughts were antisocial didn't bother him. He was committed to the success of the colony and that was all he need remember.

The crowds of people were stirring now. As usual, they moved through the square in clumps, gathering as they usually did to greet, meet and discuss the coming day or share bits of gossip about the goings-on in the colony. Many of them stared openly at Chandy and Caleb as they passed. Chandy and Caleb overheard snippets of conversation, making it obvious to both of them that their adventures looking for the Kellers had become a prize topic of conversation, made all the more so by the lack of specifics about what had happened. They looked at each other in shared discomfort.

"Feel conspicuous?" said Caleb.

"Like I'm on display. I bet if I yelled 'boo!' at one of these people they'd run like skitters."

They both laughed at the thought, but it did little to relieve their angst.

"Heard the news?" a passerby asked genuinely.

Caleb looked up and recognized a neighbor from his street.

"What's that?" he asked.

"There was a theft last night. Can you believe it? Somebody actually stole something from one of your neighbors, Chandy."

The boy frowned. "Are you sure?"

The man facing them, whose name Caleb could not recall at the moment, was obviously pleased to be the first to share this particular bit of news with the hunters. He looked down at them, dramatically grave, frowning and puffing up like a strutting turkey. "Oh, yes. Everyone's talking about it. Someone sneaked into the Shea storehouse and made off with a large cheese and some jayberry wine. He took a fresh pan of buns as well."

Caleb and Chandy looked at each other having obviously reached the same conclusion.

"Any idea who did it?" asked Chandy.

"No one seems to know. No one heard or saw anything last night at all, er, except for Lucy Green who said she saw you, Caleb, walking the streets after the moons were down."

Caleb nodded. "I was coming back late from dinner with the Crones." The man looked both startled and delighted. No one visited Donald Crone's house, at least not in recent years. This was better gossip than the theft.

"Is that right?" he said. "Well now. How is your father, Chandler?"

"He's well," Chandy said, avoiding the subject as best he could.

The neighbor gave them an oily smile. "Well that's fine, Chandler. That's just fine. And what brings you two here this morning? Shouldn't you be getting ready for the picking or something?"

Caleb stood. "We're here to see the Keeper at his request. Perhaps you'd like us to give you a full report so you can announce the details to the whole town?"

"Well, no. I mean...now just a minute. I'm just trying to be friendly, you know. Just passing the time of day. There's no need to be rude."

"Something you'd do well to remember," Caleb said deliberately. The man turned and left, mumbling to himself. He had barely crossed the plaza when he spied someone he knew and struck up conversation with her as well.

"Who is that anyway?" asked Chandy.

"Just some gossip. I don't remember his name."

"Well, he's a glasseater if ever I saw one."

"You know this for a fact or is it just gossip? Can I tell others?"

Chandy looked over at his companion still frowning, then laughed.

"I got the point," he said.

It was another quarter of an hour before the gates to the Keeper's compound swung open and Jillian appeared. She was radiant as usual, her pale green tunic and matching tights fitting her in the mysterious way of being modest and provocative at the same time. Chandy was obviously enthralled immediately, and Caleb had to admit that in spite of his attraction to Kylie, he could see how Chandy had come to regard this girl as his ideal. She smiled at them gently, her eyes resting for a long moment on Chandy's, then gestured for them to come with her. They started to follow her but she slowed until they flanked her and the three of them crossed the courtyard. Pointedly, she positioned herself so that only she and Chandy could ascend the narrow staircase together while Caleb would have to follow behind. As they climbed the stairs, she steadied herself on Chandy's arm, which was clearly a gesture rather than a necessity.

"Thank you for taking me to the jayberry picking today, Chandy. You're most kind," she said.

"Um, all my pleasure, Jillian, and I mean that."

"Of course," she said rather demurely.

Caleb had to admit that she was very good at the game, even for her age. She had Chandy's heart as surely as Kylie had his own, and she knew it. He was beginning to wonder whose idea this pairing was, the Keeper's or hers. In the main room, she left them without a word and, as if on cue, the Keeper appeared from below. He nodded to both of them but seemed surprised to see Caleb.

"I didn't expect both of you," he said.

"I'm sorry, Keeper, but I need to speak to you about something that happened last night. If it's inconvenient, I can come back."

"No, no. It's all right. I was just surprised. Come and sit. I'm sure Jillian will be back momentarily with tea."

He ushered them to the large central table and settled in with them. Caleb noticed that the Keeper's joints were stiff as he sat and he uttered a satisfying groan at having gotten off his feet and he said, "I'm getting old, my young friends. It's good to know there's someone to take up where I leave off, as far off as I intend that to be. Now then, what did you want to see me about, Caleb?"

Caleb repeated the story he had told Chandy, who could hardly contain himself in his wish to interject information when Caleb skipped over some point or detail. Patiently, the Keeper listened without comment and without expression. He sat quietly for some minutes thinking and sipping the piping hot tea, which had appeared in the middle Caleb's story and which was the only thing that distracted Chandy from the telling of the tale. Finally, the Keeper took a deep breath, sat forward in his chair to rest his elbows on the table, still holding the tea.

"Many strange happenings," he said almost to himself. "This is definitely not business as usual. First the tuskers reappear and then this shadowy figure. From what you've said, I think we can safely conclude that it was he who stole the bread and cheese last night. Had it not been for the taking of the wine, I'd have suspected an animal, but animals do not steal wine. This was a man."

"One of the separatists?" asked Chandy.

Caleb and the Keeper both shook their heads.

"Do you know anyone in the separatists' village that can jump a twelve foot wall? No, this is something different. I'll have to think on this for a while. Do you think you can track him?"

Caleb nodded. "I may not be able to catch him, but following him shouldn't be too big a problem."

"Well, we'll deal with him or it in due course. For the moment, I've another task for the two of you. You're going back to the Tower."

"To the Tower?" said Chandy.

"Yes. I've relayed the information about the return of the plague to them and they've not seen fit to respond. We must impress upon them the urgency of the situation and that means someone has to go there and speak. I know it's taboo to go there, but you've practically gone that far already, and with luck, you won't run into any more of the beasts. If you do, I can't think of two hunters better qualified to deal with them."

"But...the Tower," said Chandy in a whisper.

The Keeper frowned. "They're not alien creatures, you know. They're human beings like us and from the Old World. The worst that can happen is that they refuse to talk. Just your presence may be enough to get them involved. This is very important. We must have their help to deal with this new threat. It must be done. You'll leave in the morning."

"In the morning?"

"In the morning, Chandler. You'll both go to the festival today. It's important that you be seen. Rumors are spreading about your trophy, I'm afraid. I don't think anyone knows yet, but we need the guise of normality for the moment. People are going to find out soon enough. For the moment, we need to ease their minds."

"Well, if we must, I suppose we must," Chandy said grinning.

The Keeper hid his amusement in his tea.

For the next several hours, they enjoyed a light breakfast, something that Caleb had not anticipated, and talked of anything and everything that did not deal with their problems. Jillian had already prepared sweet rolls and butter, flavored with the cinnamon spice that grew locally in the ferns, and a mulled tea with just a hint of jayberry wine. The four of them ate together. Chandy became more relaxed with Jillian as the meal wore on, and he helped her clear away the platters and bowls when they had finished. The Keeper drafted Caleb into a game of chess, one of the amusements brought from the Old World, and with a gentle summer breeze rising from the vents of the lower level; it was a thoroughly pleasant time. Finally, about three hours after dawn, they began to prepare for the festival and Caleb left to fetch Kylie, promising to meet the three of them in the fields.

He made his way deliberately back to Kylie's house, buoyed by the morning's relaxed atmosphere and the pleasant breakfast with the Keeper, et al. He wondered in passing about how he would find Kylie's father to be today and why he had not found a way to broach the subject of the man with the Keeper when he had the chance. Perhaps he didn't want to know, or was afraid to discover some dark hidden secret. Considering Chandy and Kylie's personalities, he decided that it was just abject fantasy to imagine anything other than what he had found the man to be, that is, a very pleasant, though sad, man who still grieves for his absent wife and daughter, and who loves his children. When he arrived, however, he found Kylie waiting for him at the foot of the stairs to her house.

She was dressed much as Jillian was today, wearing a bright yellow tunic and dark tights, nearly the color of fall leaves. They showed off her long slender legs to perfection. She wore soft leather boots that tied around her ankles and lower calf, and there were two of the conical hats that doubled as carriers slung beneath her arm. Caleb had never seen her figure so provocatively displayed and it brought a stirring in him that was both disconcerting and wonderful. In that moment, he wanted her to change so that only he would realize what a perfect woman she was. Yet what detracted from the perfection of her appearance was the look of worry on her face. She brightened slightly when she saw him and forced a smile but the concern still remained.

"Good morning," he said. "Looking for somebody to pick berries with?"

"Thanks, no. My lover is coming to get me."

Caleb winced. "Someone is going to believe you when you say that, you know. We're not lovers."

Kylie giggled and handed him one of the conical hats.

"I hope you don't expect me to wear this thing. It's bad enough carrying one around."

"Don't be silly. That's for the berries and you know it. Besides, it would never fit that big head of yours. I brought us some lunch as well." With that, she reached behind her and produced a wicker basket, which she also handed to Caleb.

"I thought they were going to feed us lunch at the picking."

Kylie smiled a bit too demurely, looking up at him from a slightly bowed head. "That's if we eat with everyone else, isn't it?"

Caleb gave a wry smile in return and cocked an eyebrow. "It's going to be a good day, isn't it?"

"I hope so."

"Is your father in? I wanted to say hello."
She frowned. "I don't think that would be a good idea, Caleb. He's in one of his dark moods, I'm afraid. Let's just go."

"Anything...you want to talk about?"

She shook her head and took his free hand. "Let's go, mister Master of the Hunt."

"I'm not Master of the Hunt," he said.

"No, but you probably will be. Now let's go."

They made their way toward the town gates, mingling with larger and larger crowds of people on their way to the festival. Everyone was smiling and in a joyous mood, and no one seemed to notice the chiefs and other clan leaders carrying rifles slung over their shoulders. They carried them casually, but there was little doubt in his mind that this was not just some simple gesture in hopes of bagging an unexpected dinner in the bush. Besides, they were already well-stocked for the winter with much preserved food and other stores. So many casual hunters could not really be casual. Caleb berated himself for not thinking to bring his own.

When they reached the fields, they could see the ring of brightly-colored jayberry bushes, all in full glory and covered with berries so thickly that only their amber fruit could be seen. They had only a week to gather the fruit before the overripe berries turned to seed, and the competition to pick them was great. Those who knew nature always chose the date to pick the fruit. A few days earlier and they would be sour and bitter-tasting. Three or four days later, the fruit would be overly ripe and ready for the jack darts to swarm. Today it was the colony's turn to pick, and pick they would.

Long slabs on triangular supports were already being readied for the noon meal and the older women were scurrying about preparing huge cauldrons for cooking or laying out delicate cakes and pastries made for the occasion. Though no official contests existed at the festival, everyone knew that there was an unspoken competition among the matrons as to who would produce the finest-tasting pastries. Caleb's own mother had been the acknowledged winner several times. They walked purposefully toward the bushes to the left, knowing full well that this is where the foliage would be deepest just inside the forest and therefore afford them the most privacy, which was also the unspoken purpose of young couples today.

Younger children were already scurrying among the bushes, skinning the lower branches as quickly as they could and eating as many berries as they picked. Their yellowish lips and chins dripping with juice gave evidence of their enthusiasm and Caleb thought of the stomachaches and loose bowels that would plague many of them tonight. It was all part of the fun, he thought. It was all part of the experience. In a few days, the young boys would be bragging and arguing about who picked the most, ate the most, and whose stomachache was the most severe. Kylie spotted her brother and Jillian and suggested that they join them, promising to make the encounter only brief enough for propriety before sneaking away into the forest. As they angled toward them, Caleb spotted his father coming toward them and waved. Jonathan walked casually their way, carrying two rifles slung over his shoulder and third one in his left hand. He looked like an arsenal and very much out of place in this setting. When he reached them, he greeted Kylie with a huge smile and made some offhand comment about the festival. Then he pulled the two rifles from his shoulder and handed them to Caleb.

"You and Chandy both forgot your rifles," he said meaningfully. "You never know when you'll have an opportunity to bag some meat, even here."

Caleb took them and nodded, accepting his father's unspoken chiding for being so thoughtless.

Then the Master of the Hunt nodded again to Kylie with a smile and was off.

Kylie looked after him, puzzled. "Now that was odd."

"Oh?" Caleb said casually.

"I mean, I know you're both hunters and good ones, but can't you forget it for just one day?"

Caleb shrugged and took her by the hand, again walking toward Chandy and Jillian.

"That's just my father," he said. "He's just that way."

Kylie studied his face and said nothing.

When they joined Chandy and Jillian, Caleb handed one of the rifles to Chandy.

"What's this?"

"It's a rifle,"

"Well I know that, Caleb, but what's it for?"

"In case we see something interesting. You know, something for the larder. You never can tell what you'll run into in the woods."

Chandy got the message. "Um, yeah. I hadn't thought of that. Thank your dad for me."

"Thank him yourself when you see him," Caleb said. "You'll be returning the rifle tomorrow, I imagine."

Kylie eyed the two of them but did not pursue the subject. Instead she said, "Let's get to picking."

Chandy and I are expected to bring home enough for the year, you know." With that they were off.

They gathered jayberries for nearly three hours, returning to the tables several times to deposit their harvest into larger containers to be taken home at the end of the day. It was a glorious day for the festival with bright skies that sported only fleeting wisps of high clouds and a cooling breeze to mollify the effects of the summer sun. Music could be heard everywhere, either from clusters of children singing chants only sung at the festival or from flutes and bagpipes played by musicians who practiced all year for the opportunity to show their skill on occasions like this one.

Everyone was in motion, flowing back and forth from the harvest to the tables like waves crashing on the seashore and receding only to return again. On the last trip Kylie picked up the wicker basket and gave Caleb a knowing smile. They skirted around a cluster of completely picked bushes and walked deeper into the woods. One of the advantages of being a hunter became immediately clear as Caleb led Kylie. They moved along an almost invisible trail to a small clearing beside a creek some quarter mile from the edge of the fields. They were deep in the wood, much deeper than anyone else would think to come, and the isolation was not lost on Kylie.

No sooner had they arrived than she took the basket from Caleb's hands and set it beneath a tree, then turned and kissed him long and deeply. He pulled the rifle from his arm and propped it against the same tree and then pulled her to him. Together they lay on the soft carpet of fresh, young feather grass, still supple in its immaturity. She pushed him back and slipped one leg over his, curling up against him and kissing him again. He rolled her onto her back and hovered above her, looking into her eyes. She smiled up at him and slipped the belt loose from her tunic. He knew he could deny this woman nothing. He leaned down, kissed her and they both gave in to the moment. For more than an hour they taught each other and learned from each other the exquisite pleasure of their love, gently yet urgently allowing their bodies to express themselves without restriction.

Caleb couldn't imagine anything so perfect ever existed and he thanked the Universe for this gift, given and received. At last, when they were both totally exhausted, they lay in each other's arms. The warmth of the sun shone on them through the opening in the canopy above the clearing. They lay silently, holding tightly to each other as if to let go would end a beautiful dream, and they listened to the sound of the small creek, gurgling and tinkling beside them. Finally, Kylie sat up and walked to the stream. Caleb followed her perfect naked body with his eye and wondered at its beauty. He decided that a woman's body was the most perfect expression of beauty on this or any other world. Nothing could be more graceful or lovelier to behold.

Kylie hunkered down beside the stream and looked over her shoulder at him, "Would you hand me that cloth in the basket," she said shyly.

"Sure," he answered and picked up the cloth. He brought it to her, starting to sit beside her, but her look said that she needed privacy. He turned and sat beneath the tree.

"How do you feel?" She asked.

He grinned. "Like paradise just opened up for me. How do you feel?"

"Like a woman. It feels wonderful, thank you very much, but I'm a bit sore."

"I...did I hurt you?"

"No, my love. It's expected the first time."

"Oh," Caleb said. He suddenly realized that the thought had never crossed his mind. He didn't know if Kylie was a virgin or not, and it didn't matter. He knew she was his and that was all that mattered. So it had been the first time for both of them.

"I'm glad it was you," she said.

"I'm glad it was you," he said in return.

She looked him again over her shoulder and tears filled her eyes.

"What?" he said, wondering what he'd done wrong.

"Its okay, Caleb. It's just so perfect. It makes me cry with joy."

He leaned back again and absently stroked the feather grass, straining it through his fingers and feeling its softness as if for the first time.

"Yeah," he said. "I know what you mean.

They spent a long time dressing, each watching the other with appreciation. At first self-conscious, Caleb soon discovered that he enjoyed her watching him, as if to say there's nothing to hide from you. I want to know all about me. She seemed to have the same feeling and dressed with a surprising grace and ease. He felt himself stirring, which brought giggles from Kylie, who just continued to dress, but she obviously appreciated his attention to her. When they had finished, they gathered their things and started back toward the fields. Between them they decided to pick at least a few more berries in hopes of camouflaging their absence, and Caleb led her to a cluster of untouched bushes that no one would have found unless they traveled these woods. They quickly filled the conical hats and much of the wicker basket and were back among the others in no time. Each looked around for Chandy and Jillian but to no avail. Apparently they were not the only ones to go berry picking in the deep woods this day.

By mid afternoon the colony had picked enough for the winter, for an abundance of wine and for well into next year. At the insistence of the keeper they picked enough for the separatists as well, either for their use if they came back or for trade if they were successful in their new village. It even occurred to Caleb that there would be enough for making some of that distilled wine that Donald Crone had offered him. What had he called it? Cognac? A peculiar name but delicious beyond compare. It had been a good day and that was all that need be said about that.

People were packing and loading the harvest into carts drawn by oxen, readying the bounty for transport back to the town. Several bonfires had sprung up and musicians were joining into groups around them to play together. People were dancing, some in squares or circles, others individually. The children played games ranging from Crack the Whip to Tag, games so old that their origins were lost in the mists of time. The hunter sat for a long time on one of the makeshift tables, his love by his side, and soaked in the day. He reminded himself that there might not be many more like this one in their future unless they did something about the evil that lurked beyond the edge of the wood. For now, he was content.

"You know that we've broken the rules of our people, Caleb. Does that worry you?"

Caleb looked at Kylie with a mock frown. "What are you talking about, woman. We broke no rules."

"We've made love." She said seriously. "I mean to say, it doesn't bother me. I wanted it more than anything, but it is taboo for us to do that."

"Not so. We've done nothing against the taboo."

"Oh?"

"Hmm. As I understand it, a man is not to lay with anyone but the one he spends his life with, the mother of his children, his wife, and a woman is not to lay with anyone but the father of her children, the one with whom she spends her life, her husband. Isn't that right?"

"Well, yes, but..."

"Does this mean you don't intend to spend your life with me, Kylie?"

She grinned. A moment later, she frowned. "Caleb Grant, are you proposing?"

"Um, I think I did that in the woods."

She sat silently for a long moment, staring at the ground with a faint smile on her lips. At last she said "Okay. You certainly have changed a lot."

He laughed so loudly that those around them stopped to see what was happening. Kylie tried to shush him but to no avail.

"I think that's the first time I've ever seen you without much to say on a subject. I didn't know you were capable of such a thing. That's the kind of thing I'd do, not you."

"There's a great deal you don't know about me, Caleb Grant, including the extent of my temper, so just keep that in mind. This is a beautiful moment. Don't spoil it."

He took her hands in his and leaned over to kiss her. She hesitated for only a moment and then kissed him back.

"Well I guess that does it," she said. "Now you'll have to marry me."

CHAPTER 13

It was well after nightfall when Morg and those carrying George McCallum arrived at the colony. They moved hurriedly through the streets to the Keeper's compound and banged on the gate. After some moments they heard someone cross the courtyard, stop at the gate and slide back the bolt. When the door swung open, the Keeper stood there, peering out at them.

"Is that you Morgan?" he asked.

"It is," Morg said with as much dignity as he could muster.

"Well what is it?"

Morg swallowed. It galled him to ask for anyone's help, but to ask for the assistance of the Keeper was the ultimate degradation.

"We have an injured man here. It's more than we can handle. My grandfather told me to bring him here to see if your healers might be able to do something."

The keeper looked past Morg at the body on the stretcher. His eyes widened and pulled open the gate door.

"Bring him in. Send one of your people for his father and another for the healers. Do any of you remember where to find them?"

"I can get his father," one of them said.

"I know the house of the healers," said another.

"Good. Then get him inside," and as an afterthought, "You're welcome in this house."

Once inside, the litter was placed beside the table and the Keeper called Jillian to come and help.

She appeared almost immediately but hesitated on the stairs when she saw the scene below. Morg looked up at her and openly stared.

"Hello, Jillian," he said. "Remember me?"

"All too well, Morgan Culhane," she said coldly. She crossed to the litter and knelt beside the ashen George McCallum. Jillian felt for a pulse, then looked at his eyes as best she could in the dim light and then at the arm. "Grandfather, this man may die," she said. "I'll prepare some herbs and some tea, but I don't know. I'm not sure I can do anything for him."

Morg looked from her to the Keeper, who waved his hand at the young man dismissing his concern. "She's training to be a healer. She knows what she's saying, but don't worry. If we can do anything, we will. How did this happen?"

Morg briefly related the tale of how George McCallum came to be wounded. He filled in as much detail as he could, but had to admit he knew little about the tuskers that did the damage since he didn't actually see them. He noted the Keeper's lack of surprise at the news.

"You say this happened in the wood beyond your village?"

"Yes."

"Well, that's it. You and your separatists will have to come in. We can't protect you out there in a half-built village."

Morg almost laughed. "You're serious? You'll try anything to get us back here, won't you? Well we're not coming. We can defend ourselves very well. All we ask is that you tend to this man."

"You don't understand, my boy. This is not just a matter of the McCallum boy. It's much more serious than that. You need to understand the extent to which you and your friends are in danger. These beasts are mindless carnivores. They will attack anything that moves."

Morg's eyes narrowed as he studied the old man. "You have seen this before?" he asked.

"Just recently. You say you've never actually seen one. Well, I have the skull of one in the workroom below. Chandy Crone and Caleb Grant killed it three days ago."

"You knew about this and didn't send word?" Morg snapped.

The Keeper shook his head in agitation.

"The one they killed was over to the east by the Tower. It killed three members of the Keller clan and almost killed Caleb and Chandy as well. There were three of them and the skull is from the one they brought back as proof. We had no reason to believe that they had gotten as far as your village. This is bad news indeed."

"Well, I don't care. We're not coming in and that's all," Morg growled. It seemed to be the only thing that he heard the Keeper say.

"If you don't," the Keeper said, " you'll all be dead before winter."

Morg absorbed this. His worried look convinced the Keeper that he was finally getting through to the young man. Then Morg seemed to have a new thought.

"You say you want us to come in for the winter."

"Yes. You must!"

"And in the spring you expect us to stay?"

"In the spring you can do whatever you wish. I just don't want to see you all die at the hands of these things. If we don't work together to kill them now, we're all at risk. Don't you see that?"

"There may be a way," Morg said almost slyly. "My grandfather asked me to discuss another matter with you when I came. It may be that we can reach agreement on both issues, but we need to speak privately."

The Keeper didn't like the boy's attitude, but he decided that it wouldn't hurt to listen.

"First we take care of young McCallum here, then we'll talk. You and your friends can stay here tonight and if it's privacy you want, we can talk downstairs."

"Agreed," said Morg, smiling.

CHAPTER 14

"Wake up, Caleb."

"Mmphft," was all that Caleb could manage. He opened his eyes a bit and peered out into the dim light of predawn. Why was his father waking him up at this hour?

"Wha...what's going on?"

"It's morning. Time to go. There's tea and cakes on the table and your kit is packed. Be dressed in fifteen minutes, and don't forget where you're going. Be dressed for the trip."

Caleb rolled over and shook himself awake. His skin itched from not washing last night before crawling into bed. He and Kylie had waited as long as they could to part, and he could still taste her skin in his mouth. It was a delicious taste.

"I've gotta wash or I'll be red as a kettle fish by noon," he announced, but his father had already left the room. He rolled out of bed and started to fill his washtub but found it already three-quarters full of steaming water. Thankfully, he slid into the hot water and sat. If only he had more time. He could use a good soak right now, but a quick scrub would have to do. Five minutes for a bath and ten to dress didn't leave him much time to think, but he knew his father, and if Jonathan Grant said fifteen minutes, he meant it. Still, it was awfully early. Something must have happened in the night. Another visit from the shadow figure? Who knew? He scrubbed hard and fast, removing as much of Two Moon's glassy dust as he could, then slipped into his long undershirt and pants, both of the protective native cloth, then into a pullover sweater and pants of the same material but a larger weave. To this he added a leather tunic, cinched at the waist with a wide belt that held his knife scabbard. He slipped the knife into the scabbard, grabbed his hunting gloves and shoes and stepped out into the central room. His father was waiting for him, sitting at the table.

"Your kit is by the door. I'm giving you my new rifle and two extra gas cylinders. There are three extra boxes of caps beside the two you usually carry, and a length of rope. Here. Put on these heavy socks. There's no way to tell what you'll run into out there." With this, he tossed a pair of heavy woolen socks at his son and poured him steaming hot tea from the kettle.

"What's happened?" Asked Caleb.

"Morg Culhane arrived last night with an injured hunter. One of the tuskers got him yesterday. They're over on that side of the valley too. This could be worse than we imagined. The Keeper wants you two on the road now."

Caleb nodded, woofing down his breakfast of soft cakes and hot tea. He grabbed two extra cakes, one for his own lunch and one for Chandy's. It was going to be a long day.

"I'll get Chandy and be on my way," he said, thinking that he hoped Kylie was up this morning.

"No need. Chandy's been fetched. He'll meet you at the gate."

Caleb looked crestfallen. His father softened and offered a slight smile to his son. "I'm sorry, Caleb. You'll have to skip your goodbyes to Kylie. She'll still be here when you get back. Don't look so surprised. After that public display yesterday everybody in the town knows you two are as good as mated. It's not the first time that's happened at a picking."

Caleb felt he should be protesting, but instead he just grinned and nodded. Chandy was waiting at the gate. He was carrying one of the new rifles as well, and his kit was bulkier than usual.

"You know they've got me carrying five days of food in here? That's a lot of weight, Caleb," he said. "Don't they think we know how to hunt for our supper?"

Caleb helped him on with his backpack, then adjusted his own and signaled the gatekeeper to unlock the gates from above. "I have a feeling that they're thinking we won't have time to hunt, and besides, if we have to wait for the Tower to acknowledge us it may take a few extra days. It's a good idea. I'm carrying the same. I guess all that training is going to come in handy."

Chandy offered one of his wide grins. "Well if we see one of those things again you're going to have a very hard time keeping up with me at a dead run. I'll tell you that right now."

"We see one of those things and you'd better do your running up the nearest tree."

Chandy's grin disappeared. He turned and followed Caleb out the gate. Even in the predawn they found their way easily. Desolation was up and shining, for which they were thankful, but the fact that it was alone, and so soon after the two were in conjunction meant that a long period of dark nights was on the way. They'd be spending the last several nights of this journey in total darkness. It was an unnerving thought. With only the pinpoint lights of stars to go by, they both realized there would be no night travel then.

They skirted the lake and entered the fens as before, picking their way through the soft spongy mass of undergrowth and hoping that they didn't find any holes in the carpet that could soak their shoes or worse. It was still dark when they entered the swampy fens and that made their going very slow. By daybreak they had cleared the lowlands and were on the edge of forest.

"What time do you think they got us up today?" Chandy asked.

"About three, I think. I checked the stars when we left the town and it couldn't have been much past three thirty then."

"Too damn early," Chandy noted.

"Maybe. If the tuskers hunt by day and sleep by night, and that seems to be the case, it's not a bad idea though. We need to make good time today. It's going to be getting through the far edge of the forest that'll be tough."

By noon they were nearly as far as they had been at the end of the first day on their last trek, partially because they knew the way and partially because of their early departure. They rested at their old campsite and ate, deciding to shinny up the closer of two trees and rest for the two-hour noon break. Being in a hurry was one thing, but running themselves into a state of exhaustion in the noonday sun was another. No one kept watch. They each fell quickly to sleep, fully convinced that if anything disturbed their surroundings they would hear it and be quickly awake. Caleb was thankful that neither of them was known to snore. If a predator heard it, it would give the beast an edge. If either of them heard the other, they'd miss a good nap.

When Caleb did awaken, he came slowly out of his slumber. He stretched and looked around, then over at Chandy, still sleeping soundly. Using the sun as a gauge, he calculated that he was asleep for about one and a half hours, then he remembered that he had heard something. Carefully he reached for his rifle and chambered a cap. He pulled back on the small stud that delivered the gas charge to the reservoir and it did so silently. He lay motionless in the crook of the tree and listened. There was no sound now, yet there had been something. He was sure of that. He waited a good five minutes before finally jostling Chandy with his foot. The boy didn't move, but his eyes opened, fully alert. He looked at Caleb expectantly.

"I think we had a visitor," he mouthed silently.

"Still here?" Chandy mouthed back.

"Don't know. Just be alert. Is your weapon primed?"

He had to repeat this several times before Chandy could read all of it, but when he finally understood he nodded. He was sleeping with the weapon across his chest, his hand on the trigger guard. They stayed put and listened. Still no sound. Finally, after a full fifteen minutes of listening, Caleb signaled that he was going to drop to the ground. Chandy shifted to cover him as he did so, then followed while Caleb covered Chandy. A quick look around convinced them that there was nothing. Each picked up their gear and prepared for taking up the trek again.

"Hey," Chandy said. "Where's my sweet cake?"

"What sweet cake?"

"The one you brought me this morning. I was going to have it for desert."

"Hell I don't know. Where was it?"

"On top of my pack."

They looked around but found nothing.

"Well, if we did have a visitor they were very quiet and had very good taste. That's all I can say."

Chandy frowned. "But it got my sweet cake!"

"Be glad it didn't get you. We'd better be more careful. It looks like we're not alone."

For the next few hours they cautiously moved through the underbrush, taking their old trail where they could but avoiding any clearings that offered no immediate escape routes or climbable trees. At one point they came to a wide meadow that they had not seen on the last trip and skirted it rather than crossing it, a strategy that added nearly an hour to their travel time but afforded them more cover. On the far side, they stopped to rest and again climbed a nearby tree, this time taking their gear with them. It seemed like a great deal of trouble to go to for a fifteen-minute break, but the alternative seemed equally dangerous.

They had been sitting in the lower branches of the tree for only a few minutes when Chandy sat up straight and looked out over the meadow. Caleb followed his glance and watched the tall grass toward the far edge move purposefully. Something was crossing the meadow and it was moving quickly. After a moment, a second disturbance started, paralleling it and moving even more quickly. It was converging slowly on the first figure, angling to intercept it about midfield. They watched in fascination as the predator stalked its prey, but neither of these two were clearly the aggressor. Perhaps they'd learn something about how the beasts work, since the second figure moving through the grass was obviously the right size and speed for it. As the beast approached its prey, the first traveler stopped. Seconds later, the beast stopped as well. They sat in their tree transfixed by the drama playing out in front of them, though the only thing they could see were the paths cut through the grass by the two creatures. Finally there was a shift in the wind and the beast was able to calculate where its prey was. It turned suddenly and charged, leaping at the last moment and clearing the cover. It was one of the tuskers for sure, and it lunged, mouth open, yellow teeth bared and two huge clawed front legs outstretched. Caleb and Chandy hardly had time to notice this before the beast suddenly convulsed and fell back as if slammed by a great blow. It screeched as it fell and remained lifeless. The first figure barely hesitated before it resumed its journey, quickly crossing the field and disappearing into the wood.

Caleb and Chandy sat there with their mouths open.

"What the hell was that?" Chandy whispered.

"Damned if I know but I wouldn't want to meet it on a hunt. It moved like my shadow figure.

Maybe it's one of them."

"Well it's gone now. What do we do, Caleb?"

Caleb shrugged and jumped down from the tree. "We keep going, I guess."

By nightfall they were deep in the forest. As nearly as they could determine, they were to the north and beyond the point where they found the Keller camp but it was too dark to go further and no acceptable campsites lay behind them. With the last rays of the sun, they hoisted their packs up a large tree with long overhanging branches and limbs twice the size of a man's trunk.

Nestled into the crook of two strong limbs with their backs propped against the tree trunk, they covered themselves with their blankets, tied themselves to the limb with rope and called it a day.

As before, each slept with their weapons at the ready, the only difference being that the slings were secured to their bodies to prevent dropping them during the night. Bastion rose soon after half night. Alone it offered feeble light and was not truly illuminating until it had risen directly overhead four hours later. With another two or three hours until dawn, Caleb woke himself long enough to look around and satisfy himself that they were in no immediate danger, then slipped back to sleep. The rest of the night passed uneventfully. At dawn, they stirred and repeated the ritual of the previous day, sitting and listening for a good quarter hour before loosening their ropes and dropping to the ground. Nothing stirred other than the expected early morning sounds of the world coming to life. Once they had their bearings, they were off again.

Almost immediately they became aware of how close to the forest's edge they had been the night before. No more than a quarter mile further along they began to see blue skies beyond the trees and the further they went, the more the thick growth of evergreens and crystal trees gave way to clear skies. In an hour they found themselves on the far side of the eastern forest, further than anyone had been in recent memory.

Before them was a valley that Caleb estimated to be nearly three miles across and stretching north and south for what seemed forever. Beyond that lay the wall of cliffs and mountains that marked the edge of their part of this world. The cliffs rose majestically toward snow covered peaks or flat craggy mesas that must be a mile or more above them. Caleb and Chandy stopped for a while and just stared. Not even in legend had there been a hint of anything so beautiful. It was a whole other world, one that the separatists could colonize for centuries without ever coming into conflict with the colony, and on the side of the nearest cliff, directly opposite them, was the Tower. It stood before them like a bronze monolith, tall and graceful with an obelisk-like taper that came to a blunted point at the apex. Except for a few minor signs of corrosion high up on its face, it showed no signs of deterioration at all. Vines were apparently beginning to surround the base but not a single one had begun to climb its sides. Near the zenith was a series of three dark windows stacked one upon the other, and if each proved to be on a separate floor, this Tower must be more than a thousand feet in height. For Caleb and Candy, it was beyond comprehension. Not even in their wildest fantasies had they imagined such a structure.

Caleb followed the line of a roadway meandering from the Tower toward them. Its white surface glistened like feather grass in the morning light. Wide and relatively straight, it defied the lay of the land, crossing ridges and small canyons on spindly bridges and continued on to the very center of the small valley in front of them. Once they reached that road, Caleb knew, it would be an easy trip to the Tower itself, and hopefully to the aid they so desperately needed.

"Aroo!" Chandy said, eliciting the victory cry of a hunter.

"Aroo!" Caleb replied. "Not what I expected."

"Uh-huh," said Chandy.

"Well, we're wasting time here and wasting daylight too. Let's go."

They picked their way down the slope and into the valley, watching for any signs of the beasts, but saw none. The ground was different here, covered with a green carpet of short bladed grass unlike the feather grass nearer home and unlike the fodder grass of the meadows surrounding the lake. This was either native to the planet or an import from the Old World that they had never seen. It was soft underfoot and gave easily. To their surprise and pleasure, they didn't slip on it or have their feet slide out from under them as would have happened with the thicker cover plants by the colony, with their thick blades and waxy covering. It was a pleasure to walk on.

They made their way easily, able to see long distances in all directions and spot any oncoming danger that might present itself. This was a benign and beautiful place and they could feel it. In less than an hour they had trotted along the entire distance to the roadway and stepped out onto its hard surface.

"It's like rock," Caleb noted.

"Not at all like the ceramic of the colony."

They tested it with a few tentative steps to be sure that it would not slip out from under them or send them skidding along one of the many dips ahead. It was firm and gripped well and looked as pristine as the first day it had been made, or so they thought. Again they broke out into a trot and headed out across the other side of the valley.

CHAPTER 15

When they finally reached the base of the Tower, its true size became apparent. From one edge to the other it spread out before them for nearly half a mile and they could tell from what they could see as they approached it, the adjacent sides of the structure was equally long. It appeared to be a hexagon and featureless on at least the three faces that they could see, except for a small alcove where the road ended. They decided that this must be an entrance of some kind, but of what kind they couldn't imagine. Inside the alcove there were no doors or passages, only a single plate on the central wall with a red circular button and a sign that read, PUSH TO TALK. After some discussion, that is exactly what they did, but to no avail. They tried pushing the button and speaking while holding it down. They tried pushing it and then releasing it to see if that would work. Vainly, they hoped that merely pushing it would alert those inside to their presence and the waited for someone to speak to them first. All this was to no avail. Still, he hoped that they were communicating because each time Caleb pushed the button there was a low hum that came from all sides of the alcove. Something was happening, they could make no sense of it. Finally, in desperation, Caleb pushed and held the button in while stating why they had come and asking for a reply. When nothing happened, he repeated the process by pushing then releasing the button, elaborating a bit in the second telling. Still there was no reply. Finally in desperation, he announced that they were going to stay out there until hell froze over or someone spoke to them, and with that, he and Chandy went about the process of setting up their camp for the night.

Fortunately, the alcove was large enough for the two of them to spread out their blankets and stretch out. They gathered some fens and dead limbs from the surrounding cover and built themselves a small fire, which was quite adequate to warm them against the night chill. Then they settled in and waited. When Bastion finally showed itself, crossing above them from off the mountain ridges as it began its solitary journey across the night, they accepted that no one was going to speak to them, certainly not tonight. They settled in, rifles at the ready as usual. Caleb figured if he began to feel a chill, it would wake him and he could bring the coals back to life. That being done, he pulled the blanket up over him, scratched the irritated skin around his neck and fell asleep. They passed the night peacefully enough, awakening long enough to stoke the fire a few times, always together, and by morning, there were still a few glowing embers to nurture into a small fire for brewing tea. Once it was brewed, they drank the tea and ate some of the wheat cakes and dried meat from their stores. It was the first time they noticed that they had apparently been skipping meals, as there was a great deal of food still available. That was good news if they were forced to stay here for days.

After breakfast, Chandy walked to the small stream some hundred yards from the roadway and washed the utensils, refilling their water jugs and staying long enough to wash away most of the grit from his body. When he returned, Caleb did the same. In all that time, the Tower made no move to acknowledge their presence. By midday, they were both on edge.

"We just can't sit here, Caleb," Chandy said at last. "They must know we're here."

"Probably, but what can we do? If they won't acknowledge us, they won't acknowledge us and there's nothing we can do about it."

"Well, I, for one, do not feel like just sitting here doing nothing."

Caleb looked up from his cleaning kit. He had just finished bringing his rifle back to pristine condition.

"What do you suggest?"

"Well," said Chandy, frowning, "we could walk around the other side, couldn't we?"

Caleb thought about this for a moment. "What if they open up while we're gone?"

Chandy shook his head. "It seems to me that anyone who can watch the colony from here CAN watch what goes on around their own tower, don't you?"

Caleb thought about this for a moment and decided he should have thought of it himself. "I suppose you're right. Let me finish up here and we'll take a little walk. Unless we run into heavy brush I think we should be able to circle the base in a few hours, even with close inspection, don't you?"

Chandy nodded, and got up, putting a few supplies together for the trek. By the time Caleb was ready his young companion was already in motion. They walked to the left, a habit they had developed from hunting, always circling in the same direction when quartering a field. At first there were no surprises, just more featureless walls, but when they reached the third side, the one opposite their camp, they found another alcove with an identical button and sign. Expecting nothing, they repeated the routine that they had tried on the other side and had the same results. These people simply refused to even admit that the visitors existed. Discouraged, they started out again, still moving to the left on the way back to their camp. It was when they turned the next corner that they finally made progress.

On the fourth face there was an opening in the skin of the Tower at about ten feet. It was a square of about six feet in height and perhaps four in width with a screen over it, and the screen was flapping gently in the breeze coming off the mountains behind them. From the look of it, it was not supposed to do that at all.

"Looks broken," offered Chandy.

Looks like an air intake," said Caleb. "I'm surprised that they let it stay in this state."

"Well, what do you think?"

Caleb was already removing his small day-pack and uncoiling his length of rope.

"I think we need to see where it leads."

"Absolutely!" said Chandy, who looked around for a stout length of wood.

"Well, I don't see anything to heft through the opening around here and it?s too far to reach, even if I stand on your shoulders. How do we get the rope in place?"

"We'll have to use one of the rifles."

This was a dangerous decision. If the rifle were damaged in some way it would cut their firepower in half, and even if this valley were safe, which was still questionable, the return trip to the colony would be twice as dangerous. Discussing it further, they agreed that there was no other way. They used Chandy's rifle, as it was the smaller and less powerful of the two, and Caleb tied his rope around its middle. He stood back a few feet, gauged the distance to the opening, hefted the rifle one last time to determine its weight and balance, and launched it like a javelin toward the opening. It hit the side of the Tower just below the opening with a thud and fell back toward them. Chandy reached out and caught it before it could hit the apron. He handed it back to Caleb with a worried look. Caleb shrugged, added a few feet more line to the coil in his left hand and tried again. This time they were successful. The rifle passed through the center of the opening and clattered against the side of the Tower's shell below the hole. With a sigh of relief, Caleb slowly reeled in the excess line until he heard the rifle catch across one side of the shaft. They were in.

Chandy went first since he was smaller and lighter. He bounded up the side of the Tower pulling himself forward hand over hand and quickly disappeared inside. The line jiggled a few times as more slack was taken inside, then his head appeared over the edge with that usual boyish grin.

"It's secure. Send up the packs."

Caleb did so, then climbed the rope as Chandy had done, stepping into the opening with Chandy's help and settling onto a framework of girders just below the rim. It was here that Chandy had tied off the rope. They looked around. They were in a shaft, approximately six feet in diameter and featureless except for the ladder rungs built into the wall opposite the opening and leading upward. There did not appear to be any rungs descending below their position. Whatever the shaft was, they were definitely at its lower extremity. They peered up into the darkness, unable to see more than a few feet above their heads.

"So you want to go first or shall I?" asked Chandy.

"Let's think about this first. This shaft may go up for more than a thousand feet. Do you have any idea how long it would take to climb that far?"

"Nope, but unless we're willing to find out, we might as well just leave and head home."

He was right, of course, but it irked Caleb to admit it. This young boy was outthinking him, something he wasn't used to and wasn't comfortable with either, but he had to admit that Chandy was right. "I'll go first," he said. You follow, and if anything goes wrong, I hope you're ready to catch me."

"No problem," Chandy said.

They slipped the packs onto their backs and tethered themselves together with Chandy's rope. With the rifles slung across one shoulder to the opposite side, they started up into the dark. To Caleb it seemed like an eternity before they found anything but just another ladder rung above them. He estimated that they had been climbing for nearly half an hour with two breaks to catch their breath, and from counting the rungs, he calculated that they'd risen some five hundred feet above their starting point. It was then that they discovered a second set of girders much like the one at the entrance below. They slipped out onto the supporting beams and took a breather.

"This could go on forever," Caleb said, panting.

"Or at least for another thousand feet or so. Maybe this wasn't such a good idea after all."

"Well, we're into it now, Chandy. No sense in going back now."

After a few moments they resumed their climb, more slowly now, but just as deliberately, and this time they were rewarded with another set of girders after only some fifteen minutes. Gratefully, they stopped for another rest. While they sat, feet dangling over into the void, they began to feel a vibration. It became more pronounced and increased until they were being gently shaken, accompanied by a dull whine that was getting louder and louder. It was coming from above. A light showed itself above them and to one side, descending toward them. It lit the outer skin of the shaft and they began to see where they were. There were actually two shafts, the one they were in being the smaller of the two, and the one next to them, which was really a framework with some translucent material separating the two. As they watched the descending light, it became clear that it was a chamber or conveyance of some sort. It passed them rapidly, dropping away into the darkness below. Chandy and Caleb looked at each other, speechless. They had no idea what they had just seen.

"We should have picked that shaft," Chandy quipped.

"If we could have, we would have. Let's get going. I want to see where this all leads."

They were off and climbing again. In another fifteen minutes they found another resting point, and another one some twenty minutes later. Caleb decided the support girders were placed at equal distances and the time difference was nothing more than their progress being slowed by their fatigue. They pushed on toward the next resting point, relieved to feel cooler air at this height. There was actually a breeze coming from above, and it made the going easier. At about the time that they expected to find another set of braces, they found themselves at the top of the shaft. Above them was a ceiling of louvered shutters through which the air was flowing strongly, and to the side another opening and grating, this one also torn loose. Behind the grating was a metal plate that gave easily when they pushed it. Light streamed into the shaft from the other side. It was a brilliant white, not like the bluish color of sunlight. They both covered their eyes, attempting to adjust to the brightness, and when he looked again, Caleb announced with relief, "Chandy, I think we've arrived."

CHAPTER 16

C aleb was first into the chamber, scrambling out through the hole and jumping down at least five feet to the floor. Chandy soon followed. Both panting from the recent exertion of the climb, Caleb was surprised at the burning in his legs. He was used to climbing mountains, but the shaft was different. His arms were trembling in spasms, as were Chandy's. They must have come further than he thought.

They looked hurriedly around the room. It was roughly circular, with featureless white walls and a number of cabinets arranged in two semicircles opposite each other, close to but not touching, the walls themselves. They could easily pass between the walls and the rear of the cabinets if they had wished. Gemlike protuberances dotted the angled face of the cabinet's tops, each clustered around a frame of some kind. The framed areas were of glass or some similar material and uniformly gray.

Chandy sat roughly into a nearby chair. He found it supremely comfortable, probably because of the cushioned seat and backrest. To his surprise, it seemed to mold itself to his contours and a yellowish light shown down on him from some indeterminate point on the ceiling. Caleb hesitated, then joined him in an adjacent chair.

"Is this how the watchers live?" asked Chandy.

"Who knows? I've never seen anything precisely like these cabinets before. They don't seem to make sense."

"Or we're too dumb to understand the sense they do make," Chandy offered, and began twirling in the chair in delight.

"Quit fooling around," snapped Caleb. "This is serious."

Chandy stopped twirling. He was now facing one of the openings between the two banks of cabinets and noticed the faint outline of a door for the first time. Without thinking, he rose, walked to the door, and touched it. It slid into the wall and disappeared.

"Whoa," he exclaimed. "That was weird."

Caleb stood, lifted the two packs and the rifles down from the opening in the wall and handed one of each to Chandy. "We've got to be careful," he said. "We don't know anything about this place or how anything in it works. Watch what you touch from now on."

Chandy gave him a contrite smile and said, "You'll get no argument out of me."

Caleb came closer and examined the opening in the wall. On the other side was a small platform and stairs that led upward. He peered in, twisting to look up the stairs and then retreated to the room again.

"Just a set of stairs. I think we need to go up. Maybe everybody's above us."

"I wonder how they get down from here," Chandy said in passing. Caleb thought about this for a moment. It was not a silly question. The room seemed to have no other doors, and the only staircase led upward, not downward as well. Certainly they didn't need to take the air shaft. Perhaps it was the strange box they had seen descending in the adjoining shaft. Cautiously, they climbed the stairs to the next level, where they found another opening, and like the one below, when touched, it slid aside, disappearing into the wall. Simultaneously, the door below closed with a whisper. Chandy walked into the adjacent room without hesitation, which sent shivers through Caleb, but what was done was done. So much for caution, he thought. He followed.

This room was identical to the last, but its contents were very different. Instinctively, each slung his rifle from his shoulder and released the safety. Opposite them and to the left was a single cabinet resting against the wall. To their right were four beds arranged in two sets of two, one bed attached above another. None of this was particularly startling, but in between these two structures was a pile of shattered and gnawed bones. They were human. In the center of the room was a huge mass of animal spoor, long since turned hard as stone. It unlike any spoor they had seen before.

"The tuskers?" asked Chandy, nodding toward the pile.

"Can't be anything else. They've been here. 'Must have come through the shaft, like we did. That explains why it was pulled out to begin with."

"Yeah, but how long ago?"

Caleb stepped closer to the spoor and leaned over it, sniffing. "A very long time, I'd say. It could be years."

Chandy sighed deeply. "No wonder they never acknowledged the Keeper's calls. They were all dead."

"I don't know. That still doesn't explain it. Surely others would have come from the Old World when these didn't report. They must have had regular relief teams come in to trade out the duty of watching. Why didn't anyone know about this back on the Old World?"

They wondered at this silently, investigating the room further, pulling what appeared to be personal belongings from the top beds to examine them. They seemed the least damaged. Everything below four feet had been shredded or gnawed, including bedding, pallets and stray bits of wood and metal. There appeared to be nothing of value or even of understanding, except for some undisturbed clothing made for someone decidedly broader and shorter than they were. It was all most peculiar, but not very enlightening. When they had satisfied themselves that there was nothing further to be learned from the room, they searched for another doorway and found it, as before, opposite the one they had entered. Now holding their rifles at the ready, they passed through the opening into the small platform as before and ascended yet another floor. They hesitated at the new closed door and listened.

Neither of them had spoken for some time, Caleb trying to make sense of this new information and what it meant for the survival of the colony, Chandy in an apparent state of curiosity over everything they saw. Now they faced the possibility of more unknowns. No sound came from the other side of the door and no vibrations passed through either walls or floor. Caleb wondered if they would even be able to hear anything from the other side. For all he knew, the walls were totally baffled, which, as it happened is exactly how he felt at this moment.

At last he took a breath, brought the rifle to his shoulder and announced, "Here we go. Watch your back."

Carefully, he reached out and touched the wall. Obediently, the door slid quickly and silently to one side and a dimmer, reddish light bathed them from within. Caleb slowly slipped into the room, turning his torso right and left as he did, always sighting along the barrel of his rifle.

Chandy followed and moved to the left, positioning his back against the wall beside the doorway and scanning the room from top to bottom, then side to side.

"Last stop," Chandy said at last.

"Think so?"

"I think so. Look at the ceiling. It's shaped like the top of the Tower, and there are small windows around the walls. This must be the top observation room."

Caleb changed his perspective and began noticing things other than possible movement and had to agree. They relaxed a bit and brought their rifles to waist-high but still ready, spotting the equipment at the same time. "Check outside," snapped Caleb, nodding at one of the small observation windows. Chandy moved quickly, going from window to window. Caleb crossed to the pile of boxes and knapsacks stacked beside yet another door to one side. This was newer equipment, not at all of the same vintage of what they had seen below. There were three large boxes of some translucent material, lightweight and smooth with sheen to their surface.

Inside these, Caleb could see variously shaped parcels, all neatly packed and stacked, ready for transport. Beside them were two soft travel packs of some woven material that he could not identify. Symbols and identifying phrases were printed on each, but most of it made no sense to him. The most he could make out were bits and pieces, such as 'In Case of Emergency', and 'Authorized Personnel Only'. He pulled the tabs on one of them, which came away with reluctance. Inside he found more parcels and a set of boxes marked 'Rations', whatever that meant.

There were also five cylinders and a hand instrument of some sort with a trigger device and short tubular protuberance. Pulling the tabs on the other pack yielded similar items, as well as several apparently electronic devices. He speculated that it must be a weapon of some kind, considering its design, much like his own rifle. Caleb only recognized the other devices from their similarity to artifacts displayed at the foundry in the colony, the only technology still remaining intact from the original colonizing of the valley.

"No sign of anyone or anything," reported Chandy. He came to stand beside Caleb and stare down at the new find.

"This stuff looks new," he commented.

"It is new, but who does it belong to?"

As if on cue, they felt a deep vibration in the floor and a familiar sound coming from the last unopened door, standing just beside the pile of equipment. It was the conveyance in the other shaft, returning to the top of the Tower. They moved back to flank the opening, weapons at the ready. They looked at each other nervously, and then concentrated on the door and the hum coming now louder and louder from behind it. Finally, the sound stopped, as did the vibration in the floor and after a moment's hesitation, the door opened with a whir.

The passenger stepped in and stopped with a start, reaching from something at his belt. Caleb and Chandy stiffened their hold on their rifles and both drew a bead on his forehead. His eyes moved from one of them to the other, his body frozen as if in some surrealistic tableau, and then he moved his hand away from the object at his side and let his shoulders relaxed, and gave them a wry smile.

"I see my expectations of you two were well-founded. You're not the cerebral Neanderthals I had been led to expect."

Caleb looked at the man carefully. He scanned him from head to toe, noting anything that might represent a threat, from his stance to the position of his feet, to the dilation of his eyes and what he was wearing. From what he could see, the man was no particular threat. He was a squat man, more than a foot smaller than either Caleb or Chandy, but he was broad of shoulder and thick of leg. His torso was a bit hard to determine beneath the rather billowy dark green shirt that he wore beneath a leather vest covered with pockets, trousers that fit loosely over apparently large thighs, and boots made of some unfamiliar shiny material which covered half his calf. They appeared to close with snaps and a fast-release buckle at the top. He had a round face, not exactly pudgy but showing a fleshiness that comes from too much good food, and his complexion was ruddy. Whether this was from exertion or was his natural coloring was hard to determine. What most struck Caleb were his eyes. They were dark and small, like black beads, and they stared at each of them unflinching. The man clearly thought of himself as in control of the situation, and had no intention of revealing too much, or so Caleb reasoned. Yet he appeared to be caught so totally unawares by their presence that he had no intention of fighting back.

"May I come in?" he said quietly. "Technically, I am the host here and you the visitors, so I do wish you'd lower those threatening devices." Without waiting for an answer, he slipped past them and crossed to one of the chairs opposite the now closing door. He sat with surprising grace for such a large man and smiled up at them.

"Oh do relax, gentlemen. I promise not to eat you."

Chandy lowered his rifle. Caleb hesitated for a moment and then did the same. He inspected their visitor again. It became apparent that not only was he shorter than either of them, but that he was shorter than any adult in the colony. Though his arms were massive, his hands were relatively delicate, with long narrow fingers and virtually no calluses that Caleb could observe. When he had crossed the room Caleb noticed that he walked with a slight stoop, as if he were carrying a heavy load, and his back had a natural arch to it that thrust his head slightly forward. Even his feet were different, turned in toward each other, and they were short but wide. Around his waist was a wide belt which held several pouches, including a large one in back, and two square containers, one on each hip. The handle of one of the weapons that Caleb had seen in the packs protruded from the one on the man's left.

"I can understand your consternation, gentlemen. I'm hardly what you expected to find at the Tower, but quite frankly, it appears to me that anything you found would be a surprise, considering you're not even supposed to be here. What are your names?"

"You first," Caleb said roughly.

"I? I am Professor Skylar Fylfot. It's a silly name, really, but I blame my parents, not myself for that. I hope you'll do the same. And you?" Caleb found himself angry at the man's lack of fear. Here he was, facing two armed hunters with rifles pointed his way, and he seemed as relaxed as a patriarch in his own home.

"My name is Caleb...Caleb Grant. This is Chandler Crone. Now who are you and what do you have to do with the Tower?"

"Ah. Chandler Crone. You would be the descendant of Thomas and Regina Crone. And as for you, Mr. Grant, I assume your ancestors include Ben and Sarah Grant?"

The two hunters looked at each other.

"You seemed surprised? I've read the records, you see. It's a necessary part of my research."

"You're...a watcher?" Caleb asked, almost giggling.

"A what? A watcher? Oh, yes. That makes sense. That is what you'd call someone from the Tower, isn't it? Not really, my boys. I'm quite beyond that program. I'm an historian. Why are you so amused by that?"

Caleb and Chandy looked at each other and nearly burst out laughing. "Well, you're not exactly what we'd come to expect a watcher to look like,"

"Hmm? So? You were expecting perhaps some ancient robed figure of a man with a long white beard?"

"Um, something like that."

"Ah well. Sorry to disappoint. No, as I said, I'm just an historian."

"Like the Keeper?" asked Chandy.

"If I understand your nomenclature, yes. I'm here to chronicle the history of the colony."

They both lowered their weapons entirely and relaxed a bit. None of this made sense yet, but at least there was some foundation for trying to determine what was going on. Caleb tried to put this new information into some sort of rational context, but he was having a hard time doing it.

After all, anyone from the Tower was more legend than real, and Fylfot was nothing like any of his expectations.

"I don't understand you, er, Professor Fylfot. Where are the watchers?"

"The watchers!" Fylfot exclaimed. "They've been gone for a century or more, I suspect. When I first arrived, I thought that they might still be here. You know, as part of some secret government project, but no one's here. No one watches anymore."

"But the experiment," said Chandy. "If it's over, why are we still here?" Fylfot shook his head and sighed. "Of course. You know nothing of any of this, do you? Very well then. If you'll have a seat, I'll try to explain. Would you like some tea? I've brought a particularly fine Oolong with me. No? So be it." Fylfot stood and opened one of the packs, extracting a small box, which he opened, and removed a short cylinder. He pulled on the top, which caused the device to expand and immediately a pungent steam began to rise lazily from the now-apparent opening.

"Sure you won't have any," he asked? They both refused the offer. Sliding his ungainly bulk lightly into the chair again, he took a long pull on the tea, leaning back, eyes closed and face smiling contentedly. "There's nothing quite like a genuine Oolong, you know. It's hard to come by these days. Well, that's quite enough of that.

Let me explain your position. "This colony was abandoned, I'm afraid. I'm sure that comes as a shock to you, but due to the machinations of the kakistocracy that grew out of the Great War, what was left of civilization simply wrote off the whole colonization affair as untenable, indefensible in principle, unmanageable, and unnecessary."

Caleb and Chandy looked at each other, hoping at least one of them had understood what this man was talking about. They looked back at him quizzically.

"Ah. Let me put it this way," he said in exasperation. "There was a great war that destroyed a goodly portion of the total population of the planet. We were reduced from a population of nearly nine billion starving people to less than one billion, and it all happened over a period of several weeks. There was little physical destruction since the weapons used were almost entirely biological, and the only reason the nearly billion survivors lived was because of their natural immunities and the short half-life of the bugs. Hence we were no longer crowded and experiments involving the extensive colonization of other worlds were unnecessary. As for being untenable, even if we had wanted to, we had all but lost the knowledge and technology to carry out such transports, and thus any desire to continue the project was indefensible in principle for the government in place, which was, as I mentioned government by the utterly inept. Stupid leaders make stupid decisions, which, as it happens, have become our saving grace. It has led to utter inaction by the governments of the world with the populations under those governments ignoring their dictates. We've come back to individual initiative and voluntary cooperation in the cultural behavior of our people and are doing quite well, thank you, as a result. Now do you understand?"

Caleb frowned. "I...you're saying that there was a war, there's no good government left, which you like, but which means no one can make any decisions about the colonies, and who needs them anyway since the population is so small."

"Well, essentially, I suppose you could put it that way. It's a bit simplistic, but then so was my explanation. Now do you see?"

"No," said Chandy. "If that were true, why weren't we told? Why weren't we brought back home?"

Fylfot took another long drink of his tea, slurping it noisily as he did so. "That's a very good question, my boy. Actually, there was a great deal of sentiment to do so, and we could have, directly following the conflict. We still had enough expertise and, for a brief period of time, we still had the power production to do it. In fact, an attempt was made, particularly when the...watchers, as you call them, began to see signs of the rats returning."

"Excuse me, Professor Fylfot, but you know about the rats?" asked Caleb.

Fylfot looked at him in utter horror. "You thought that we wouldn't?"

"I've never talked to a watcher. I don't know what to expect."

"Why, it was the rats that ate your crops and threatened the colony. It was the rats that evolved into those monstrous predators you see in the forest today, and they're about to become a very serious threat again."

"Rats," repeated Chandy.

"Exactly, my boy," said Fylfot. "Rats are simply larger and more aggressive mice. Over one hundred years ago, watchers reported an increasing problem with mutating rats left over from the original extinction. It was decided that they would keep an eye on them and if the problem worsened, they would be exterminated again and the colonists removed. The team was never heard from. Another team was sent, but it too was never heard from. At that point, it was decided that the colony must have been destroyed and the Tower as well, and the experiment was shut down."

"If that's so," Caleb asked carefully, "then what are you doing here?"

"Ah. Well, you see, as an historian, I have an interest in the events of the entire prewar colonization project, and I came to see what I could learn about the colony's final days. It was only recently that we've regained the ability to transport on sight and as soon as I could, I took advantage of it. It was a great surprise to me to arrive and find myself in the midst of that demise as it happens."

Caleb felt a cold chill run through his body. "You're saying that the colony is going to be destroyed?"

"No doubt about it, Fylfot said without emotion. He could have been lecturing about ancient history for all his emotion, but he looked up at them out of the corner of his eye, as if awaiting their reaction. "The rats are gathering and they are hungry. Winter's coming, or so I am assuming from the activities I've observed, and they'll descend on the colony before the windy season, then when the winter arrives, they'll feed off each other until spring, the strong devouring the weak, as you would expect from an evolving social creature. It's no different than what humans tend to do in similar circumstances. We just don't eat each other in the process."

"No!" shouted Chandy. "We'll wipe them out!"

Fylfot calmly smiled at the boy. "You can not. They are too many and you are too few. Of course, I could probably destroy them, but as an impartial observer, it's not my job. I'm just here to watch," he said sipping his tea and watching their reaction closely.

"The best you can do is hide in your tepees and hope they don't break in. I should warn you though. If they can break into the Tower, which is built like a true fortress, they'll have little or no trouble breaking into your puny homes. It really is quite, hopeless, you see."

He smiled politely, leaned back in his chair again and took another sip of the tea, seemingly content. When neither of them had responded to this for some time, Fylfot looked up from his tea, apparently distressed. "I've upset you, haven't I? I can see why. Let me make up for it. I can take you two back with me. That should make up for the shock, eh? You'll both be safe, you'll be exposed to a wonderfully advanced world, and you'll survive."

Caleb reached out and slapped the man, hard across the face. He did it without thinking and felt no compunction about having done it. Fylfot fell back in the chair and glared at him, then gathered himself, straightened his collar and brushed spilt tea from the front of his garment, which seemed to have absorbed not a single drop of the liquid.

"No," he said. "I suppose that would not be acceptable, would it? My apologies. It's just that everyone thinks you are all dead a century ago and I have a hard time thinking of any of you as living beings, which you obviously are. Historians must be objective, you know.

Emotion has no place in the discipline. Considering your plethora of kedogeny at this moment in time, I can forgive the aggression. I do not recommend this as a repetitive method of communication."

Chandy groaned. "What the hell did he say?"

"I think he just tried to apologize but warned me not to do it again."

"Oh," Chandy said, almost disappointed.

Caleb suddenly made a decision, the roots of which escaped him. All he knew was that it was the right thing to do. He moved back a few paces, looked through one of the small observation windows at the still high sun and announced, "We're leaving. All three of us are going back to the colony."

Fylfot's reaction was immediate, reaching to his belt for his weapon. Caleb was too fast for him, grabbing Fylfot's wrist. To his surprise, the man was incredibly strong, drawing the weapon in spite of Caleb's grip. As he raised it to fire, the barrel pointed directly at Caleb's forehead, Chandy delivered a blow with the butt of his rifle that left the man slumping and seemingly lifeless.

"I hope I didn't kill him," Chandy said.

"'Not sure I'd mind if you did," Caleb hissed. Damn, that man's strong."

In moments, they had piled the professor, his supplies and weapons, and their own gear into the conveyance and were on their way down to the base of the Tower. As they descended, Chandy firmly bound the professor's wrists and stripped him of anything even remotely looking like a threat to their safety. They both agreed that it was going to be a very long trip home.

CHAPTER 17

O nce he revived, and after some superficial doctoring for his considerable headache, Professor Fylfot proved to be a very effective beast of burden. He convinced them to release him long enough to change into a one-piece garment, loose fitting and drab gray in color. It looked very utilitarian. Remembering the strength that the man had demonstrated when Caleb had grabbed his arm, they double bound his wrists in front of him and loaded as much of the boxed supplies into their own packs, stuffing the rest into a single large crate which they promptly secured to the professor's back along with one of the packs. They took turns carrying the other extra pack, reluctant to leave behind anything that might be of value to them and realizing that as soon as they cleared the forest, it could be transferred to a travois that the professor could pull behind him. As for the good professor, his former amiable personality had understandably soured.

Carrying his load in silence, he periodically punctuated the trip with mumbled curses and an occasional 'ummph' as they mounted some steep slope or traversed a small ravine. For the most part, he proved even sturdier than they would have expected. Caleb noticed that there was something in his gait that looked familiar and decided it must resemble the stride of some obscure colonist that he had observed on the city streets. Still, the familiarity of this man worried him.

By sunset they had made good progress, being nearly halfway home, and the easier part of the trip across the thinning forest lay ahead of them. They settled in to two large trees whose cradling branches offered good purchase and a nearly luxurious floor of broad, smooth barked wood to support them. All of the baggage was deposited on smaller yet still quite substantial limbs above them. Fylfot was tied to the trunk of a vertically soaring branch between them. As Desolation rose slowly over the crest of the mountains, a process that took longer and longer as the days wore on toward the windy season, they curled themselves up in their ground cloths and blankets and settled in for the night.

It was late when Caleb was awakened by that inner sense that sometimes roused him from sleep. He could smell danger, and in this case, he could literally smell it. The musty, rancid stench of a rat filled the air. Silently he felt for his rifle, afraid to move more than an inch or two and slowly turned his head to peer down at the foot of the tree. There, sniffing the ground at the base of the tree, its nose twitching back and forth, whiskers scratching at the tree trunk, was a very large specimen of the beast. It was larger than the one they had brought back by some twenty pounds, and its naked tail was shorter compared to its body than he expected, the tip having been chewed off by some predator or one of its own kind. It appeared old, with patchy fur that stood up like the bristles on a brush, and its pinkish red eyes stared searchingly wherever its head faced.

Caleb chanced a glance toward Chandy and found him equally awake and alert. He hadn't heard a sound, but the boy had shifted his weight to face Caleb's direction and his rifle was at the ready. Together, they watched the beast move about below them. In a moment, he was joined by two more of the beasts, then by a fourth, and finally by two more. With each new adversary, Caleb's heart pounded a little more until he thought that the tuskers must surely hear it thumping in his chest. They lay as still as they could, hoping that the predators would leave, and in time, the pack seemed to lose interest and turned away to forage elsewhere.

The last of them, the old leader, was almost out of sight when it happened. "Mphh! What the hell's going on?" snapped Fylfot, raising up and looking about.

"What's that awful smell?"

Immediately, the leader turned and let out a squeal that so startled Caleb that he nearly dropped his rifle. The huge rat charged back toward the tree and the others followed on the run. Without the slightest hesitation, it leaped onto the side of their tree and began climbing toward them. Two shots rang with a double hiss and it exploded both at the shoulders and just behind the skull. With a great thud, it fell backward and for a moment, the others milled around, snapping at each other and tearing at their leader's body.

"Let me loose!" shouted Fylfot. "Cut me loose and I'll kill them all!"

"No way!" shouted Caleb and he fired at another beast, crippling him in the hindquarters. He cursed and reloaded as Chandy sent another projectile into the beast's spine to finish him.

From there it was chaos as the remaining four rats began working their way up the trunk of the tree toward them. Chandy dropped a third with a shot that went precisely down its throat, but as it fell, another replaced it nearly level with their position.

"Use the pistol!" shouted Fylfot.

"Use what?" growled Caleb, trying to force a jammed chamber to function on his rifle.

"The handgun that you took from me! Just aim it and pull the trigger!"

Two tuskers remained and were nearly on them. Caleb threw his rifle at the lead rat but it didn't slow it down.

In desperation, he reached for the strange weapon, grabbed it by the handle, assuming that the barrel was to be pointed at the target, and squeezed the trigger. There was a flash of light and the beast fell from the tree, a small hole having bored through him from nose to mid back. He fired again and the last rat jumped from the tree, squealing. Chandy fired his rifle, wounding it at the base of the spine, and it clawed its way toward a clump of bushes, dragging its back legs. Without thinking, Caleb aimed and fired, sweeping the weapon from left to right, not sure of its accuracy at this range, and the beast's head fell away, burned through by the beam of light emitted from the barrel.

Breathing hard, he looked around the entire circle of the tree to see if there were any more of the creatures, but except for his own panting and that of Chandy, the only other sound was the dripping of urine on the ground below. Professor Fylfot had unceremoniously chosen that moment in time to lose control. He was curled against the tree between them, grasping the trunk and making small whining noises, like a whimpering child.

"I think it's over, Caleb," Chandy said shakily.

"I sure as hell hope so. Are you all right, Professor?"

The professor looked over at him, tears filling his eyes, and nodded. With what appeared to be extreme effort, he calmed himself.

Caleb looked at the weapon appraisingly. He turned it over in his hands, examining everything except the end of the barrel.

"Is there some sort of disabling lever on this thing?" he asked seriously.

"On the right side. It's a little stud. Once you put your finger on the trigger it automatically releases."

"That's good to know," Caleb said with remarkable calmness. He slipped the device back under his belt.

"As I remember, we packed four of these, didn't we?"

Fylfot nodded. "There are also two heavier rifle versions in cases in the large box.

They've been broken down for easier transport."

"That's six altogether. What were you going to do with all that kill power?"

Fylfot thought for a moment, his eyes shifting to the left and down. "You can't have too much protection, you know."

"So it would appear," Caleb said evenly.

In an hour, Desolation began rising quickly to the north nearly at the farthest shift in its wandering orbit, and with Bastion still shining brightly in the sky, they decided to give up in their vain attempts to get any more sleep.

Between the adrenaline and the stench of the corpses below, it was obvious that they were not going to get any more rest this night. As close as it was to dawn, they descended from the trees, loaded their 'mule' once again with the large box and one of the backpacks and were off. Chandy had retrieved one of the hand weapons from the sack that he was now carrying and seemed to be much more at ease as he took the lead. Caleb was glad to see that he still moved with the caution of a hunter, however, and decided that the boy was truly worthy of the title. They'd be home by mid-afternoon at this pace, and he was glad of it. The Keeper must be told of all this, and Caleb was sure that he would have many questions for their newfound colonist.

CHAPTER 18

S torms were not unusual this time of year, often seen as the precursor of the coming windy season, but this one was as severe as any the colony had ever known. Rather than the high winds and light rain of a fall storm, it presented the three with a deluge that came straight down on them like needles. It was relentless. It arose suddenly, the dark clouds rolling in from the northwest, bringing dust and debris and the sharp crackle of lightening and thunder and then simply becoming stationary overhead.

In less than a quarter hour, the roiling cloud bank had blanketed the sky above the valley from rim to rim and obscured the two moons in the process. Were it not for the fact that dawn had broken, they would have been left stumbling in the dark as well as assaulted by the cold and soaked to the skin. They stopped long enough to strip naked, forcing Fylfot to do the same, and stood for a few moments letting the sheets of water wash over them, washing away the grit of days of travel.

Caleb thought how surprising it was that he'd not noticed the damage to his skin earlier. He had scratches and whelps on both arms, a large raw patch just above his right knee, and he was bleeding from hundreds of hairline scratches on his forehead and cheeks. Chandy was much the same, with patches of raw exposed wounds around his neck and on the sides of his body. Even Fylfot suffered, his newness to the planet rendering him particularly susceptible to the effects of hard grit on tender skin. Yet he was not much more raw and encrusted than either of them, which gave Caleb pause. The man had obviously been in the forests often since he'd arrived on the planet. As the rain eased from a driving, stinging torrent to a soft drizzle, they slipped back into their wet clothes. They would dry in the sun along the way.

"How long have you been on the planet," Caleb asked Fylfot as they started out again.

"Not long," Fylfot said curtly.

"How long?" Caleb repeated darkly.

Fylfot studied Caleb briefly, then said amiably, "About three weeks."

"That's quite a while. Have you done much exploring?"

"Um, some. I walked to the rim several times, looking for some pass or opening out of the valley but couldn't find one. I've...also explored closer to the colony itself."

Caleb nodded. No wonder their companion was as rough as they.

"I think you might want to bathe every day to avoid all the scrapes and scratches," Chandy said in passing.

Fylfot grinned apparently pleased at the change of subject. "Yes. That became abundantly apparent after awhile. I began going down to the pool in front of the Tower daily for my morning ablutions. I didn't go in, of course. There's no telling what strange denizens might be lurking about you know, but I stayed clean at any rate. That is not to speak pejoratively of the environment. I'm not saying that this is an unpleasant place. It's actually rather pleasant, or was until I met the two of you, but I found that my pernoctations, if you'll forgive my ecclesiastical reference, were best followed by a thorough cleansing of both soul and body. The delightful riparian atmosphere was a perfect crucible for burning away the dross of my nightly ills."

"Uh-huh," said Chandy, totally lost.

Caleb smiled and lightly set his hand on the boy's shoulder. "I think he's saying that he washed in the morning to get over his lack of sleep at night."

"Yes, yes," said Fylfot. "That's exactly, though somewhat imprecisely it, you see."

"Well I'm afraid you'll find the next lake you encounter a bit less pleasant."

"Oh? How so?"

"It's the rain," Caleb said. "It could swamp the fens. If it does, any attempt to cross it will be useless, especially for the next few days. We'll have to skirt around it and follow the lakeshore to get home."

Chandy stopped short and looked at Caleb over his shoulder. "That's going to take us close to the separatists? camp, isn't it?" Caleb nodded and kept walking. "Can't be helped. Once we're through the feather grass, which will be a hard trek after the rain, we'll skirt the far fields and cut back across to the shoreline. We shouldn't be near the camp for more than a few minutes. With luck, they'll never know we're there."

"Separatists? camp?" asked Fylfot with great interest.

"Just a group of colonists who want to go off on their own. They're on one side of the lake and we're on the other."

"Ah. Yes, I've seen them. They're building another village, aren't they? I thought it was simply a move to alleviate overcrowding, a common remedy for centuries back home.. So they're separatists, are they? How interesting. Actually, how fascinating. I'd like to stop and talk to them, you know."

"I'm sure you would," Caleb said," but you won't get the chance quite yet.. There's a group of only a few hundred of them and as soon as the winds start, which could be just about any time now, they'll be back at our gates, begging to come home. When that happens, you can talk to them all winter"

"Pity," said Fylfot musing, then seemed to have had another thought.

"All winter? What do you mean? I'm not going to be here all winter."

Caleb said nothing, just kept walking and prodding Fylfot to move. The bulky man fell into silence, and chewed on this new prospect. "All winter," he mumbled. Finally, he stopped dead in his tracks and turned back to Caleb.

"There's an easier way, you know," he said brightly.

Caleb was beginning to lose his patience with their beast of burden. "There's an easier way to do what? What are you talking about?"

"You seem anxious to avoid the fens and these separatists. Why not go by the river and save yourself the encounter?"

Both Caleb and Chandy offered condescending smiles.

"What?" Fylfot said at last.

"The river leads in from the opposite direction."

"From the lake it appears to, but it actually winds itself around the edge of the valley and originates along the rim not far from the Tower. It's miles longer, but it's much faster, not to mention more comfortable. I'd rather go by boat than travel on foot with all this baggage anyway."

Caleb gave the man a disgusted, crooked smile. "It's a nice thought, but there are no boats this side of the lake, and they never venture up the river. The current is too swift."

"On the contrary," Fylfot announced, puffing up like a lummox in rutting season. "I have a boat in the larger of the two packs you're carrying. It's inflatable."

Again the two simply stared at the man. Fylfot looked initially confused, and then seemed to come to some realization. "You've never seen an inflatable boat? It's made of a very thin flexible material that fills with air from two canisters and becomes rigid. This particular one will carry four people tightly or three comfortably."

"And it can take us down the river?"

"Of course."

"Even in that swift current? It's just rained for hours."

Fylfot grinned triumphantly. "It's very stable, actually, and virtually impossible to puncture or rip."

Caleb looked at Chandy who shook his head indecisively. The decision was his, and his young friend offered no help in it. For some moments he considered the idea and then said, "All right. We'll try it."

"There is one thing, though. You'll have to untie me. If you're not familiar with this particular craft, it's difficult to maneuver. You'll need me in the bow with a paddle."

Caleb thought about this for a moment and said nothing.

"Oh for heaven's sake, gentlemen. I'm not going to run away. What would I do out here without equipment or weapons? It's ludicrous!"

Caleb sighed and looked at Chandy who nodded. 'Okay," he said. "We'll try it."

"Good!" said Fylfot enthusiastically. "Then I can get this crate off my back!"

They turned to the north, following Fylfot's directions and in less than a quarter hour could hear a distant rush of water. Another twenty minutes crossing a low, wide floodplain, now soaked to a depth of several inches, they came to the deep channel that was the river. Following Fylfot's instructions, they pulled the craft from its container, a cylinder about the diameter of Caleb's calf and perhaps a foot long. Fylfot pulled a long silvery tab at one end. With a rush, the tube split open, expanding into a flat bottomed boat, narrow at the prow and broad at the stern. It was made of a thin silvery material that instantly became rigid upon inflation, and was some five feet wide at the center and approximately fourteen feet in length. Fylfot retrieved folded paddles from the center seat and pulled telescoping handles to their full length. Caleb had to admit that he was impressed. When they lifted it and slid into the current, its surprising lightness further amazed him, and the three of them found themselves scurrying to climb in the boat before the current swept it downstream.

The craft skimmed the surface of the water, skipping along rapidly with the current and picking up speed as they maneuvered it to mid-channel. It was an exhilarating ride, and Caleb let out a whoop as they lowered themselves off the boat's seats and onto its deck for greater stability. They were being tossed over the waves of whitewater at ever-increasing speed. The roar of the rushing current was deafening. Caleb watched Fylfot at the bow, easily maneuvering them through the rapids with a twist of his paddle to one side or the other, admiring his skill. When he looked at Chandy, he found the boy rigid, eyes closed, married to the loops on either side of the boat in a white-knuckled grip.

"What is it, Chandy?" he yelled the din. Chandy yelled something that he couldn't understand.

"What's wrong?" he yelled again. Chandy half turned his head and looked back at him in unbridled horror.

"I can't swim!" he yelled.

"You can't what? That's crazy. Of course you can swim!"

Chandy shook his head. "No I can't! You've never seen me swim because I don't know how!"

There was desperation in his voice. Fylfot looked back over his shoulder and grinned. He looked at his two captors and laughed.

"Don't worry, my young friend," he said. "We're not going to sink, you know. This boat has nearly perfect buoyancy and incredibly maneuverability even in the most turbulent of seas. Watch this!"

He plunged his paddle into the water on the right side of the boat and gave it a slight twist. Immediately the craft shifted to the left, careening across whitewater caps and pitching violently. Another twist on the left and the craft repeated the move in the opposite direction. The boat lifted out of the water on the left side and nearly went vertical. Both Caleb and Chandy had to use all of their strength to keep from falling out.

"What are you doing?" Caleb yelled.

"Sadistic glasseater!" shrieked Chandy.

At this, Fylfot laughed again and repeated the maneuver, this time even more violently than the first. Chandy pitched forward and then to one side and bounced out of the boat, being saved from disaster by his left arm, still firmly gripping the loop on the gunnels. Chandy was being dragged mercilessly by the current, his head dipping repeatedly into the water as the water and the speed of the boat pushed him down into the water. Caleb reached out to him and grabbed his wrist. The boat lurched again in the opposite direction and Chandy released his grip on the loop. Caleb could feel his arm starting to separate from his shoulder as the boy drifted violently from the boat and then snapped and twisted back against the hull with a loud 'umph' when he hit the rigid side.

"Hang on, Chandy!" Caleb yelled and began pulling him in. Chandy was sputtering and coughing, gasping for air. He was rigid now and the more he stiffened the more he sank into the water.

Caleb grabbed his paddle from the deck and swung it out over Chandy's body with his other hand. Chandy grabbed it with his free hand and Caleb let go his grip on the boy's wrist. Now he was pulling Chandy toward the boat and lifting him with both hands tightly gripping the handle of the paddle. He was able to twist the paddle so that the flat of its blade played against the surface of the water like a wing, lifting itself and the hapless Chandy up. Chandy took in a great gulp of air and spewed a stream of water from nose and mouth. Caleb was hauling him in now. He lifted with all his might until Chandy's head was above the gunnels and released the paddle, grabbing his shoulders. His own shoulder screamed with pain from that first jerk, but he refused to let go. Chandy reached out over the edge of the boat and tried to grab another loop on the deck. It was that moment that Caleb felt a searing pain in his leg, just behind the knee and realized that Fylfot had just delivered a sharp blow with his paddle.

Instinctively, Caleb stiffened his torso in response to the sudden anguish of the blow and pitched over the side. Chandy fell back with him and the two of them were now bobbing up and down in the current. Free of the drag created by the boat, the current buoyed them up so that they virtually skimmed the surface of the waves, a process actually aided by Chandy's return to absolute rigidity. Caleb shifted the boy, rolling him over on his back and turning him so that he traveled feet-first down through a series of rock-lined channels. He looked up long enough to see Fylfot in the distance, sitting placidly in the boat and looking back at them, grinning.

Without thinking, Caleb began using Chandy like a rudder, guiding them both toward the nearest shore. Thankfully, they were beyond the floodplains and gently sloping walls lined the channel on either side. They were slowing now, and a look ahead told Caleb that it was either get out of the water now or drown in the calm water. Without a current, it would be impossible to keep Chandy afloat.

Caleb kicked out with his feet, using his last bit of strength, now pulling Chandy's bulk along behind him. Reaching out for a branch on the riverbank, he missed. He tried again, this time seeking purchase on a low shelf, but they were moving too fast. On a third try he grabbed an overhanging vine that flexed like a bow string and swung them both up against a mossy bank. Gratefully he pulled himself up onto the low table of earth and was relieved to see Chandy doing the same. They crawled forward out of the water, each rolled onto their back and lay still, panting.

"We'll lay here for just a moment," Caleb said. "We need to catch our breath. Don't try to move."

"Just for a moment," Chandy mumbled.

CHAPTER 19

C handy was the first to awaken. It was late afternoon and he stirred, prompted by the sounds of Two Moon's creatures foraging for last bits of food before the sun set. Others were beginning to stir, preparing to begin their nocturnal hunt. Between the two, the forest and grassland along the edge of the river were alive with sound. He rolled over on his side, wincing from the pain in his ribs and along the edge of his cheek. He groaned hoarsely and tried to sit up. On the second try, after a great deal of effort, he succeeded. He looked around him.

Caleb lay beside him, perhaps six feet away, splayed spread eagle on his back, breathing steadily in his sleep. Dried blood covered one side of his chin, and his clothes were torn, not an easy feat for glass fiber cloth. One foot had lost its boot and the other leg was caked in a dark mud to the knee. Chandy watched him for a moment, satisfying himself that his mentor and friend was okay.

He turned his attention to his surroundings. They lay on a mossy embankment only a few yards from the now receding waters of the valley's river. It was wide here and rough, with rocks jutting out from the surface just downstream from their position. In the distance he could hear the roar of rapids. On the opposite shore and behind them was forest, the usual combination of carbon-based and silica-based flora, and tall trees that formed a canopy over the dense foliage like some blue-green umbrella. He detected no signs of larger animals, no scent or sound, no unusual disturbance of the underbrush or watering trail emerging from the forest in either direction as far as he could see. Satisfied that they were safe for the moment, he rolled over onto all fours and crawled to Caleb's side.

"I'm awake," Caleb announced as Chandy was debating whether to disturb him or not.

"Better than dead," he said grinning.

Caleb opened one eye just enough to look at the boy. "Hunter's humor. That's a good sign, Chandy. Have you had a look around?"

"Yup," he said. "Was that a test or are you just waking up?"

"Both. I assume that there's no immediate danger or I would have heard about it."

Caleb opened his eyes fully now and turned his head, first one way then the other. Carefully, he sat up and leaned forward, sniffing the air. He rubbed his eyes groaning.

"That was some ride," he said.

"Yeah," Chandy said, shuddering.

"Well, at least you know what it's like to drown now. Remind me to teach you how to swim."

"Humph," was all Chandy said.

They took stock of their situation in silence. They pulled off their clothes, examining each other's bodies for serious injuries, then examined their belt packs for contents to see what had been lost and what they had for tools and equipment. Miraculously, nothing was missing. Each found small half-moon cutters about two inches in diameter, several pieces of patch cloth with tins of the strong native glue so essential to colony life, several lengths of glass thread for snares and binding shelters, a fire-making kit consisting of pellets and a flat-headed tamper for slapping them to induce a flame, and a supply of concentrated dried popple berries for quick energy. In addition, there were two extra cylinders of compressed air in each kit and on their belts, the long, wide-bladed knives that all hunters carried. Most surprising and of most interest to them, they still retained their small handguns that they had confiscated from Fylfot. They had the essentials.

"Okay," Caleb said at last. "We won't starve, we can build shelter and have a warm fire, we can protect ourselves, hunt and make what we need for travel. I wish we had more repair patches, but one good kill and I'll have my missing boot. As long as we don't find ourselves in need of a ground cloth, we should be okay."

Chandy frowned but nodded. He began gathering the equipment to return to his kit and laying out his clothes to see what he could do about repairing them. He moved in jerks, tossing the precious tools back in the pouch with a vengeance. The clothes he laid out none too carefully in disgust.

"Problem, Chandy?"

"Fylfot. I'm going to kill that man if I see him again. He tried to kill us, didn't he? He damned near did it, too!"

Caleb nodded and continued his methodical inspection of his own clothes. He began patching holes in his tunic, carefully arranging the patches for maximum coverage and periodically stepped back to judge the effects of his work. He said nothing.

"Well?" Chandy said at length. "Aren't you going to say something? We let that slime trick us. We put ourselves in a bad situation and he took advantage of it. Caleb, we ought to know better."

Caleb shrugged, slipping the tunic over his head and tying together the loose ends of what used to be a sash. "We underestimated him, that's all. It won't happen again. Next time we'll be wiser and he won't have the chance to take us off guard."

"If there is a next time. He's miles from here now and we don't even know where he is."

"There'll be a next time. I don't know where he is, but I know where he's going. We'll catch him."

"You do?" Chandy asked. "You know where he's going?"

"He's going to go down river to the lake and then to the separatists? camp. He's going to try to hide from the colony there. If we go across country, we can catch him before he gets that far. I don't care how fast that boat of his is, he's going to be delayed at the cataract and the falls just above the lake, and when he crosses it, we'll be waiting."

Chandy thought for a moment and decided he should have figured out that one himself. It was a logical choice for the historian. "Oh," was all he said, and he began repairing his pants, patching the holes in the knees and the rip in the side just above the boot on his left leg.

Caleb didn't bother to tell Chandy that he didn't know where he was going. Only that his sense of direction told him to head south and east, more or less in the direction of the lake. They found the going easy for the most part, and Caleb began taking stock of landmarks and game sign for future use. This was a part of the valley that was seldom visited by either hunters or gatherers. It was too far away for hauling game, and there were sufficient supplies of nuts, berries and roots closer to the colony to avoid the necessity of foraging this far afield. Yet it was a very rich land and held great promise for the colony's future, if they were to survive the second plague of rats. Fortunately, there was no sign of the beasts in this part of the valley yet, and he wondered why.

They traveled in a more or less straight line, making their way through several thickets of crystal bush and thorny undergrowth, some of which had grown up in the hours since the downpour. It was a peculiarity of the more dangerous silica plants that rain would dissolve them in short order, only to have them spring up again more abundant and sharper-edged than ever. This took some days or weeks, of course, but even the low-lying crystalline 'buddings', as they were called, could tear at the legs and ankles.

When they heard the roar of the cataract ahead and to the left, Caleb was both relieved and elated. His dead reckoning had apparently served him well, and they decided to wait at the base of the great falls for Fylfot's arrival. The historian would spend some time trekking boat and equipment past the narrow gap in the rocks, and by the time he had completed the task, he would be exhausted and therefore more easily subdued. Caleb had not forgotten the man's prodigious strength.

When they reached the foot of the falls, they stood for some time, looking up at the mountain of water, crashing through the narrow gap in the rock cliff that separated the upper river from the lower reaches that led to the lake.

Chandy had never seen the cataract and he stood dumfounded, mouth agape, staring at the split in the rock, the tall geyser of rushing water, trying desperately to squeeze through the small space in its rush to the wetlands below. The mist curled around them, covering them with a heavy dew as they stood there, and Caleb grinned at Chandy, water dripping from his chin and nose, yet unable to affect the boy's wonder. It was much the same as his own first experience of the falls. It was a true wonder, but they had much to do, and there would be other times for admiring the forces of nature. He grabbed Chandy just above the elbow to get his attention. The boy turned, frowning and Caleb motioned to him to follow.

It took no time at all to prepare for Fylfot's arrival. They moved down stream some hundred yards, following the portaging trail that others had used while traversing this part of the river, and found a likely spot to wait for their prey. With little equipment at their disposal, they were still able to fashion two blinds, one on each side of the portage trail, and settled in to wait.

Behind them, the roar of the cataract continued its din, though not so loudly here as at the base of the rend in the natural wall, and they gave up trying to anticipate their quarry's approach by the sound of his movements. Instead, they arranged themselves comfortably in the blinds so that they could see anyone approaching.

An hour passed and Caleb was beginning to doubt the wisdom of his plan. There was still no Fylfot, and he should have been here by now. They couldn't have missed him. The historian wouldn't know how to hide his track, and there had been no sign of his passing when they arrived.

Had he somehow come ashore and doubled back to the Tower? There would be no surprising him a second time. He'd be prepared for visitors next time, and he could kill them at will as soon as they entered the air vent, assuming he hadn't repaired it by now. Could he have overturned in the current or not known about the cataract and tried to run it like rapids? If that was the case, they'd never find him or their lost equipment. It would have all been destroyed, including his boat no matter how strong it was.

He was about to break cover to talk things over with Chandy when the young hunter pelted him with a small stone. Caleb crooked his head to one side in question and Chandy pointed up the trail. Caleb followed Chandy's pointing finger and caught sight of a lumbering bent figure, dragging a strange boat, now filled with supplies and being used as a sled. It was Fylfot, and as they had expected, he was sweating, panting, and absolutely exhausted. They waited until he was just in front of them before they stepped out from their blinds, Caleb in front of him and Chandy next to the boat. Fylfot gasped and stumbled, falling forward to the ground when he saw them.

"Hello, Professor Fylfot," Caleb said with a smile. "I see you made it."

"Why, my dear boy..." Fylfot stammered. "I'm so glad to see you're alive. After that tumble into the water that you two took, I was afraid you'd been killed. And there's the young Chandy as well. This is good fortune indeed, isn't it?"

He lifted himself onto his knees and started to raise up, one hand steadying himself in the attempt, the other moving to his side.

Caleb brought his right arm from behind his back and pointed the beamer directly at Fylfot's forehead. "Don't give me an excuse, Fylfot," he said.

Fylfot's hand moved away from the holstered pistol and he struggled to his feet, grinning.

"Why, my dear boy. You don't think I was going to threaten you, do you?"

He was sweating even more profusely now, and breathing harder, much more than he would have from simple exertion. Fylfot saw himself on the edge of death and Caleb wasn't about to disillusion him.

"You will do exactly as I say, Dr. Fylfot. You will let go of the tether on the boat, sit cross-legged on the ground and put your hands behind your head. I've never killed a man before, Professor, but I wouldn't hesitate to do it in your case."

Fylfot didn't speak. He did as he was told, and while Caleb continued to point the weapon at the man's head, Chandy recovered the beamer from Fylfot's holster and tied his hands securely at the wrist. That done, they motioned for Fylfot to stand, and he once again surprised them by easily rising from his cross-legged position without any help from them. Apparently his earlier struggle to stand was just one more ruse.

"I suppose we're going to be walking from here", he said.

"I suppose so. The boat is a bit tricky, as you pointed out. I wouldn't want another accident."

Fylfot shivered slightly and shrugged. "I also suppose I'm going to be carrying most of the load again?"

"Undoubtedly you will. It should be interesting to watch when we cross the fens. They're still flooded, you know. With all that weight, you may sink. What a tragedy that would be...to lose all that equipment."

CHAPTER 20

They made their way back through a small section of forest and found themselves on the edge of the fens. Only scattered crystalline bushes and a few isolated tufts of high green grass broke the smooth surface of the ground, now completely submerged by runoff from the deluge. The clearing skies were reflected brightly in the mirror of the water. It looked as if lacy tufts of cotton were skittering across the surface, keeping perfect pace with the high clouds that were the remnant of the passing storm. Caleb frowned and let out a quick puff of breath.

"Yeah," he said, "It's even worse than I thought. We'll have to make a wide detour just to avoid the muck out there. I'm afraid we won't make it home until close to dark, and that's a good ten or twelve hours away."

Chandy mumbled low guttural utterances, the meaning of which were quite clear. Fylfot simply groaned at the thought of carrying his burden that much longer. As for Caleb, he shifted the load on his back, took the extra pack from Chandy, and turned to the left. His two companions had little choice but to follow. All understood that, with the added inconvenience of a wider detour, there would be no travois to lighten their load. It would take too long to build.

They moved along the margin of the fens, staying safely away from the water's edge and keeping watch for any lake creatures that may have found their way into the newly flooded shallows.

There were at least three species of local fauna capable of killing them. All three normally kept to the depths, but after heavy rains, they sometimes ventured out onto the floodplain in search of food. One of them, a peculiar creature about seven feet in length and shaped like an oval platter, had a habit of laying in wait at the margin of the floodplain and then leaping out to attack anything that showed movement. It used a lunging motion that allowed it to flop over its prey and kill it with stingers covering the underside of its body. Of course, humans were quite inedible to it, but by the time it had taken a taste and decided to move on, it was too late for the victim. Death was a possibility, serious illness inevitable.

The journey took them far to the south through fields of feather grass that powdered to the touch as they passed. The rain had done that. The plant thrived on sunshine but disintegrated in the presence of water much as did the larger Spanglar bushes. For the pilgrims the net effect was fine glass crystals in their clothing and misting clouds, like pollen in the air, and they covered their faces with strips of wet cloth as best they could to prevent the grit from settling on their skin and in their eyes or lungs. Caleb followed a track that brought them onto bare rock as much as possible and led them to the edge of the dense forest that lay to the north. The two hunters moved cautiously with rifles at the ready, while Fylfot was limited to scanning the flats in all directions, looking for movement. Twice they heard heavy hooves coming from the dense underbrush, but on neither occasion did anything present itself. Apparently the tuskers were not around for the moment.

Eventually they turned back to the south and into the fields bordering the territory of the separatists. They could hear the gentle lapping of little waves coming off the water, driven by the stiffening breeze and were relieved to find themselves at last in known territory. Caleb and Chandy had hunted this area often in the past few years, but the separatists now claimed these fields as their own. Grazing was being carried out here. They spotted and then approached a small herd of lummox, which eyed them suspiciously, chewing their cud steadily but continually aware of the passing strangers. Two bulls in particular shifted to position themselves between the rest of the herd and the travelers in a dance that was millennia in the making. Fylfot was fascinated by the great hairy animals, all bulk and head, with short stubby legs and short spiral horns that protruded from their foreheads pointing straight forward to help plow the earth for roots and tender shoots. Through gasps of air he mentioned it. Caleb and Chandy simply pushed the man forward when he wanted to stop and observe the creatures, one of the mainstays of colonial larders. Further along, they climbed a small knoll and stopped to rest. Caleb saw no harm in letting the outsider observe while they ate the last of the sweet cakes Caleb's mother had prepared and a box of the Old World rations brought by Fylfot. It was while they were resting that things changed. One moment they were pointing out animals to Fylfot and the next they were facing three men who simply rose up out of the high grass in front of them. Instinctively, Chandy reached for his rifle, but Caleb grabbed his arm. When Chandy turned sharply to look at him, Caleb gently pointed with his eyes to the hand weapon at Chandy's belt. Chandy relaxed.

"Good afternoon," Caleb said easily.

They all three nodded. Caleb recognized two of them as hunters he had once trained with.

He didn't know them well, but he remembered them from his initiation time. The one named Darius Fletcher was quite adept as he remembered, and very quick for his size. He was relatively tall, nearly seven feet in height and very muscular. This made it all the more amazing that he was able to approach so close to them without being detected. The other, Sean, was smaller and not very bright at all, but he was a dead shot and very quick to kill on the hunt. As for the third man, he was a youth of about Chandy's age and unknown to Caleb.

Darius stepped forward and tried to look terrifying. "What are you doing here? Are you lost?" he said coldly.

"Hello, Darius. We're on the way home. We needed to come this way to avoid the fens. Sorry if we disturbed the herd."

"Be sorrier that you disturbed us!" snapped the younger one with them. Darius half turned and reached out with his long arm, slapping the boy backhanded across the face. The boy fell backward, rolling at the last moment and shifting into a crouch, as if ready to attack.

"You're Harden, aren't you?" said Chandy, forcing a smile. "I remember you now. We used to play out behind the metalworker's compound, remember? We used to find all sorts of discarded iron pieces back there."

The one called Harden regarded Chandy, red-faced with anger. "I remember," he said sullenly.

Who's the other one with you?" Darius asked. It sounded more like a command than a question.

"Him? He's from the Tower. We're taking him to see the Keeper."

"From the Tower," snorted the one called Sean. "You're telling us that he's from the Tower? Is he a god you captured? He looks more like a ground sloth to me."

"It's...hard to explain. When the Keeper speaks to him, we'll know more."

Darius realized that they were serious. The import of speaking to a watcher was obviously not lost on him. Caleb watched his body language, his breathing, the set of his eyes and the tension in his muscles. He knew Darius was caught off guard and trying hard to regain his composure.

"I think perhaps that he should talk to Morgan first," said Darius evenly. He looked Caleb in the eye, his gaze now unwavering.

"I think not," said Caleb.

"Now who is this Morgan? Is he your leader?" asked Fylfot.

Darius shifted his attention to Fylfot and looked him up and down. "He's an elder. We have no leaders, just free men and women following their chosen paths in life together."

"Fascinating," said Fylfot to this. "I think I'd enjoy meeting him, actually."

"Then it's settled," said Darius.

Caleb shifted his rifle in his hands slightly. The meaning was obvious. "If you want to speak to this man or if Morgan does, you can come to the Keeper's house and discuss it."

Caleb and Darius stared at each other, each waiting for the other one to blink. Neither did. Caleb sought desperately for some way out of the stalemate, unwilling to give up his prisoner and equally unwilling to come to blows with these three. Suddenly, he smiled and relaxed.

"Okay, Darius. If you think Morgan would want to talk to our friend here I can understand that. After all, we are in your grazing fields, aren't we? But I insist that we be on our way in time to reach the colony by nightfall. There are dangers out here at night that you aren't aware of.."

Darius nodded. "You'd be surprised what we're aware of, Caleb. I can't speak for Morgan, but as for myself, I'll agree. You need to be on your way in good time. That should not be a problem."

The three separatist hunters led the way as the party cut crosswise through the fields toward the rising village in the distance. Chandy tried repeatedly to catch Caleb's eye, but Caleb gave no sign of what he was up to. The boy would just have to wait until later. Fylfot, on the other hand, had no compunction about sharing his thoughts. He assailed Darius with questions about the separatists and why they had moved across the valley from the main colony, pushing him for details of the history of the move and the reasons behind their decision. Darius answered his questions easily while revealing nothing of genuine substance, and in doing so gained Caleb's respect. The man was very quick to understand that this stranger was not to be trusted yet. Apparently, as with Caleb, Darius saw something out of balance with the man, some missing piece of information that left him cautious with his dealings with the man.

CHAPTER 21

T he party created a great stir when they reached the village. Curious villagers came by the dozens as soon as they were spotted. Word was sent to Morgan and Olivia immediately. By the time the party reached Morgan's platform, he, Olivia, and Yetti were all there waiting. They looked down at the group without comment, apparently sizing them up while appearing not the least rattled by the visit. Caleb walked confidently to the steps of the platform and started up the stairs. When the one called Harden moved to block his way, Morgan waved him aside as he moved back to give Caleb more room on top.

Caleb stepped out onto the platform and nodded to the three of them. "Hello, Morgan," he said, "and to you, Olivia. This is Yetti, isn't it?"

"You remember me?" she said, surprised.

"I remember your sweet cakes, and the kindness you showed my mother when she had the fever. Yes, I remember you well."

Yetti smiled, a bit flustered and obviously charmed by this, something Caleb was hoping for. Even Olivia softened slightly, no mean feat for a woman of her tough personality. As for Morgan, he smiled slightly and offered his hand.

"Nice of you to visit," he said.

"An unexpected one, I'm afraid. We were on the way home and skirted the fens after the storm, ending up in your grazing pastures. I hope we didn't disturb anything."

Morgan's expression never changed. "I'm sure you did not," he said. "But who is this? He's a stranger to me."

"Fylfot's the name, sir, Skylar Fylfot. I'm an historian, here to chronicle the demise of the colony."

Morgan raised an eyebrow and looked him up and down. "Is that so?" he said.

"Yes indeed, eh heh. Quite frankly, you and your separatists are a very great surprise to me and I simply must talk to you about it."

Morgan looked to Caleb, inviting comment.

"It's complicated, Morgan, but we were sent to the Tower by the Keeper and found him there. The watchers are gone and we are threatened in ways you can't imagine. The professor is all we found there. We were bringing him back to talk to the Keeper when we were...invited to visit the village here."

"So? The Keeper sent you to the Tower? I find that hard to believe."

"We're faced with a threat that warranted it. Believe me, the threat is real."

"We know about the beasts, Caleb. We're preparing for them now. Morg and some of his friends have been to the colony with one of our hunters who was injured by them."

"Who was it?"

"George McCallum. I understand he'll live. Does the Keeper really believe the threat to be so great??

"You've seen what they can do. There are hundreds if not thousands of them. Our friend here tells me that they are the plague returned."

All three of the elders reacted, the two women moving back a step and Morgan instinctively grasping the knife at his waist. He looked at an inanely smiling Fylfot then back at Caleb and finally at Chandy.

"You're the one apprenticed to the Keeper?"

Chandy looked surprised but nodded. Morgan thought a moment, frowning.

"Frightening thought," he said with agitation.

Chandy looked insulted.

"Not you, my boy. The beasts returning. This changes things." He turned and looked out over the village to the far partially-built wall facing the woods. Caleb followed his gaze and saw men and women digging a wide ditch while others filled it with scraps of wood and small logs. "You will stay awhile?" he asked slowly.

"As long as we can. We need to be back by nightfall. I don't want to be out on the plain after dark."

"That's very wise. Yetti, will you take these two to the commissary and feed them? I'll want to talk to our off world visitor for a while."

Caleb could do little but agree and thank the man. He wondered what Morgan was up to, but finally decided it's just more of his paranoia. The man obviously wanted to question the historian for himself.

"If I might offer a word of caution, Morgan, I'd advise weighing anything he says very carefully. He's proven himself to be treacherous since we found him."

Fylfot reddened and began rocking back and forth. "Not so, not so. It's a simple misunderstanding, an accident along the way, nothing more."

"Treacherous," Caleb repeated and said no more.

Leaving their packs and the heavy chest at the platform, Yetti led them through the myriad of half-finished houses and newly-completed foundations. Caleb took in as much as he could without appearing obvious. He found the work well underway in creating a new enclosed village and the quality of workmanship as good as the colony's. The Keeper, he decided, would be anxious to hear about all this. Occasionally, he and Chandy would exchange glances when they saw something surprising or worth noting. They hoped Yetti didn't notice.

When they reached the commissary area, they were seated at a central table, all rough wood and sharp edges, and given cakes and a bowl of stew only as Yetti could make it. Around them the aromas of cooking and earthy soil swirled, mixed with a faint odor of freshly butchered meat, but as soon as they lifted spoon to mouth, the stew itself erased all that, its own pungent spice overpowering any other odor. It was delicious and they were both glad for it. Chandy attacked it with such vigor that one would think he hadn't eaten in days. When they finished, they sipped cool jayberry wine and leaned back, their feet stretched out beneath the table.

It was then that they noticed that they were surrounded by a dozen or more young women. Each of them seemed to have some task to perform and all stayed at a respectable distance, but they were obviously observing the two with interest. For Caleb, it was a somewhat unpleasant experience, but Chandy was reveling in the attention. He smiled and nodded whenever some young lady caught his eye, and seemed to take delight in embarrassing them in the process. Caleb watched the game for a few moments, and then offered a little grunt.

"I thought you already had a woman," he said.

Chandy's smile faded only slightly, and without even bothering to look Caleb's way, he said, "Women should always be reminded that they are women. I'm just reminding them of their charming nature, that's all."

Caleb shook his head and returned to sipping his wine. "This from a sixteen-year-old boy," he said sarcastically.

Chandy turned and looked him in the eye. "This from my sister, Caleb. You might find that useful information sometime."

Caleb was about to defend himself when Chandy's expression changed. He was looking intently in the direction of a cluster of finished houses in the direction of the wood.

"What's up?"

"I...I thought I saw ... Oh, never mind."

"You thought you saw what?" pressed Caleb.

"Well, I could have sworn I saw Jillian, but that's ridiculous. What would she be doing here?"

Caleb chuckled. "She wouldn't. She has no reason to be here, and the Keeper would never allow it."

"Yeah, you're right."

"Where was she?"

"Hmm? She was over there by those buildings. I only saw her from the back, and this girl's hair was shorter. It only came to the bottom of her neck, but the way she walked reminded me of Jillian."

"And that, my friend is what comes of falling in love," Caleb said playfully.

"I suppose so, or maybe it's this good wine."

He took another gulp of the wine and refilled his mug.

"Well I see you two are causing a stir."

It was Yetti now standing behind them.

"' Must be Chandy, Yetti. They're not here to see me," said Caleb.

She laughed and threw her head back. "Was that modesty from a Grant? Now that's something new. I don't remember your father ever being that reserved with his self-appreciation."

"Are we talking about the same man?" Caleb asked.

Yetti smiled wistfully. "There was a time, young man, when your father had women following him wherever he went, and I don't remember him objecting either. You're a great deal like him, you know."

"Maybe not," Chandy jibed. "He's going to marry my sister, Kylie. I guess he's pretty much a settled old man now."

Yetti grinned and laughed heartily again. "And a wise choice, too. I guess that leaves it up to you to chase the young ladies. One thing about having such a small group here is the lack of variety, you know. That goes for women as well as men."

"There's no help here either, Yetti. I'm afraid our young friend here is in love"

"Anyone I would remember?"

"It's Jillian, the Keeper's granddaughter. I'm afraid they're a couple now."

"Is that so?" Yetti said, seeming to consider the idea. "Well I can't stay and talk any longer. Why don't you two look around until Morgan and Olivia are ready for you?"

She turned and left hurriedly.

"That was quick," Chandy said.

"Hmm. Well, she always was an odd woman. I think it comes with so much responsibility. At any rate, her suggestion's a good one. Let's look around."

They walked casually through the camp, greeting old friends from before the split and nodding politely to others whom they recognized. For all appearances, they were simply strolling, but both of them were paying close attention to everything. They walked past the kilns and by the makeshift metal shops, though where the separatists were getting metal they couldn't imagine. They skirted the edge of the fields near the wood and casually walked the edge of the rising outer wall and ditch. They were making good progress. From what they saw, there was much activity here, with fresh trenches having been dug and filled with straw and brush. Caleb could see that it was the beginning of makeshift defenses against the rats, should they attack before the wall was finished. He filed the information away for later. It looked like a very good strategy. Activity was high. Everyone was busily working at something, mostly construction and the gathering of food in all forms. Even the hunters were helping bring in the barely mature natural plants that grew in the forest and along its margin. To Caleb it looked like preparations for a siege, or at least his understanding of a siege from his history classes in school. As they completed a circuit of the outer perimeter to the West, they spotted some twenty villagers bringing long staves from the forest where they had been cut. The thick saplings had already been skinned and sharp points had been fashioned at one end. The separatists were preparing to defend themselves, and they were going to do it here. Chandy and Caleb looked at each other with consternation. They both knew that it would be a disaster to try to defend this place without walls, ditches or no ditches. The Keeper's hope that they would return to the colony when the rats began their attacks was apparently in vain.

"It's getting late," Caleb said. "We'd better be going."

CHAPTER 22

Morgan was certainly no one's fool, and certainly not a fool for this outlander. He was certain that there was more than met the eye with the mysterious stranger from the Tower, and when the strange little hulk of a man spoke of the demise of the colony, he sensed a subject that needed to be explored further. He began his interrogation of Fylfot by casually showing him what the separatists were doing, pointing out the salient points of the village's growth from the platform.

He watched the historian's reactions closely, picking his words carefully to invite comment without revealing too much to the man. When he felt that he had established some level of rapport with the amiable visitor, he began to question the man in earnest.

"You mention that you were here to observe the demise of the colony. Is that because of the tuskers? Do you believe there are too many of them for us defend against?"

Fylfot offered one of his oily smiles and shook his head. "Actually, my dear Morgan, I did not know about the tuskers when I first arrived on Two Moons. It was only after I began observing from my lonely metal tower that I discovered them and the danger they represent. I was actually expecting a higher degree of decay among the colonists after the watchers left. You knew that they left? No? Well it's true. There hasn't been anyone in the Tower since shortly after the quelling of the rat infestation all those generations ago. I'm afraid most people on the Old World don't even know that the colony exists anymore. No, I assumed that the colony had fallen into despair from a lack of support and modern technology, but you seem to be far more resourceful than I expected."

"We are resourceful, aren't we? Particularly the separatists here in the new town."

"Yes. Yes indeed. In fact, after noting this expansion and finding out that you've left for reasons of political and social philosophy, I'm beginning to think that your demise is prematurely anticipated."

"I see," Morgan said in a noncommittal tone.

"Yes. Actually, this separation is a good sign, and from what those two 'people' said, a wise move."

Morgan now looked at the man with increased interest. "And just what did they say?"

"Well," Fylfot said in almost a whisper, "I don't mean to gossip, you understand, but those people in the old colony are not really your friends."

"Speak plainly," Morgan commanded.

"Yes. Well, I suppose I must. I overheard my captors talking last night about how threatening your new village is to them and how the...Keeper I believe they call him? They were saying how this keeper person thinks that you need to be forced back to the old colony and under his control."

"Is that so?" Morgan said carefully.

"Hmm. Yes. They said that they ought to strike while you're still weak so you'll have to come back to them in order to survive."

Morgan fell silent and turned away, pretending to study the sheafs of plans on the table in front of him. Fylfot said nothing, allowing the seeds that he had just planted to grow.

"And just what did they plan to do?" he asked over his shoulder.

"Well, I understood them to say that they were going to raid or destroy your food supply so you'd have to come back to them, begging for help. Fortunately, that doesn't have to happen now."

"It won't happen now, I can assure you!"

"Oh, being forewarned certainly helps, but I can give you help very much beyond just knowing of the attack."

"You can help us?" Morgan said skeptically.

Fylfot seemed to puff up without moving a muscle. He gave Morgan a knowing look, as if he was now in control of the situation.

"Of course I can. I bring with me knowledge that you cannot possibly have, and I bring technology so far beyond that of the old colony that it would make you virtually invincible."

When Morgan didn't ask for details, Fylfot rushed to add, "You see, I have weapons that are more than a match for those creatures. I have eight altogether, both rifles and hand weapons that depend on energy plasma to destroy a target. With those weapons, we can not only defend against the rats but against the old colonists as well! Why, we could rule this planet, you and I, and I don't mean just this valley. Beyond the walls of the caldera is a whole world waiting for us, and with modern technology, there's no one to stop us. Just think of it, Morgan. You and I could rule this whole world!"

"You're an ambitious man, Fylfot," Morgan said with disgust.

"And I suppose you're not? Don't judge me too quickly, Morgan. Every society needs strong leaders, and you've already proven your willingness to take on the role. You did that when you moved away from the old colony. You're a leader and you have no choice about that. It's your nature! Think about what's best for the colony, Morgan. Think about what's best for all the people on this world, both here and back in the old town. Don't they deserve better than that overbearing Keeper? Aren't you a better choice to lead the people than he is?"

Morgan stared at the historian and said nothing. Thoughts that he had hidden even from himself were beginning to call to him, their logic impeccable as it had been all along. The off worlder was right and he knew it but he had never been willing to admit it until now. Still, this short, hulking figure was not to be trusted. If he could use him and then discard him....

"What do you suggest?" he finally asked.

"Ah," said Fylfot. "I have a plan. I have a brilliant plan for us both."

CHAPTER 23

Neither Chandy nor Caleb spoke as they walked back through the center of the camp toward Morgan's quarters. There was no need. Both were thinking of the friends and acquaintances that would be killed if the tuskers attacked before winter, and they were very sure that they would. Already there was a touch of coolness in the air, and the normally gentle breezes were becoming progressively harsher. Even the jack darts were beginning to gather along the river and in the fens, a sure sign of an early migration. It wouldn't be long now before the windy season started.

"I suppose we need to go back and prepare for these people coming home this winter," said Chandy sadly.

Caleb nodded, thinking about the tuskers. "Let's hope that there are separatists left to come home."

They walked in silence after that, passing the commissary area quickly and briefly waving at Yetti who gave them a peculiarly sad look. Caleb wondered if she was sensing the coming disaster too.

As they approached Morgan's quarters a dozen hunters came toward them, armed and looking grim. Each carried one of the newer pneumatic rifles and they held them casually but at the ready. Chandy touched Caleb's arm, but he shook his head.

"Just act casual, Chandy," he said. "Let's not overreact."

The hunters came directly to them, led by Caleb's friend, Darius.

"Going on a hunt, Darius?" Caleb asked casually.

"Morgan wants to see you. He sent us to fetch you."

"That's thoughtful," Caleb said carefully. "We need to be on our way if we're going to make the colony by nightfall. Thanks."

Darius gave no sign of having heard Caleb. He simply signaled and the group proceeded to the platform, hunters flanking them. Morgan was waiting for them with Olivia, standing at the top of the platform, looking down at them.

"You'll need to stay the night, my friends. I'm not through speaking with our guest, and our discussions could go on late into the night. We'll make you comfortable and you will leave in the morning. I've sent a runner to the colony to let the Keeper know what's happened."

There was no suggestion or offer in what Morgan said. It was a flat statement of fact, and the 'escort' was obviously here to be sure that they complied. Under the circumstances, there was no choice but to agree, but to maintain some level of control, Caleb said, "We thank you for that consideration, Morgan. Yes. I think it will be all right to stay another night. You may have some extra time with Fylfot."

There was almost a look of admiration in Morgan's nod. He had an apparent appreciation for Caleb's not-very-subtle meaning.

They were escorted to a group of dome-shaped structures near the grazing fields on the edge of the village and then ushered into one of the buildings. It was comfortable enough, clean and sweet-smelling with new straw on the floor and delicately embroidered coverings on the raised beds. A fire had already been started in the small hearth in the center of the room, and a large tub flanked by tall ceramic ewers of clear water invited them to bathe.

Caleb immediately tested the two beds with his hand, picked the harder of the two and began removing his clothing, piling it on the bed like a dog marking territory with his scent.

Chandy stood exactly where he was. He hadn't moved. When Caleb noticed, he sat on the bed and looked at the boy.

"So what's wrong now?"

"You're going to let them get away with that?"

"You have suggestions as to how we could stop them?"

Chandy shook his head, frowning.

"Look, Chandy. These aren't our enemies, you know. I'll admit they're damned rude and downright belligerent right now, but they're still our people. They're also damned scared. Wouldn't you be a little on edge out here on a limb the way they are? It just seemed easier to not make an issue of it. Besides, I could use a good bath. My crotch feels like the rough side of a Spanglar bush.

Chandy considered all this silently for a moment and then added, "We're prisoners. I'll bet there are guards outside right now."

"Or nearby," Caleb agreed. "I'm not sure that they're willing to totally insult us yet, but I'm pretty sure we're being watched. Think of it as added security. We have our own guards now."

"I guess," Chandy said without much conviction. "Hurry up with that bath. I've got more sand in my navel than hair on my head."

They bathed and exchanged their clothing for long robes provided by a middle-aged woman who was only vaguely familiar. She had entered without knocking while Chandy was standing in the tub and Caleb was beside the bed, both completely naked. It didn't seem to faze her at all, but Chandy sat down so quickly that he bruised his rump painfully. Without ceremony, she gathered their clothing, set down the robes, and as she left, commented, "They'll be cleaned and back in the morning." Without further conversation, she was gone. For the most part, they were both too tired to care, and after slipping the

robes over their heads, they nearly fell into the two beds
and fell into a deep sleep.

It was well past half-night when the sounds outside
awoke them. Chandy was up first, fumbling for wood to
put on the fire and lighting a candle from the nearly extinct
flames of what remained among the embers. Caleb was on
his feet nearly as quickly, rifle in hand. They looked at
each other, listening to the commotion outside.

"What the hell is all that?" Caleb said.

"I don't know, but they sure are noisy about it."

Chandy now grabbed his rifle and the two of them
stepped out into the night. There were indeed two hunters
outside their doors, looking only slightly less confused than
they were. When they saw the two emerge from the
doorway, they turned and barred the way.

"You need to stay inside," one of them said.

"What's going on?"

"We're not sure," the other one said, "but I think there
are tuskers at the far end of the compound. Everyone's
gone to fight them."

"So why are you two still here?"

The two guards looked at each other, obviously
conflicted. "We're...here to protect you two. We have orders."

"You've got orders to keep an eye on us and be sure we
don't sneak away, right?"

They looked at each other again, and one finally shrugged. "That's basically it," he said.

"Good. Then keep an eye on us and don't let us sneak away while we all go see what's going on over there where the yelling is."

Without even waiting for a response, he set off in the direction of the wood, the tails of his robe flapping around his knees. The others quickly fell into line behind him. They made their way as directly as they could through the camp, dodging piles of discarded materials and half-finished homes. Caleb cursed who ever laid all this out, noting there were no direct routes through the maze that he could see. Maybe Morgan wanted it that way to slow down the 'invaders'.

Flames were beginning to rise into the air along the trench line. People were shouting and milling around, unable to decide how best to handle the situation. Morgan and Olivia were prominently silhouetted against the red of the flames, pointing and barking orders, trying to organize some sort of plan of defense. As they approached the chaos, they could see that it was giving away to order, little by little resolving itself into groups of villagers stationed along the low wall.

Caleb and Chandy, their guards in tow, joined the nearest and smallest cluster. They found themselves wedged in among a clutch of hunters, all armed and all looking grim. Caleb looked out through the flames. Some twenty yards away, at the margin of the forest, hundreds of red glowing eyes stared back at them. Looking quickly left and right, he saw a solid line of beastly eyes, held at bay for the moment by the fire.

For a while, no one did anything. It appeared to be a standoff as long as the fires could be kept going. To Caleb, that was the fatal flaw in their plan. He turned and looked for Morgan, who was close by.

"Morgan!" he cried. "We need more wood!"

Morgan looked his way, hesitated briefly, then growled orders at a cluster of villagers who he had held in reserve and they were off to find anything that they could that would burn. Caleb looked back, seeing still more pairs of glowing eyes joining those already on the edge of the wood. There were many hundreds of the tuskers now. Without thinking, he brought his rifle to his shoulder and fired. A tiny flame shot up between two of the eyes facing them, and with a squeal of pain, the beast fell forward into the light, his skull split at the back. Suddenly more hunters were firing, and more tuskers fell in heaps all along the line. With each volley, they dropped huge numbers of the beasts. People began to shout and cry, both in elation and defiance. For the first time in his life, Caleb experienced what could only be described as a war cry, as he felt his body fill with rage.

There were tusker bodies everywhere now, beginning to pile up among the low brush of the forest's edge, but in each case, the ruddy beacons were replaced by others from behind them. By now, it appeared that there were thousands of them, all waiting and screeching angrily at the fire in the trench.

Everything that would burn was sent tumbling over the wall into the trench to keep the flames going. The battle continued like that for nearly two hours, but little by little, the flames began to subside. Fuel was getting short. Suddenly, the pairs of glowing eyes began to decrease as more and more of them disappeared back into the forest. It was going to be a near thing, Caleb decided, but the beasts seem to have their fill of the slaughter as the flames subsided even more.

From the left there were screams of terror. Caleb looked around in between shots to see a dark undulating mass making its way toward the defenders from the side.

"They're flanking us!" someone cried.

"Pikes!" yelled Morgan, and a group of women and old men shifted to the left carrying the long poles cut the day before. They had been sharpened and the tips fired hard until they were deadly. They lined up with surprising speed, planted the butt of the pikes into the ground, and braced themselves. The dark mass resolved itself into

individual tuskers, frothing at the mouths, their long tusks
scraping the ground as they ran. When they hit the line of
pikes, the whole mass shuddered and came to a sudden
halt, but it soon began to move again, some tuskers leaping
over the defenders, others riding up on the backs of the
dead in front of them and attacking the villagers savagely.
Caleb saw one old man's head severed completely from his
body and a young woman pierced through the chest with
two long fangs. As if on command, the entire group of
hunters around him shifted and began moving toward the
new battle, firing and reloading as they advanced,
concentrating on the tuskers in front, awaiting the ones
behind to kill them in order.

They presented a withering fusillade, dropping the
beasts as easily ascything wheat and in moments, the few
remaining alive retreated, or stood in frustration, their tails
whipping, front limbs sweeping arcs threateningly into the
empty air as they were methodically cut down by the
hunters.

Almost immediately there was another roar from the
trench line and the hunters returned to their station on the
run. The entire line of rats was moving forward, slowly
but building speed as the flames had all but disappeared
below the edge of the trench. Caleb's heart sank. They
were all low on projectiles and there were more tuskers

here than they could handle. They were going to lose the battle. Chandy stood up on the wall, rifle at his waist, and began firing blindly at the oncoming horde. Others joined him, ready for one last desperate fight before they died. It was then that Yetti appeared with four lummox drawn carts filled with large urns, sealed at the top with leather drum heads.

"Make way!" she cried. "Give me room!"

Villagers and hunters alike stepped aside as the carts were brought up along side the wall.

Simultaneously, Fylfot appeared, coming on the run from the village accompanied by seven hunters armed with the Old World weapons he'd brought with him. Suddenly Caleb remembered his own pistol and drew it, abandoning the rifle. Chandy, still atop the wall saw it, grinned and did the same. They began sweeping the horde, severing legs and splitting backbones or heads wherever the thin thread of light touched them. Fylfot's hunters were on the line now, doing the same, but even with this impressive increase in firepower, the tuskers came on.

Yetti barked orders of her own and two hunters lifted one of the urns from the cart, resting it on the wall. Yetti quickly cut the retaining rope around the drum head and pitched the urn forward into the ditch. Instantly, white hot flames erupted from the pit and began flowing left and

right from the spot where Yetti stood. Others lifted still
more urns into place and began pouring the contents into
the trench as well. Caleb laughed and looked at Chandy
who stared in disbelief.

"The cooking oil!" Caleb yelled. "They're dumping
Lummox oil in the trench!"

The tuskers had just reached the trench when the oil
burst into flames, incinerating many as they leaped toward
the wall. The rest quickly veered left and right and
retreated into the forest. They braced themselves for
another attack, reinforcing those with pikes on each edge
of the walls. They waited, but another attack didn't come.
Finally, Caleb turned and sat heavily against the wall,
resting his head on the cool smoothness of the ceramic
coating and breathing heavily. Chandy jumped from the
wall and slid into place beside him, remembering too late
his bruised cheeks. They looked around. Bodies and parts
of bodies littered the ground around them. More beasts
had gotten past them than they realized, but they, too, lay
dead, some only yards from where they sat. Around them
the living slumped and panted, offering smiles and nods to
those by their sides. Caleb looked into the eyes of the
hunters and villagers who had stood with him and he saw
that they mirrored back the respect he was feeling for
them. In the distance, the sun was beginning to peak

above the rim of the valley, adding to the ruddy light that colored everything that they could see. Even the lake in the distance was a thin sliver of pinkish glow in the shadows. For a long time, they didn't move. For a long time, they tried not to remember the night.

CHAPTER 24

"It's time for you to go," Morgan said flatly. It was late afternoon by now and much of the horror of the night's attack had been cleared away. Bodies had been gathered and many already buried, rubble had been cleared and more brush from the forest piled into the trenches in case of another attack. Chandy and Caleb had joined the others in the effort, preferring hard work to thinking about what they'd experienced. In all, some sixty villagers had died. Three more were missing and presumed carried off to be a meal for the beasts. They had been very lucky and though no one said it, it was obvious that they all knew it. Greatest among the losses experienced that night had been Yetti, who was killed by a single large rat who launched itself over the flames just as they subsided, and neatly removed her head. It was sad, and a heavy blow to the village and the colony. There would be many who missed her and many who could not forget how she had saved them all.

Morgan had Caleb and Chandy escorted back to the platform by their two guards as soon as things began to calm and now they stood before him and Olivia, who was looking very dark and very stern.

"It's time for you to go," Morgan repeated.

"I agree," Caleb offered. "As soon as we can load up and Fylfot shows up, we'll be on our way."

"Professor Fylfot has decided to stay with us," Morgan said. "We'll also need your backpacks and supplies, your weapons, and all that Fylfot brought with him. These hunters will see you safely back to the colony."

For a moment no one spoke. Caleb could feel the tension in the gathered group and for once, Chandy had the good sense to hold his peace. Finally, Chandy made to protest, but before he could speak, one of the hunters shoved him toward the path to the lake and pointed his weapon.

"Are you certain this is what you want to do?" Caleb asked evenly.

"I'm quite sure," said Morgan. "You are no longer welcome here, and you can tell that to the Keeper as well. We've beaten the creatures. They won't be back. We are a separate community now, and we've proven that we can defend ourselves."

"How are you going to survive the winter?" Caleb asked seriously.

"Our food supply is safe. We will gather more fuel and with fewer people to feed and house, we can cut back on the number of houses that are needed by the windy season. Most importantly, the people now have a new sense of their own power. We'll be fine. I'll send word to the Keeper regarding our decision."

Morgan turned his back on them and crossed to the small table at the opposite end of the platform. Their escort took their rifles and their back packs. They were each given a small gourd of water and herded toward the lake. Caleb was pleased to see that none of those with whom they had shared the battle the night before were among this escort. It would have been the final humiliation. When they started off, Darius led the way.

Neither of them said a word on the journey back to the colony. They walked silently, eyes on the path ahead, mechanically placing one foot in front of the other as if their only concern was to reach their destination, which, as it happens, was not far from the truth. They sensed that their escort would be delighted to find some excuse to treat them badly and they could not allow that to happen. For Caleb, this was a time to sort out what had happened. What Morgan had done could have extreme consequences for all of them. This was no job for him. He was anxious to report back to the Keeper. As for Chandy, he was breathing harder than his walking would demand. He was obviously feeling the humiliation of being turned out without his belongings, like some sort of criminal to be banished from society. Periodically one or another of the escorts would prod one of them with a rifle butt or a barrel to encourage them to keep pace. It was all Caleb could do to not take a weapon away from one of them and return the favor.

Yet there was one overriding fact that helped him remain calm. At his side, and at Chandy's side, they still had the hand weapons that Fylfot had brought with him. Somehow, no one had thought to check them before they left. At least that small victory would be theirs, and he could imagine Morgan's reaction when it was discovered. Thrust and parry, Morgan, Caleb thought. Deception was not exclusively the prerogative of those in control of a situation.

When they were near the gates of the colony walls, the escort stopped. Darius turned to the two. He was conflicted and it showed.

"Morgan says neither you nor anyone else in the colony is to come to our side of the lake unless invited. Anyone who does will be considered a trespasser and treated accordingly. Do you understand?"

"Why are you doing this, Darius?" Caleb asked simply. Darius looked away, trying to regain his composure.

"You are to tell the Keeper that..." here he swallowed hard and continued to look away, "his days are numbered. He is superfluous now."

"What!" snapped Chandy?

"Caleb," Darius said, ignoring Chandy, "You'd best go now. I don't think we'll speak again."

"This is ridiculous!" said Chandy. "You can't just decide this on your own!"

"It is decided, boy," Darius said now looking at Chandy. "You'd do well to keep your mouth shut now and go."

Caleb rested his hand on Chandy's shoulder.

"Let's go, Chandy. We can't do anything here but get hurt."

"Before you go..." Darius said. He handed each of them their hunting knives. It was a gesture of respect, one hunter to another and all knew it. For Caleb, it was almost an apology. He nodded and took his blade, sheathing at his belt. Chandy did the same, somewhat mollified by the gesture.

With that they turned and walked toward the gates of the town. The sun was just above the rim of the valley and sinking quickly, the dark beginning to engulf them in the absence of Bastion and Desolation, still hours away from rising.

The Keeper was in a dark mood and had been ever since he'd heard the message from Morgan. Caleb sat silently in the cellar study and watched him, waiting for the flood of questions that he knew would come. It had been this way for the past three hours.

When they had entered the city, Chandy had stormed off toward his house, tears in his eyes with rage and shame. He refused to go to the Keeper, preferring to disappear into his own world to lick his wounds Caleb was at least able to exact a promise from the boy to explain to Kylie where he was and that he would come to her when he could. For his own part, he wished that he'd had the luxury of running away like Chandy, but his duty lay elsewhere.

To his surprise, the Keeper had shown little emotion when he related the story of their journey to the Tower and of their discovery of Professor Fylfot. He sat silently listening, intently holding Caleb's gaze and offering no sign of recognition or reaction. It was only when Caleb related the last of their saga, the seizing of their weapons and the ejection from the separatists' village that he began to ask questions. To Caleb's surprise, they were not the questions he had expected.

"How far along are they on the construction of the outer wall?" he had asked. "How many houses have they completed? Did you have an opportunity to see their food stores? Are they secure? What about weapons? How many do they have? How did the people seem? Were they wary of you two or friendly? Do you think they could withstand another attack by the rats?"

He sought details on the layout of the new village and on the activities of the people, as if the whole incident of ejection and the theft of the rifles were inconsequential. At least he did ask to see Caleb's new hand weapon, which he studied carefully, then handed back to him. That was all an hour ago. Since then neither of them had spoken. All in all, it was a very uncharacteristic response. Finally, the Keeper looked over at his guest, seated across the table from him. "You must be hungry. I'll see what I can find," he said, and rose.

"Er, where's Jillian? I would expect her to do that. If she's away, I can wait until I go home."

The Keeper's mood darkened even further. "She's not here, Caleb, which is why I'm glad Chandy isn't with you. If he'd come, he would have asked that question long ago. It would complicate things."

"I don't understand."

The Keeper turned around and faced Caleb. "She's in the separatists' camp. She's going to marry Morg, Morgan's grandson."

"Wh...what! She's what?"

The Keeper appeared more troubled than ever. "She's going to marry Morg. When he was here with George McCallum, he brought a message from his grandfather. Morgan suggested a marriage between one of their leaders and someone in the hierarchy here to cement relations and ensure that we maintain friendly ties. Morg brought specific offers and assurances, and as Keeper,

I could not find fault with his logic. He's always cared for Jillian anyway. It appeared to be a natural solution to the strained relations between the two groups."

"But she's in love with Chandy!"

"She's fifteen. She doesn't know what she's about yet, and Chandy doesn't need the distraction. It's not wise for a Keeper to have a spouse at any rate. It's too much of a distraction. I thought their attraction for each other to be nothing more than a flirtation, so I allowed it. Both of them need some experience of the heart, though for different reasons. As my granddaughter, she is bound to do as she's told, and she obeyed my instructions."

Caleb stood abruptly. "I can't believe you did that," Caleb snapped. He was surprised at his own anger with the Keeper.

The Keeper smiled looked pained and nodded. "At the time it appeared the perfect solution to many of the colony's concerns, and the colony is my first duty. If it meant stability and success for the colony, I'd try to marry you or anyone else off in a similar manner, and, I dare say, you'd do it, though you'd probably hate me for it. At any rate, it appears I may have made a bad bargain."

Caleb slumped down into the chair again. "I don't know how Chandy's going to react to this."

"I know, Caleb. I know. I thought the wound would heal in time, but it appears we haven't much time, do we? This is not like Morgan. It's not like him at all. He's stubborn and independent, but he's no fool."

"It's like Fylfot, though," Caleb said. "The man's devious. He's evil. I haven't trusted him from the first and his trying to drown us just made me even surer of his evil. He's the one that's influenced Morgan. I wonder what he told him about Chandy and me. I wonder what Fylfot told him about the colony."

"It's an unusual name, Fylfot. Do you know what it means?"

"Um, no."

The Keeper simply nodded.

"Keeper, what are we going to do?"

"Well, and this is just between the two of us, what I'd like to do is go somewhere and drink too much of Donald Crone's good brandy, but that's not going to happen. This may still work out. Morgan has to know that I've made the most conciliatory move that I could by agreeing to Jillian's marriage to Morg. Maybe he'll come around. As for Fylfot, we'll have to wait and see. Right now, I have too much to do to worry about my personal feelings. With the watchers gone and the project abandoned, we are totally on our own and we have to behave accordingly. In the morning, we'll start preparing to defend ourselves. We'll need trenches, brush barriers, more rifles as soon as they can be made, and we'll need to strengthen the houses as well. I've a few ideas that might work as well."

"Do you really think the separatists would attack us then?"

"The separatists? Of course not. As soon as they find out what it will be like to deal with those rats, they'll be back here looking for our protection. It's the rats I'm concerned with. If they move on the colony before winter, we are going to be in serious trouble. What happened in the separatists' village proved that. That reminds me. We may need to ration food as well. Another three or four hundred mouths to feed this winter could be a problem."

"What...can I do?" Caleb asked, marveling at the Keeper's ability to shelve his personal problems for the sake of the colony.

"You can do nothing more until morning. We'll need to call a council of the clan chiefs and organize things. They'll want to question you and Chandy. For now, go to the boy and see what you can do to prepare him. He'll need as clear a head as he can muster by tomorrow."

The Keeper stood and crossed to Caleb, placing his hand on his shoulder. It was a gentle touch.

"I know it's a lot to ask, Caleb, but these are dangerous times. You'll have to take care of Chandy as best you can. Frankly, I don't have the time now."

Caleb moved mindlessly through the back streets of the town, too busy sorting out all that had happened to be bothered with watching where he was going. He thought about the changes of the past week, when his entire world had been turned upside down. What was that phrase he had read in school? 'Serving to make the whole world turvy.' That's how he felt now. His whole world was turvy. The Tower, once the ultimate taboo, was now no more than an abandoned building. The watchers were long gone and the colony was totally on its own. There was an alien from the Old World passing among them, and the Keeper, long the revered authority on everything, had shown himself to be a fallible old man, no longer sure of himself. It was all more than he could handle.

As he passed through a narrow alley between two buildings, he heard the distinct slap of a jack dart against a building. He looked up in time to see the lifeless body fall from a height of some ten feet to land on the pavement with a peculiar clapping sound. They'd be swarming soon, their carapaces hardening for the migration to the other side of the valley walls before the coming of winter.

When the winds came, they'd carry them high into the air and out over the rim into the outer world. Somehow he wished he could do that now. He'd like to be lifted by a great wind and taken far from this place; far from the confusion and heartbreak of what was coming. It did indeed serve to make the whole world turvy.

He made his way slowly through the streets, finding more jack dart carcasses and a tightly-closed world. No one stirred in the pale light of the two moons, finally high enough in the sky to dimly illuminate the night. He was reluctant to reach his destination, yet anxious to get there. The thought of seeing Kylie again spurred him on, while the thought of Chandy's reaction to the news about Jillian made him want to turn and run. If only he could fly away, he thought. If only.

As he approached the Crones' house, he saw Kylie waiting for him, seated on a low wooden bench beside the staircase. She stood when she saw him and he was once again struck by her beauty. She wore an off-white gown that covered her from the neck down, with laced half-sleeves. It was buttoned half the length of the dress from neck to midsection. It was perfectly straight, totally shapeless, but it draped her body with grace, inviting fantasies of what lay beneath. It took his breath away. She smiled softly at him and took several steps toward him. Her eyes glistened in the moonlight with tears.

"Hi," he said softly.

"Hi," she replied. "Rough journey was it?"

He nodded. "I'm glad to see you. I need some stability in my life right now. I need to talk to Chandy."

She took his hand, guided it around her waist, and wrapped her arms around his neck. Her head rested on his shoulder and she sighed deeply. "He knows. I told him when he arrived."

"Oh," was all Caleb could think to say.

A moment passed in simple embrace. She pulled away ever so lightly and looked into his eyes. "You must be very tired," she said, "And very hungry. I assume you've been with the Keeper all this time."

"Yes. I was with the Keeper."

"Come inside, my love. Father's asleep and Chandy's hiding in his room. I'll see what I can put together for supper and what I can do for your wounds."

It was such an innocent statement that he didn't even wonder at it. He simply allowed himself to be led up into the house and sat on the broad-back settle to watch Desolation pass in the night sky. Behind him he could hear her setting a place at the table, pouring something into a glass and padding softly about the room. He was glad for the respite. It had been a long, terrible day and a worse night. He needed to heal and he knew it.

At length, she came to him and led him to the table where he found fresh fruit, some of that spice bread that she did so well, and a large bowl of soup, mostly broth and only lightly seasoned. It was exactly what he needed. She sat and watched him in silence, not wanting to intrude. Occasionally he would look up and see her looking back at him, not as someone watching so much as someone in attendance. It was all he could do to not cry at her tenderness.

Halfway through the meal, he said, "I love you."

"And I you," she said and fell again into silence.

After that moment, he began to feel better. Caleb had no idea how hungry he was until he began to eat, and he devoured every morsel with relish, finishing it off with the still-steaming tea in his mug. When he had finished, he leaned back, released a single involuntary belch, and chuckled.

"Well, that wasn't very polite, was it?" he said.

"I found it endearing. You should hear me do that some time."

Caleb frowned. "How did he take it?"

"Not well, but not too badly. At least he didn't try to go see the Keeper. He's very angry, Caleb. We all are. What the Keeper did to Jillian is like a betrayal of all that we stand for. It's seriously divided the people."

He nodded. "I'm not surprised. Still, the Keeper never does anything unless he thinks it's for the good of the colony. He has his reasons"

"He's a senile old man!" Kylie said.

"He's sharper at his age than I'll ever be, Kylie. I don't like what he did any more than you, but we've never had a situation like this before. The separatists have divided us. They've broken off from the colony. Now we have to deal with them as what they are - another community. That's never happened before. We're on very new ground with all this, and no one is going to be sure of their footing for a while. Did Chandy tell you what happened to us?"

She gave him a pained expression. "I cannot think of anything more humiliating for a hunter than what they did to you. It was like castration!"

"Yes," he said, thinking of how apt the image was.

"What could they be thinking?"

"The Keeper says that they're just scared. They're striking out because they feel so helpless. I can see his point, even sympathize with them, but it's no excuse. It can't be allowed."

"What are we going to do?"

"Not we, Kylie, just Chandy and me. It's our problem to solve. The colony can't get involved."

Kylie rose and carried bowls and platters to the counter. She stood facing the wall, then slammed them down and turned. "Caleb Grant, you've got the most incredible ego of anyone I've ever met!" she yelled.

"Um, what?"

"It's your problem, is it? It's your problem and Chandy's? What about the rest of us? Those rifles belonged to the colony as much as they did to you two. They took your equipment, they took your Old World man, and they took your power. That reflects on the whole colony and everyone in it! Don't you see that? This is about all of us, and you can't call it your own! How dare you?" He stared at Kylie open-mouthed. She glared back, waiting for an answer. He felt as if he'd been backhanded. He was jolted to the core. His mind raced. In the end, he closed his mouth and sat up straight. He gave her one of those curt nods that his father used when he'd made up his mind about something.

"You're right, of course," he said, "And you're incredibly beautiful when you're mad. Your eyes have a fire in them."

She sputtered, softened a little, and turned away.

"Don't change the subject," she said.

They both chuckled and crossed to the settle. Neither of them spoke for a very long time.

CHAPTER 25

Caleb awoke the next morning curled up on the settle with a crocheted blanket over him and a soft, goosefeather pillow under his head. He could hear the movement of several people in the room, but what had awakened him was the aroma of breakfast cakes fresh from the stove. He sat up, stretched, and rubbed his face with his hands. He must have fallen asleep some time during the night. Standing, he folded the blanket neatly and placed it on the bench with the pillow on top of it. A quick sweep of his hand through his short hair, and he was ready to face the world.

Stepping from behind the settle he found Kylie at the table, huge skillet of breakfast cakes in hand, smiling at him.

"It's about time," she said.

"Hmm. How'd I know you were going to say that?"

"Because she's a woman," said Donald Crone, standing just long enough for courtesy, and then returning to his breakfast.

"Good morning, sir."

"And good morning to you. Now sit down and eat before it gets cold. The tea's already poured."

He attacked the cakes with gusto equal to last night's dinner and silently thanked the Universe for falling in love with a good cook. Donald continued his own meal, mostly ignoring the guest except to ask for sweetener or cream. Kylie joined them and Caleb watched her eat, all gentile and proper.

"Where's Chandy?" he asked as casually as he could. "He's not up yet?"

"Up and gone," said. Donald. "He left at first light to see the Keeper."

"I don't like the sound of that. You do know what's happened, I suppose."

"'Knew it before you did," Donald Crone said. "Its okay, Caleb. He's all right this morning. I'm pretty sure that the Keeper will straighten him out."

"He was awfully angry, Father," Kylie said.

"Hurt and shamed, I'd say, and with good reason. There's one thing about that boy, though. Once he calms down he makes a decision and then carries it out. He's not going to do anything rash, at least not without you along, Caleb."

"I hope not," said Caleb, finishing the last bite of cake and downing the last of the spiced morning tea. "I suppose I should go and see what I can do though."

"Sounds like a good idea," his host said.

"Would you like me to go to see your parents and tell them you're all right? They may be worried," asked Kylie.

Caleb reddened, realizing that he hadn't spoken to them since all this started. "It would be a big help. I'll probably see my father at the Keeper's, but my mother could use the company. She needs to get to know you better anyway, don't you think?"

Mr. Crone looked up at both of them. "Well," he said passively, "that's settled."

Caleb rose and stepped out into the morning light. He gave Kylie a parting kiss and was off. He found himself dreading this day as much as he had last night, but there was nothing to do but to wait and see.

To his surprise, the clan chiefs were not gathered in the Keeper's compound. The sun was already over the rim of the valley and rising, yet they had not been summoned. Caleb sensed something new in the air. Something had changed dramatically here and he could feel it. He climbed the stairs to the Keeper's house and knocked hesitantly on the door. There was no response. He knocked again, and slowly the door opened. The Keeper stood before him, looking more fatigued than Caleb could ever remember seeing him. He must have been up all night, planning and organizing his response to what had occurred. Across the room, Chandy sat at the small table beside the stairway. He looked totally dejected.

"Come in, Caleb," the Keeper said. "We have news."

Caleb entered and joined them at the table.

"I've something to tell you," the Keeper said.

"Have you and Chandy talked?" Caleb asked.

"We've talked, and I think we've come to an understanding," the Keeper said looking at Chandy, who nodded agreement.

"What's happened?"

The Keeper rubbed his eyes. He let his hands drop to his lap. He was obviously in pain.

"I've been thinking through the night and I've reached the conclusion that Morgan is correct in his assessment of the situation. My days as Keeper are done."

"What? What are you saying? You are the Keeper. That can't change!"

The Keeper shook his head. "Think about it, my young friend. The purpose of the Keeper is to keep the records and to be a go-between for the watchers and the colony. Well there are no watchers. There is no experiment, no test colony and no program to seed the universe with our progeny. It's all over. That means that we are truly on our own, and I no longer have the right to instruct or control any part of what happens here, beyond what I personally do."

Caleb said nothing. He just stared at the old man, unable to formulate a single coherent response.

Chandy looked up from examining his hands and smiled weakly.

"No more Keepers, Caleb. There's no more power in the title, no reason for people to listen to him."

"And no further need for prohibitions on pair bonds between colonists. The population is large enough now to not worry too much about genetic matching. I've lost my reason for existing in the position. From now on, we will have to develop some new form of governance."

"Like Morgan's dictatorship?"

"No, Caleb. That's out of the question. We need to develop self determination by mutual agreement. What form that takes is up to the people, but no dictators, even if the people want it. It's too easy to give up sovereignty over one's own life for the sake of convenience. That is one thing that I'll fight to the end. Other than that, whatever the colonists want, they can do."

"You're giving up," Caleb said, the words sticking in his throat.

"I'm being realistic."

"What about the separatists? Do we just let them keep us out of that side of the valley?"

"If they want that, then we will have to agree to it. I don't imagine they'll want to remain isolated for too long.

There simply aren't enough of them to survive without good relations with us. They'll see that in time."

Caleb's heart sank. The Keeper gave him a weak smile.

"The old ways are gone, Caleb. It's over. At least you two will be hunters as you always wanted. Chandy doesn't have to worry about learning to be a Keeper.

"Besides," Chandy sneered, "now that Jillian's gone, I don't really care anymore."

When Caleb left the Keeper's compound, he was dejected beyond belief. The whole structure of his world had collapsed around him. What was once a mystical icon was now just a deserted tower. The colony had split, both philosophically and physically, the Keeper was being challenged for leadership, and his best friend had lost his lady to politics. He simply didn't want to think about any of it right now. It was too much.

He made his way through the town to the Crones' home and virtually pulled Kylie away from her work to take her up the hill as he had promised. He needed the company, and he needed the peaceful seclusion of a more rarefied environment. Maybe he could find some solace on the mountainside with his love. They climbed by a gentler route than he and Chandy usually took, out of consideration for Kylie, but it proved unnecessary. She moved easily along the trail, outdistancing him as she ran ahead to look out over some ledge at the valley below, or

hurried to some small plateau to pick wildflowers and clumps of multicolored feather grass along the way. For all her own worries she was almost giddy out here in the open, and Caleb was grateful for it.
It lifted his spirits more than he could have imagined.

In no time at all, they were at the summit, looking around at the fantastic vista that the height afforded them. To the east lay the valley rim, reddish in the sunlight, with green and silver clumps of vegetation sprinkled in crevices clinging to its sheer walls. To the north and south the rim continued, and to the west, the great expanse of the valley, with the great lake in the center and the beginnings of the separatists' village near the western wall. Kylie took in a deep breath when she saw it, then calmed herself, studying the whole circle of land and sky around them. She seemed to take in every detail, cataloging features and places in her mind.

"I had no idea," she said in a whisper.

"Few do. I don't think anyone but Chandy and I actually come up here anymore."

"Anymore?"

"There's a small abandoned stone hut on the other side of the crest. It's very old and fallen into bits and pieces, but at one time they apparently came up here to keep watch. I don't know for what."

"Perhaps for the coming of the plague."

Caleb looked at her with unspoken question

"Chandy told me all the details," she said, smiling.

"Does it frighten you?"

She thought for a moment, and said, "Not really. Especially when I'm with you." They sat silently, looking out over the valley. Neither dared to speak for fear of breaking the mood. They just spent the time enjoying their world, feeling the cool breeze on their faces and watching the wispy clouds that portended the coming of the windy season, scudding across the sky.

"Where's the Tower from here?" she asked at last.

"Over there by the Eastern rim. You can't see it from here. It's hidden in the trees."

"And the new village? Is that it over there?"

Caleb nodded, "That's the place," he said, glancing to the west.

"What's that moving by the lake? It looks like small dark clouds.

"Jack darts," he answered. They're starting to gather for the swarm. For the moment, they're pretty harmless, unless you run into them on the fen, but, then again, who in their right mind goes to the fens unless they have to?"

"You," she said playfully.

"Only if I have to. In another six weeks, they'll all come out of the forests and swarm. By that time, we'd better be buttoned up. It only takes one blindly running into you to kill."

She shivered. 'It's such a violent place, Caleb," she said in a near whisper.   "I hate that about it."

Caleb squeezed her hand gently. "Only this time of year. The rest of the time it's pretty friendly...or was."

Again neither of them wanted to speak. Caleb watched the flittering clusters of jack darts for a few moments and then turned his attention back to the forest. He saw movement on the edge of the wood.

"Kylie," he said carefully, "Look over at the forest and tell me what you see."

Kylie turned to look. "I see trees and bushes, feather grass clearings and Spanglar bush tangles. I see some jack dart flights and the way the wind plays along the tops of the tall trees."

"Anything else?"

"Something's moving in there. In fact, there's a bunch of 'something's moving in there. Some of them are close to the edge and coming out into the fields. Behind them is a larger movement, slower but darker. What is it?"

Caleb stood and took Kylie's hand, lifting her to her feet.

"Rats!" he said. "They're chasing the animals out of the forest. There must be thousands of them!"

At the edge of the forest, hundreds of animals could be seen scurrying about in chaos, running to and fro along the margin of the forest while others further in were slowly being overtaken by a mass moving over them like a tidal wave. The wave advanced all along the forest as far as the eye could see. For all their sluggish progress, they were unwavering in their advance.

"They're eating their way through the wood. We've got to warn the colony!"

They made rapid progress down the mountain, Caleb leading Kylie along the steeper trail that he and Chandy trained on. In no time, they were out onto the flats and sprinting toward the colony. Caleb was torn in his mind, wondering if he should send Kylie on ahead to the colony while he warned the village but decided to see her safely inside the walls first. There was time, he decided. The tuskers could not reach the fields before sometime tomorrow. There was time.

Charging through the gates, he found the colony already in a state of alert. People were scurrying around, reinforcing both the inner and outer city walls. Hunters lined the outer wall near the gates while the herds of domestic animals and farmers were rushing in with the last of the harvested crops. As they approached, Caleb spotted Darius and three others hurrying away from the town toward their own village. Obviously it was unnecessary to warn them of the new danger. Once inside, Kylie hurried off to her home to help her father close up while Caleb made his way to the Keeper's compound. He found the clan chiefs gathered and his father barking orders. The Keeper signaled him as he entered the compound to join him along with Chandy, who was already armed.

"You've seen the rats?" Caleb asked, trying to catch his breath.

"Darius told us."

"I'm glad they already know. How soon will Morgan and the others be coming in?"

"They're not coming in, Caleb," the Keeper hissed.

"What?"

"They said that they beat the beasts once and that they can do it again. They demanded...demanded that we join them at the village. They also demanded that you and Chandy give up your energy weapons. Apparently it finally dawned on them that you have them. I refused, and they threatened to come take them."

Caleb had never seen the man in so dark a mood. He was seething with rage, shaking slightly as if doing his best to contain his ire. He looked at the two of them with grim determination.

"Tonight, you two will bring my granddaughter back home," he hissed. "Do whatever you must do, but get her home."

CHAPTER 26

By nightfall the colony was well on its way to being prepared for the coming struggle. The old trenches, now no more than indentations in the earth outside the walls of the town, had been cleared and deepened and were currently being filled with spangle brush. Near the gates, where the trench was weakest, cooking oil was stationed along the walls and every rifle that could be made to work had been issued to the defenders. Pikes and torches were gathered strategically along the outer wall, and the inner wall was being reinforced, a process that would take all night and well into the next day.

In the midst of this, Chandy and Caleb prepared to slip quietly away as soon as it was dark. They traveled light, each carrying only a rifle, energy pistol and knife, and they were dressed in thick clothes of silica fiber for protection against flora and fauna alike. Chandy carried a second set of clothing in his small shoulder pack for Jillian as well. As they waited for the brief period of total darkness between the setting of the sun and the rise of Bastion and Desolation, Caleb thought back to another night when he was watching a mysterious figure leap the full height of the wall and disappear into the darkness. There had never been a satisfactory explanation for that. Indeed, few people had believed him, but then, who would have believed rats the size of hogs until this last week?

"Almost time," Chandy said.

Caleb smiled to himself. The boy had grown in the past few weeks. He was sure of himself and more audacious than cocky. Caleb was glad to be in his company, glad to have the young hunter as his companion. He was a man to depend on.

The sun finally fell below the rim of the valley to the west, its ruddy glow quickly shifting to blue, then purple, and as the night creatures fell silent, it finally shifted a faint violet glow on the horizon. The valley was totally dark and would be so for some twenty minutes. It was time to go. Ropes were lowered over the wall to the north, and the two figures dropped swiftly down onto the narrow strip of ground between the wall and the trench. The smell of curing enamel on the newly-repaired wall filled their nostrils. The freshly-turned earth gave slightly beneath their feet, but its softness muffled any sound of their footsteps. Silently, they made their way to the gate and out along the causeway to the main road. A sharp jog to the right and they found the slight impression of the ancient game trail often used by hunters out to practice their tracking skills. By day it was undetectable. By night, it was the feel of it that led them toward the lake and the forest beyond. They broke into a jog as soon as they could, hoping that no night creatures were stirring as of yet.

Behind them the oil lamps were lit at the gates of the colony and the town itself began to glow with the internal lights of street lamps and houses. There would be no silence and no rest in the town tonight. By morning, their precious and limited electrical power would light up the entire perimeter of the outer walls, but for the moment, it was all lamps, torches and fires.

The two moons crested the rim of the valley exactly on time and bathed their world with their pale yellowish light. The brighter Bastion stood like a beacon while the dimmer Desolation glowed a cool greenish blue, further distorting the landscape. It was enough for Caleb and Chandy. Any movement along the way would signal danger before they encountered it.

Jogging at a near run, they covered the distance to the village quickly. They skirted the edge of the lake, racing along its shore and watching for predators, but it was too close to the windy season for most danger, and what few lake dwellers ventured out of the slime this time of night were harmless vegetarians looking for an easy meal of fen grass or swamp weed, or so they hoped.

Well before the moons were at their zenith they were approaching the village. They slowed and crouched behind one of the more forgiving varieties of Spanglar bush to catch their breath. They could see the village clearly, lit up around the perimeter with torches, guards posted every twenty yards or so, all facing outward, all at the ready. People within the village itself were bustling about much as they were back at the colony, gathering in foodstuffs, reinforcing their hovels as best they could or putting the finishing touches on newly completed conical homes. There were scarcely thirty of these structures up and fully half were not ready for habitation. If the tuskers were to attack tonight, they would quickly overrun the defenses.

The two decided on a plan of attack. They would make their way around to the edge of the ditch where they had fought off the tuskers before and slip in at one of the many breaches in the wall. With luck, they could find entry at a point guarded by a villager rather than a guard and never be heard or seen. Neither of them had much faith in the plan, but with the whole area under guard, it was the best they could come up with.

Nearly an hour passed before they were in place. Before them was a gap in the wall with a single farmer, pike in hand, guarding the breach. The two of them moved cautiously, first crouching then crawling literally on their stomachs until they were against the wall some ten yards to the north of the breach. The farmer guard was nodding. It was almost too easy. Chandy led, creeping toward the opening, rifle over his shoulder, hands held close to his body. Caleb followed in a similar manner.

There was a soft "ooof!" sound and Chandy disappeared. Caleb froze. The boy had simply vanished, as if swallowed by the ground. He listened closely, trying to pick up any sound at all, but except for the deep sawing breaths of the still dozing guard, he heard nothing. He eased his way forward carefully, testing the ground with one hand. Three steps and his hand reached out into nothing.

"Down here," Chandy whispered.

Caleb looked down into the void. He reached forward again and again his hand met with nothing. Carefully he felt the ground in front of him, finding the edge of a trench of some sort and silently lowered himself into it, stepping on Chandy's leg as he did so.

"Watch it!" Chandy whispered.

Caleb shifted and settled in beside his friend.

"What the hell is this?" he whispered.

"From the aroma I'd say it's a drainage ditch.

Caleb sniffed the air and caught the odor of decay and human waste. He snorted. "More like an open sewer," he hissed.

"Well, whatever it is, it leads right into the village, and I don't see anything to keep us out."

"Okay," Caleb whispered. "Let's get it done."

They crawled along the length of the ditch, which led to the animal pens, a discovery that did little to cheer the two rescuers. Apparently it wasn't human waste they had smelled, but the fetid output of four-legged oxen and hogs. Caleb made a mental note to disinfect when they got back. Looking up from the trench to get their bearings; they were deep in the camp near the butchering tables. The surrounding areas were completely deserted.

"Everybody's getting ready for the next attack," Chandy said.

"At least there's something to be grateful for. Now where did you see Jillian when we were here?"

Chandy pointed to a small cluster of makeshift huts not far away. They also seemed deserted. They looked at each other thinking the same thing. What if she was out there working on the trench or the wall? They'd never find her.

"Well we're not going to find her sitting here," Caleb said. "Let's check it out."

"'Good a place to start as any," Chandy agreed, and they were off.

At this point, they walked. They did it as casually as possible, sure that in the dull light of fires and torches they would be little more than silhouettes anyway. Everyone was too busy to bother wondering about two hunters crossing the village. They came to the hut that Chandy had seen Jillian enter and after listening for a moment, went in.

Jillian was curled up on a small pallet, a light blanket covering her. Her recently-cut hair was just long enough to cover her neck, and the blunt edge caused it to cascade down along her cheek, nearly covering her face. There was something unnatural about they way she was laying. Chandy knelt beside here and Caleb turned to watch the door.

"She's not waking up!" he said aloud.

"Shhh!" snapped Caleb. He looked back over his shoulder at the two, then back to the door. No one was around. "They probably gave her something to keep her quiet. It sounds like something Morg would do. Is she dressed?"

Chandy carefully pulled back the blanket and moaned. "The bastard! I think he raped her!"

"Don't jump to conclusions. There could be lots of reasons that she's naked. She is naked, right?"

"Yes."

"Well that's going to make it easier. Get the clothes on her that you brought and let's get out of here."

Chandy did as he was told, making soft sobbing sounds as he did so. He dressed her quickly but tenderly, and sat beside her, holding her in his arms.

"I'm gonna kill that pig," he whispered.

"First things first. Let's get her out of here." Caleb took one last look through the door and froze.

Morg and two other hunters were coming toward them. They were laughing, and it was obvious that the two companions were teasing Morg. Caleb pulled the pistol from his belt and stepped back into the shadows.

Chandy didn't need to be told what was happening. He crouched between Jillian and the door and drew his own pistol. They waited.

The three stopped outside the entrance and from the sound of it, passed a flask of wine among them. "Hell of a time to get married, Morg. We may all be dead by morning."

Morg laughed aloud. "Can you think of a better time to get married? I'd hate to leave a widow without any memories." At this they all laughed and passed the flask again.

"You two get back to the wall, and take my rifle. I've going to use a different gun tonight. I'll be along."

Again they laughed and as the two drunken hunters headed off in the direction of the trench.

Morg stepped through the door. He stopped dead in his tracks, staring down at Chandy's grinning face. Caleb reached out from behind him, grabbing him around the neck and covering his mouth. Morg's hands went up to his neck immediately and his pants, already loosened, fell in a heap around his feet. Chandy hesitated for a split second at the sight and before he could fire, Caleb had slammed Morg's head into a post and followed with a punch to the jaw that dropped him.

"Why'd you do that?" Chandy demanded.

"It's not nice to marry the widow of the man you kill," Caleb said grimly.

"But now what? We can't leave him here like this."

"Do you really want to murder him in cold blood, Chandy?"

Chandy just looked at Caleb for a moment. "Damn!" he said.

He rose, lifted Jillian over his shoulder, and with only a glance at his friend, stepped over the still body on the floor and out into the night.

"Well," said Chandy, hefting his load higher on his shoulder, "how do you want to play this?"

Caleb slipped the light blanket over Jillian. From a distance, Chandy would look like someone carrying a large sack rather than a body. "It's certain that we're not going back through that ditch. There's no way we can drag or pull her along that way. I say we just walk straight out of the village. If we look like we know what we're doing, maybe they'll be too busy to notice."

Chandy grinned. "I like it. Even if it doesn't work we'll be legends for trying it."

They turned and walked straight through the village in the direction of the colony. No one stopped them or even looked up as they walked by. As Caleb had said, they were all too busy. Near the outer perimeter of torches and guards, they angled their course between two posts, putting them ten yards from either of the sentries. They easily passed through and out into the grazing field. No one gave them a second glance.

In the distance they could see the final hurdle coming into view. A single scout was coming in from the direction of the lake, making his way carefully along the edge of the fens. The scout was intent on where he was stepping and was not paying attention to the two of them and their burden approaching. As he got closer, Caleb's heart sank. It was Darius. He'd know that walk anywhere. He reached for his pistol, praying that he'd not have to use it, but knowing that if Darius recognized them, he would. Quickly Caleb changed course and moved further out into the shallows along the lake. It was either that or the fens, and he was not about to set foot in that mire at night if it could be helped. They were a good fifteen yards to one side when a voice called out.

"You two! Where are you going? What have you got there?"

They recognized the voice but it sounded too much in command - too strong and vital.

"Fylfot," Chandy whispered.

"Just keep going. I'm not as worried about him as I am about Darius. He's the real problem."

Darius finally looked up and spotted them. He started to raise his rifle and thought better of it. He looked back and forth between the two with their burden and the approaching Fylfot, now boldly striding in their direction. "You there, hunter," Fylfot snapped. "Stop those two! Stop them now or I'll have your hide!"

Darius turned his full attention to Fylfot and stared. As for Chandy and Caleb, they kept a steady pace toward the lake.

"Did you hear me?" Fylfot repeated. "I said stop them!"

Darius began angling toward Caleb and Chandy. Caleb's heart sank. He had no wish to confront this man. He was too good a hunter and was once a good friend. By now, Fylfot was also trotting in their direction. He held an axe in his right hand and looked ready to use it.

For a moment, it was an odd tableau in the night, all these people converging on one spot, but at the last moment, Darius swerved aside and brought himself between Fylfot and the others. Caleb and Chandy turned to look, as amazed as Fylfot, but they kept moving.

"What are you doing? Didn't you hear..." Fylfot never finished his sentence. Darius' rifle came suddenly up and he slammed it into the historian's forehead, dropping him on the spot. He turned to Chandy and Caleb. He nodded with a satisfied grin and they nodded back, passing him quietly. Caleb kept the man in the corner of his eye, trying not to be obvious. He saw Darius stop. Turning and pulling the rifle from his shoulder, Caleb turned full to face him and pointed his own pistol at the man's head. Darius hesitated. Darius started to lift his rifle but lowered it, and shook his head, pointing at the stirring body of the off worlder lying at his feet. Grinning strangely, he let out a loud guffaw followed by a shake of the head. Darius waved, turned and trotted off toward the village. Caleb and Chandy loped off into the darkness, burden and lives intact.

CHAPTER 27

C aleb lay on a small pallet near the cooking fire at the Keeper's home. The predawn morning light was beginning to peek through windows, bathing the room with an eerie bluish light that mixed strangely with the reds of the glowing embers of yesterday's cooking fire and the result gave an almost sickening pallor to the room. He rolled onto one side, alleviating the cramp in his right shoulder and thought of their adventures last night.

The Keeper had been angry when he saw them arrive, and shocked to see the limp form of his granddaughter. Without a word to either rescuer, he had taken her to her bed and examined her, assuring himself that she was only lightly drugged and that she would sleep it off. The darkness of his countenance when he turned to them was frightening. He had said bluntly, "Tell me everything." They had talked for hours with the Keeper interrogating them as always, pulling every detail and nuance from their memory including things that they didn't even realize that they had seen. Caleb reported everything as methodically as he could while Chandy excitedly shed the effects of the rescue's rush by babbling on excitedly. The Keeper showed little patience for Chandy's hyperbole, cutting him short whenever he strayed from hard fact. His manner was cold and absolutely on purpose in his questioning. It was as if a switch had been thrown as soon as he had determined that Jillian was going to be all right. From that moment on, he was completely absorbed in the task at hand. By the time they had finished, it was well into the night and the Keeper ordered them to rest. Chandy had spent the night at Jillian's bedside, sprawled on a long bench retrieved from the entryway while Caleb accepted the pallet by the fire gratefully. His head still buzzed from the intensity of the Keeper's questioning, yet somehow the experience broke the spell of fear from the night before. Rolling over a final time, he sat up, stretched and stood, looking for a kettle or pot to begin heating water for tea.

"I'll do that, Caleb. Don't bother."

Caleb turned and found Jillian near the staircase, smiling at him.

"You're up," he said. "I didn't think you'd be on your feet this soon."

She crossed to the fire and began rebuilding it from a kindling box on the right of the firebox.

"I've been up for several hours. Chandy's told me what happened. Thank you for coming for me."

Caleb nodded self-consciously.

"Where is Chandy?" he asked.

"He's upstairs with my grandfather. I actually came down to start the tea and awaken you. I see that you've already gotten up."

"Just barely," he said. "Thanks. Are you sure you don't want me to do this? You had a pretty rough time last night."

She gave a slight shutter and said, "No. I'll be fine. Besides, all I did was sleep and let you two carry me. How frightening can that be?"

Caleb didn't pursue the subject any further. Whatever Jillian had to endure in the camp with Morg was her business, not his. He smiled weakly, moving the pallet back onto the side wall where it had been the night before, and went up the stairs to the main room. He found the Keeper and Chandy seated at the table, deep in conversation, with Chandy doing most of the talking for a change.

"Ah, you're awake," offered the Keeper. "Come and join us. Our young friend here was just telling me about Darius. You failed to mention that it was Darius that saw you leave the camp."

"Did I?" asked Caleb. "Sorry. I guess it didn't seem important."

"On the contrary, my friend. It may be very significant. Darius seems to take some sort of leadership role in the village, perhaps threatened by Fylfot. From what Chandler has said, that animal was barking orders as if he was in charge. If Darius is willing to confront Fylfot and let you escape, it may mean that there's disagreement among the separatists at Morgan's decisions."

Caleb frowned and nodded. "More likely it shows his displeasure at how Jillian was treated and how much he resents Fylfot." He chuckled. "Fylfot's gonna have a hell of a headache this morning. I wonder if he could tell who hit him in the dark. Darius is a good man, Keeper, but he's loyal. It would take an offense to his basic code of behavior to provoke him to break the trust."

"Really," the Keeper said, raising an eyebrow. He rose and began pacing the room, contemplating this. Both Caleb and Chandy knew better than to interrupt him. In the end, he walked to the latest Colony Chronicle, sitting open on top of the book case where the books were kept. Without looking up he said, "I'm impressed with your maturity, Caleb, and with yours, Chandy.
It's good to know that you have wisdom beyond your years. If the fight goes badly for us and people die, it's going to take that kind of wisdom to lead the colony out of this."

"We'll have you, Keeper," Chandy reminded him.

"Hmm," he said, but for how long? The next few days are going to be quite perilous."

Chandy shook his head. "Not that perilous, I hope."

"Ah," the Keeper mused. "Blessed be the confidence of youth." With that he sidestepped to the open door and looked out over what he could see of the town, his hands clasped behind his back. No one spoke for a very long time.

After tea and morning cakes, the Keeper led the pair out into the compound and on to the inner gate. Jillian was left to tidy the house, which she did silently. There was no indication of strain between her grandfather and herself, but his tone seemed more solicitous than usual and he promised to help her prepare the house for the winter as soon as he could return. She had kissed him gently on the cheek as he left and he embraced her in a warm hug. To Chandy and Caleb, it was the most intimate expression of feeling that they had ever witnessed from the Keeper.

The Keeper inspected the gates and the immediately adjacent walls. He questioned workers carefully about the progress they were making and offered several suggestions as to how to increase the strength of the barrier. He also ordered glass shards to be embedded in the soft rim of the wall itself to further discourage any rats that may decide to climb them. Satisfied, he moved on, his two young companions in tow, into the outer ward and onto the outer gates.

Here, too, he inspected the work and discussed the situation with the construction crew. Outside the walls the ditch was complete and Spanglar Glass bushes were being planted. Many had been set in place earlier and were beginning to grow, their chaotic array of crystalline leaves, all pointed and sharp, serving well as an additional barrier to entry. Only the road before the gate was free of Spanglar, and here picks had been erected as a secondary barrier, their sharp, black carbon tips ready to impale oncoming tuskers. As a final precaution, he climbed to the top of the wall, peering out over the plain and lake beyond. Chandy and Caleb stood on either side of him, still silent.

"What do you think?" the Keeper asked at last.

Chandy was the first to answer, "If the attack is the same as we experienced in the village we should be able to do fine, but there were only some five or six hundred tuskers in that attack. What if there are more?"

"That, Chandler, is what I'm asking you."

Chandy shook his head. "It would be close."

The Keeper looked at Caleb questioningly.

"I agree. It could be a near thing, Keeper. Thank heaven we've got the inner wall. We may need it."

"What do you see happening here?"

Caleb thought briefly, then said, "Well, the ditch and Spanglar will stop them for a while. If they rush in, many in front will die, but the rats are cunning. They think about things. It won't take them long to find a way over or around the ditch and then they need to climb the wall. Those walls are slick, but we haven't had to build them with this kind of attack in mind. They'll dig their way in eventually and start climbing."

"I think they'll try for the gate, too. It's just wood and won't take long to go through," said Chandy.

"What else, Caleb?"

"Well, we'll be firing down on them from the walls the whole time, and that will slow them down considerably, but if there are really thousands of them they can come on faster than we can kill them. When they get to the inner wall, it will be the same thing all over again, except that there is no trench. We'll have to stop them there or it's over."

Chandy nodded in agreement.

"Then it will have to do. I think we'll save the oil for the inner wall. It will make a nice surprise for our visitors if they get that far."

"There are shops built right up against those walls. The shopkeepers are not going to be happy about losing their shops," said Caleb.

"Well they'll have to! It's either the buildings or their lives. We can't have those shops giving the rats something to climb onto to get over the walls, at any rate. It will add to the fire." He looked back out over the wall toward the lake. "I would have liked to have the separatists with us here, but I suppose that's impossible. They'll be the first to die, I'm afraid. Caleb, I want you to supervise the inner wall. See to it that oil is stationed around the entire perimeter and that the gates are reinforced. Clear out all the merchants, by force if you have to, and tell them to take what they can inside the inner wall.

"Chandy, I want you up on a hill, watching... Take two hunters, some of your close friends that you can depend on, and see what's going on closer to the lake. If you see anything at all, come back immediately. As for me, I'll meet with the clan chiefs. Jonathan is organizing those townspeople who can shoot into a militia. We need to be sure everyone knows what to do. Any other ideas?"

Chandy cleared his throat. "I'd...like to spend some time with Jillian before all this happens."

The Keeper looked hard at the boy. "After you see what's going on out there near the lake.

"Caleb, you need to see your mother and father and if you can find time, talk to Kylie. She worried while you were gone. Now go. The sun's already up and we have much to do before tonight. I think that's when they'll come."

CHAPTER 28

P reparations went well. Both the outer and inner walls of the town were now completely fortified and the population organized into groups of workers according to expertise and what needed to be done. The meager electricity output of the power plant had been diverted from producing recycled metals to supplying power to strings of lights along the inner wall. Over the generations, little of the technology that the colonists had brought with them continued to function, and the number of colonists who knew how to repair or, for that matter, use much of the modern machinery had dwindled to only a few. What knowledge had been retained was for immediate, practical tasks, which did not include advanced technology. At the appropriate time, the lights could be turned on, but no one knew how long they would last, or if they would actually work at all. Even testing had been vetoed for fear of burning them out before they were needed.

The people took surprisingly well to Caleb's barking orders at them, particularly after his father and two of the clan chiefs arrived affirming his right to do so. They resented being ordered around by a mere hunter, but after the process of preparing the walls had begun, the logic of his orders became apparent, and complaints gave way to enthusiasm. By late afternoon, they were essentially ready for the night, but kept working, trying to improve the strength of their makeshift fortifications and to be sure that they hadn't missed anything. It was as much to keep their minds off what was coming as it was to prepare.

It was during this last stage of preparation that Kylie came to the wall. She found Caleb above the gate, inspecting the perimeter and directing workers, and she climbed the steps to the watchtower without comment, waiting for him to notice her. When he did, she smiled mildly. Caleb was strangely proud to have her there. He was in his element as a leader and for Kylie to witness it seemed appropriate. She was looking on with approval.

"I hope I'm not in the way," she said.

"No. I'm glad you're here. I was going to come to your house, but, as you can see, I found myself suddenly busy. I'm sorry if I worried you."

"Once I knew you had returned," she said, "I was fine. I knew you would find me when you could."

"Oh?" he said. "Then why are you here?"

"Um, I couldn't wait. Besides, I wanted to see what you were doing."

"I only hope it's enough."

Somehow that single phrase said more than anything he could have said. She knew exactly what he meant, felt his concern and his pleasure at his job here. She thought to herself that they would always have this rapport, needing few words to convey how they were feeling. It was like he was a part of her and she a part of him. Even in the midst of this crisis, it made her happy beyond belief to see that.

He looked at her and smiled, as if reading her thoughts. He crossed the small platform and held her in his arms. "I won't be much longer," he said. It was all she needed.

Caleb watched her walk away toward her house, reluctant to end the moment. In the end, he scanned the walls a final time and told everyone to see to their families. They would be needed again soon enough. He could hear the commotion at the outer wall as the colonists there were completing their own preparations. He turned and looked out over the outer ward at the stream of people now moving down the main street, burdened with whatever they could carry, abandoning their houses for the safety of the center of the city. He looked beyond the walls to the plain in the distance and noticed a single column of smoke rising from the direction of the separatists' village. More preparations, he thought. They were also taking last-minute action to face the beasts. Perhaps, he thought, the rats will have had enough of them and bypass them on the way to the city. A second column of smoke rose into the sky to the right of the first, then another to its left. In quick succession, more and more fires were being lit out there at the village until soon there was a curtain of dense, dark smoke all along what must be the outer boundary of the village itself. He was halfway down the wall when Chandy came running toward him.

"They're at the village!" he cried as he ran.

"I saw," said Caleb. "I could see the smoke from the watchtower. What happened?"

Chandy stopped to catch his breath, then turned and began running back toward the outer wall.

Caleb followed.

"We saw them coming," he shouted over his shoulder. "We were up on the ridge at the old lookout. I was on the edge of the hill and I saw them moving through the woods. There must be thousands of them this time. They came from three sides at once and they moved at an incredible speed. I could hear what sounded like thunder. When we came off the hill, the ground was shaking, like a herd of bullocks stampeding. "

"Slow down!" shouted Caleb, as Chandy kept running and yelling.

"There were thousands of them, Caleb. They completely surrounded the village, circling until escape was cut off, then all of them turned in at once and attacked.

That's all I know. We just started running. There was nothing we could do, and if we were seen..."

"Have you told all this to the Keeper?"

Chandy gulped for air and nodded. "He knows."

"Then go find Jillian. It may be the last chance before tonight."

Chandy slowed and then came to a sudden halt in the middle of the road. It was such a sudden change in motion that Caleb ran into him, sending them both sprawling. When he stood again, he was still breathing hard, but the excitement had left him. He helped Caleb to his feet and gave him a worried look.

"Do you think we can stop them, Caleb?"

Caleb shrugged and felt foolish. "I don't know, Chandy, but if we don't, I'd hate to go down thinking I hadn't spent time with Kylie before it happened."

Chandy nodded, then walked slowly away in the direction of the Keeper's compound. His arms hung limply at his side, his breathing still labored from the running, but he seemed almost slumped-shouldered, like a beaten man.

"Go!" growled Caleb, and Chandy picked up speed, trotting off to find Jillian. By the time they reached the outer wall, Caleb found his father and most of the clan chiefs gathered in the larger of the two guard towers with the Keeper. He bounded up the stairway to the broad opening at the top of the tower and stood beside his father. The Keeper spotted him and looked his way only briefly before concentrating his attention on the village in the distance again.

"Aren't you supposed to be at the inner wall?" he said absently.

"If I'm going to fight these things, I have to know what I'm up against," Caleb said.

"If anyone knows what we're up against, Caleb, it's you. I put you in charge of the inner wall for a reason. You and Chandy have the only really advanced weapons in the colony and have experience using them. If the tuskers get into the city, you're our only hope for the colony. Where's Chandy?"

"He's looking for Jillian."

The Keeper nodded. "Good. As for you, your father and I can handle things from here. You can stay for awhile, but I think Jonathan will agree that when the attack comes, we don't want you here."

"It's true, Caleb," Jonathan Grant said seriously. "When it starts, you'll have to be at the inner wall. They'll need a leader there or they'll panic."

"What about one of the clan chiefs? They'll respond to them. I'm just a hunter. I don't want to lead anyone."

Caleb's father put his hand on his son's shoulder, looked at him gravely, and said, "You have been a leader since you were a child. Everyone knows it but you. Why do you think you were chosen to sponsor Chandler? Trust me when I say that they will listen to you and they will respond to you. We need all of the clan chiefs here on the wall."

Caleb said nothing. He looked out over the wall to the fields beyond and the columns of smoke in the distance, trying to take it all in. It would take some adjustment, but in his heart he knew that his father was right. For some time, no one said anything. The wind was beginning to shift toward the colony, bringing with it acrid smoke and the stench of burning oil and flesh. Caleb hoped sincerely that it was the flesh of the tuskers. Specks were appearing out on the plain, moving rapidly past the lake toward the colony. At first they thought they were tuskers, already rushing to the next battle, but the way in which they moved and the lagging speed of their movement was more like that of humans than animals. They moved in a group, erratically shifting with the terrain as they came. Jonathan called out to those at the gate below and the great wooden doors swung open. A group of some twenty hunters charged out, running to meet the incoming refugees. Caleb searched the lake edge for pursuing tuskers, but there were none to be seen.

It was deathly quiet when the party arrived at the gates and they quickly passed through. The great doors closed with a resounding boom and were sealed. Looking down from the gate house, Caleb counted heads. There were some forty-five separatists in the party, mostly women and children. He recognized Darius and several other hunters on the perimeter of the group but his concentration was on Fylfot, prominently standing in the middle of the crowd. He looked tired and a little scared, but by no means cowed by his experiences at the village. He swaggered about in an exaggerated attempt to look in control. He even tried issuing orders to Darius and the others and was promptly ignored.

"Is that your professor?" the Keeper asked.

"Yes," answered Caleb without further comment.

"I'll see him."

Darius looked up at the small group in the gate house tower and waved. He smiled weakly, acknowledging gratitude for their momentary salvation and made for the stairs.

Fylfot noticed, and quickly surged ahead, cutting Darius off and mounting the stairs ahead of him. "I am Professor Skylar Fylfot," he announced, looking directly at the Keeper. "I assume you are the one they call the Keeper?"

"I am," said the Keeper flatly.

"Good. Since you seem to have some remnant of your former authority, I will address my remarks to you. It is a pity so many had to die in the conflagration that has taken place at the village. Many good men and women died out there, in no small part due to your refusal to come to our aid. We will note that at a later time, when such facts are more relevant. For the moment, the exigencies of the times dictates that such accountabilities be set aside in favor of swift action. I can see you've done a reasonable job of preparing to save yourselves, but now that I'm here, we can do much better. I'm sure you'll agree."

The Keeper looked down at the puffy smiling face of the professor with monumental control. "I think not," he said.

"Sorry?"

"I think not. If anything, you've demonstrated a total lack of understanding of the situation, and, though I assume you are a competent historian, you have no concept whatever of either tactics or strategy. In short, Professor Fylfot, you are lucky to be alive, fortunate that we have taken you in. You should be glad that we haven't left you to the tuskers."

"Really, sir!" Fylfot bellowed, puffing himself up in as commanding a posture as he could muster. "I do not think you understand your position. You are no longer in charge. There are no Keepers. If anyone here is in a position to lead, it is I. I hold in great disdain your attempts to usurp my rightful position, gained by virtue of superior intellect, superior knowledge and official status, as the new leader of this colony. We need to organize this rabble immediately into a cohesive fighting force, capable of opposing the horrendous evil that confronts us and avoid a repeat of the debacle that has just taken place out there. Do you wish to destroy what is left of the colony as well?"

The Keeper hesitated momentarily, then nodded. "You are correct in your assertion that there is no Keeper now. The purpose of the office is gone. However, by unanimous agreement among the clan chiefs, I stand as Premiere of the colonial entity. As such, I am in charge. As for your superior knowledge and expertise, that is an obvious fabrication. Now if someone would please remove this obsequious sycophant from the tower, I would like to confer with Darius on what happened at the village." The Keeper turned his back on the little man and walked to the tower's edge.

Fylfot stood his ground, his mouth moving though no sound came out, trying to formulate an answer. Finally, he screamed, "Obsequious sycophant? You dare to say that to me? You can't do that! I'm in charge! These are my people now!"

"Get him out of here," the Keeper said calmly, not bothering to look at the man again.

Fylfot reached for his belt, producing one of the small energy pistols and aimed it at the Keeper. Before the professor could speak again, Darius had grabbed both his arm and the weapon and struck him with his knife, puncturing him just under the ribs, thrusting upward to the heart. Fylfot collapsed at their feet.

"I suppose I've done murder now," Darius said.

"I'd say you've merely killed another rat," the Keeper replied.

Caleb retrieved the pistol and handed it to Darius. The hunter looked down at the weapon in his hand and studied it for a moment, then slipped it under his belt and with his other hand, wiping the blood from his blade onto his pants. He replaced the knife in its scabbard and turned away. Once the body was removed, no one spoke of the incident again.

CHAPTER 29

Darius' account of the fight at the separatists' village was brief and to the point. The tuskers had come at them from three sides, charging out of the wood before anyone even knew they were there. They had barely enough time to light fires in the pits before the tuskers were on them, and while the separatists' attention was at the low wall, others tuslers came in from the sides and finally from the rear. Darius and the survivors had escaped only because of the smoke and the confusion. Once inside the village, the rats began a frenzied attack, mindlessly striking out at everything that moved, including their own kind. The hunter estimated that perhaps fifty or sixty rats were killed by their own, another two hundred by the villagers. In the end, the hopelessness of the situation was evident, and the survivors had made their way through the thick smoke in twos and threes, and headed for the colony.

"What about the energy weapons?" the Keeper asked.

"They did their work, but they were in the center of the wall defenses, where the tuskers hit first. Those with energy rifles swept their weapons back and forth along the line of rats, but it didn't help. They were overrun in less than a minute."

"Did any of your people escape with energy rifles?"

Darius shook his head. "Not a one," he said. "At Fylfot's orders, I was directing defenses at the rear of the village, or I would have been cut down with the first wave."

"And where was the good professor while all this was happening?"

Darius spat. "He was supposed to be at the wall, but as soon as the attack started, he ran. He said he was going for help, but when I saw him, he didn't even slow down at the village edge. He was running full out."

Jonathan nodded. "Well, he's no longer an issue now. What about Morgan and Morg?"

"Morg was at the wall. He was one of the first ones killed. I saw a tusker take off his arm, and another one his leg. He was still alive when they started eating him. Morgan stood his ground at his platform. He and Olivia fought them to the end. The last I saw of them they were being pulled down by a swarm of really big ones. After that, I never looked back. I just kept running like the others."

"And a good thing you did," said the Keeper. "You'll be of more use here and alive than back there, dead."

Darius swallowed hard and coughed. He was fighting to keep his composure.

"How soon do you think they'll be coming?" asked Caleb.

"I don't know. I don't think they'll attack very soon. They're...feasting," said Darius.

"Hmm," mumbled the Keeper. "And after that they'll sleep. I don't think they'll be at us until late tonight or tomorrow. I suggest we all get fed and get as much rest as we can. Everyone who cannot fight will go inside the inner wall. Jonathan, please get them started. Caleb, I want you back inside the inner wall now. You need to rest. Leave someone else in charge there in your absence. As for you, Darius, you and your men can choose your own ground. We're glad to have you back with us."

"For that I thank you. I think I'll go along with Caleb. I still want to know how he was able to get into the village to fetch Jillian."

Caleb laughed. "Not me, my friend. That was Chandy Crone. I was just there for the fun."

As refugees and colonists streamed through the inner wall gate, Darius and Caleb looked over their defenses. Caleb was impressed with Darius' understanding of their position. He made several suggestions that no one else had thought of, including the creation of a Spanglar weed funnel that would force the charging tuskers to focus their attack on the wall just to the right of the gate itself. That way they could concentrate their burning oil at one spot for maximum effect.

With Darius' help, preparations were completed in a very short time, and they decided that they had done all they could to prepare. Caleb decided to ask Darius to take charge of the inner wall in his absence, and to his relief, those manning the wall accepted him without dissent.

Caleb headed for the Crones' house and Kylie. He hadn't seen Chandy since he'd sent him off to find Jillian, and he had no idea if Kylie even knew what was going on. Her father had been at the inner wall, helping to reinforce the tiles on the outside surface, and they'd hardly had a chance to nod hello in passing. He was still there now, refusing to leave as long as there was any possibility of tuskers attacking without warning. Caleb was tired and he was hungry, but most of all, he wanted to see Kylie before all this started. His mother, he knew, would understand. The wife of Jonathan Grant was used to long hours of waiting. He'd see her on the way back.

The house was open when he got there. Inside he could hear Chandy's voice, high pitched with excitement. From his rhythm he was obviously relaying some tale of danger and adventure, probably to Kylie. Caleb was always amused by Chandy's ability to shift into his imagination at the most inopportune times. Faced with possible annihilation, he chose to tell tales. Caleb envied his young charge's ability to do so.

He climbed the steps to the entrance and stood for a moment and peered in. Chandy was pacing with his back to the door. He was gesticulating wildly as he related the rescue of Jillian in detail that went far beyond fact. Kylie and Jillian were seated at the table, listening in rapt fascination. Neither noticed Caleb standing there.

"So I lifted Jillian into my arms and we set off through the camp, bold as a bullock. No one even paid any attention to us until we were on our way to the lake. Suddenly we saw hunters coming our way. 'Just act naturally,' I said to Caleb. 'Just act like we know what we're doing.'"

"And that's when we had to swim the lake to save our lives!" said Caleb, entering the room.

Chandy spun around, sputtering. His mouth kept working as if he was saying something, but nothing came out.

"Oh, that's silly, Caleb," said Jillian laughing.

"Um, uh, yeah. That's not what happened at all," Chandy stammered.

"The way it did happen," Caleb said, "was that Chandy saved Jillian. That's all that needs to be said. He was amazing to watch."

Kylie stood and threw her arms around Caleb's neck, kissing him hard. "I thought you'd never get here," she said.

"For a while there, neither did I. I would have come earlier, but I've been a little busy."

"It doesn't matter. You're here now," she said, and led him to the table.

Chandy settled into another chair and poured Caleb a cup of steaming tea from a large pot. Taking it gratefully, he began sipping it slowly.

"Can you stay?" Kylie asked.

"For awhile. I suppose Chandy told you about the village and what happened there."

"He told us," Jillian said solemnly, "Only forty survivors."

"Forty-seven by actual count." He saw the worried look on Kylie's face and added, "But we're better prepared than they were, and in a much more defensible position. No need to worry."

She smiled weakly and reached out for his hand.

"I think we need to go," Chandy said, and stood. Jillian stood as well and gathered her shawl about her shoulders. They walked to the door.

"I'm going to take Jillian home to get some things. She'll be staying here with Kylie for a while."

"Ask my mother to come too," Caleb said, then to Kylie, "If that's all right?"

Kylie smiled sweetly. "Of course it's all right. We'll find out all there is to know about you two while you're...elsewhere."

"Everything?" Chandy asked.

"Everything," Kylie answered, with an impish look in her eyes.

"Oh hell," he groaned, and they all chuckled.

Jillian looked back as she left and said, "We'll be several hours."

When they'd gone, Kylie stood and cradled Caleb in her arms, pressing him to her breast. "Have you eaten?" she asked.

"Why are women always trying to feed me? It must be some nurturing mother kinda thing."

"You rest," she said, ignoring the jibe. "Chandy told me how hard you've been working. I'll fix you something. Perhaps I should make enough for my father as well."

"He won't be back for a while, Kylie. He won't leave the wall until this is over. He's a good man, you know. I've never seen him so focused; so self-assured."

"That's the way he always is in a crisis, Caleb. It helps him forget Mother. I think it's one of the few times that he's really happy. He has so much to give, and so much pain."

She began to cry. Caleb settled her in his lap and held her. They sat for some minutes like that, each holding the other, each with their own thoughts, grateful to be in each other's arms. Somehow the idea of eating slipped away and they found themselves making love on the settle with the moonlight streaming in through the great window. Caleb finally slept, head cradled in Kylie's lap, but his dreams kept intruding on his peace. He found himself surrounded by the tuskers, weaponless and trapped. He could smell them, feel their breath on his skin. He heard them roar like thunder. Over and over they cried out, yelling like thunder...like thunder.

"Thunder!" he cried, suddenly bold upright on the settle. Kylie stirred beside him, startled by the outburst.

"Caleb?" she said. "What's wrong?"

"I hear thunder."

They looked up to find the night blanketed with clouds, streaks of lightening snapping from cloud to cloud and ground to sky. It was an awesome display, and continually there was thunder.

"It looks like quite a storm," Kylie said almost soothingly. "There'll be lots of rain and I can't think of a better place to pass a stormy night than in your arms."

"It's the rain I'm worried about, Kylie. The Spanglar in the trenches will all melt away. By morning, we'll be vulnerable!"

He leaped to his feet, slipping his trousers on with one hand and grabbing for his tunic with the other. Kylie was up, reaching for his boots and knife belt. Caleb grabbed them on the fly, slipped into his boots, and bolted for the door.

"Find Chandy and Jillian," he called. "Find them and my mother. Tell Chandy to meet me at the wall and the rest of you stay here, in this house. Pull up the ladder steps, bolt the door and stay here, no matter what. Understood?"

He didn't wait for an answer. He ran through the streets, drenched in the downpour that started just as he emerged from Kylie's house. Others in the street were busily seeking shelter or running to the walls as well. He wasn't the only one that realized what was happening. When he arrived, he found Darius and Chandy already on the small guard tower above the gate, staring out at the flood.

"How bad is it?" he asked when he joined them.

"Bad enough," said Darius. "I can just see the outer gate from here. The Spanglar had grown pretty well around it, but it's all gone now. That means the trenches must be cleared by now as well. It picked one hell of a time to rain."

"We've still got the oil, and the walls are solid. Maybe it will hold them," offered Chandy.

Caleb shook his head. "It won't be enough. I'm going to the outer wall. I want you two here. We may have a lot of people coming this way if that wall gets breached. I'll be back."

He nearly leaped to the ground and squeezed through the gate as the gatekeepers swung it open. He ran flat out, splashing great sprays of water along the way, oblivious to the blinding downpour that pelted him. At the outer wall, he mounted the tower and found his father and the Keeper staring over the edge. Caleb peered down into the darkness. In the dim light of the torches, miraculously still fluttering; he could see the outline of the trench, now empty except for a layer of tiny crystals, glistening in the firelight.

"That was fast," he said.

"It doesn't take long once they get wet, does it?"

"Now what do we do?

Jonathan said nothing. He just continued to stare down at the ditch. "If this ends quickly and the trench drains well, and if they don't come until morning," said the Keeper, "We may be able to lay down more Spanglar weed. It won't be very high, but it might make them think twice before coming on. It should give us a little time to eliminate some of the first to arrive."

"That's a lot of ifs, Sirius," Jonathan said. It was the first time Caleb had ever heard anyone address the Keeper by his name.

"It's all we've got. Caleb, I'm glad you're here. You need to start gathering all of the Spanglar crystals you can find. I don't care if they're ornamental. We'll throw everything in the ditch when it's dry enough and hope for the best."

Caleb grunted agreement and ran off to organize the job. Within half an hour, and after the end of the downpour, dozens of citizens were converging on the outer gate, small containers of Spanglar in their hands. All of the tiny crystals that could be found were gathered and deposited in an urn. When all was said and done, it was no more than half full. Caleb carried the urn to the tower and placed it on a small table beside the Keeper.

"There's not much here," he said.

"It will have to do. Now all we can do is hope for a bright morning and a drying wind."

CHAPTER 30

Everyone slept at his post that night. Anyone who was old enough and strong enough to fight was either on the outer or inner wall, huddled in their blankets against the hard ceramic of the parapets or standing guard. At quarter hour intervals, the power plant would direct electricity to the lights strung along the perimeter, checking to see if anything stirred beyond the town. Nothing did. In between these brief moments of illumination, the town lay in total darkness. In the inner ward of the city, those who could not fight were crowded into houses and barricaded against the obscenity outside. Both Bastion and Desolation had passed well in advance of the storm and were now far below the horizon. They would not be back before the next nightfall, and it was generally assumed that by then, the outcome of the struggle would have been decided. Caleb awoke before dawn, as he generally did. He propped himself against the wall sleepily and looked over at his father, standing guard. His father looked over at him and smiled, then bent and retrieved a wet cloth from a shallow pail at his feet. He handed it to Caleb, who took it without a word and slapped it against his face. The water was ice cold.

"Has anything happened?" he said.

"Nothing yet, son. The trench has dried well. As soon as the sun is up we'll try seeding it, at least around the gate, but it's pretty hopeless. The Spanglar will never grow quickly enough, even with a good clear sky."

"The Universe will protect us."

Jonathan stared down at his son for a moment, and returned to watching the fields. "I didn't know you were that religious, Caleb."

"It seems foolish to not believe in a higher power. All of nature screams its existence. I just don't talk about it very much."

"A wise decision on both counts," Jonathan sneered.

After that, they were silent until well after dawn. By the time the sun had been up for several hours there was still no sign of the tuskers and the ground had dried completely. All of the Spanglar crystals had been used to seed the ditch though they did not go far, and they were only just beginning to grow. It would take several full days before they were at a useful height. Still the act of seeding was valuable in itself. It kept the people busy doing something to protect themselves, even if it yielded inconsequential results, and it kept him thinking about something other than the coming conflict.

The Keeper had been back and forth between the wall and meetings with clan chiefs, designing and redesigning strategies and coming to agreement on what they should do when the attack began. He stood now looking down hopelessly at the smattering of small crystalline plants lining the ditch in clumps. He was frowning. "I suppose we've done all we can," he said. "I wish we had more Spanglar."

Caleb suddenly had a thought and reached for the pouch on his belt. He had totally forgotten the Spanglar crystals dropped by the apparition he'd chased over the wall. He reached into the bag and withdrew a handful of them now. He knew it would probably not help, but he reasoned that they wouldn't hurt either. Absently, he tossed them over the wall into the ditch.

"I forgot I had some Spanglar seeds," he said to no one. "I'm sorry."

"They're coming," the Keeper said. Everyone looked in the direction the Keeper was pointing. Along the edge of the lake, a dark mass was forming. They were still too far away to see clearly, but it was obvious that they were tuskers, massing for the attack. There were literally thousands of them. Even if they could not have been seen, the wind was blowing in the direction of the colony, and the stench was appalling. It was the smell of rotting flesh and feces, wet and moldy and putrefied. Several defenders vomited over the wall in response. Most grabbed whatever cloth they could find to cover their faces. Caleb grabbed the cloth he had used to clear his head, dampened it and put it over his mouth and nose. Only Jonathan seemed unaffected, though his eyes began to water.

"Posts!" yelled Jonathan. "Look to your front. They'll be on us on all sides!"

They were coming on now, moving quickly across the fields. They sounded like thunder and the ground shook with their passing. It was just as Chandy had described it happening at the separatists' village. The wind began to blow hot, a precursor to the windy season, and the stench increased until it was nearly overwhelming.

Absently, a minute corner of Caleb's consciousness wondered if the odor emitted by the tuskers was an adaptation to render their prey helpless.

There was another sound filling the air as well, a closer sound like a rustling or crackling. Caleb looked down to the trench and gave a muffled cry. The Spanglar was growing and expanding faster than he had ever seen. It was spreading along the ditch, traveling like a living thing, already rounding the corner of the wall to the sides, and climbing into the air, some six feet in height. This was no ordinary Spanglar. There was no random nature to it at all. It grew straight and produced sharp barbed crystals that faced outward and upward, but only on the side away from the wall. This was a vicious, deadly barrier rising from the ditch and it had to have been cultivated to grow this way.

"Where did you get those seeds?" cried the Keeper.

"From the creature I chased over the wall that night. It dropped a pouch of them."

The Keeper laughed. "It seems we have an ally. Is there any more?"

Caleb nodded.

"Spread it around the inner wall. Be sure to leave a barrier at the gate or we'll never be able to get in if we need to. Go!"

Caleb was off and running. One last look over his shoulder told him that the oncoming tuskers had already covered nearly a quarter of the distance from the lake edge to the outer wall. As soon as he was inside the inner ward, the gates were closed and he climbed to the ramp, walking along the edge and sprinkling crystalline seeds as he went. He walked a quarter of the perimeter, then turned and began sprinkling on the other side of the gate. Darius and Chandy looked at him as if he'd lost his mind, but he had no time to explain. When he had finished, he raced back to the guard tower and peered over the edge. The Spanglar was already taking root, rising from the ground and from the sides and tops of buildings nestled against the inner wall itself. It began to form a solid impenetrable mass. Cheers rose from the defenders on the walls and looking around, Caleb could see them following the progress of the growth as it raced along the wall until the entire inner ward was surrounded with a hedge as high as the wall itself. He looked back at Darius and Chandy who were now standing, staring at him open-mouthed.

"The Universe protects its children!" he yelled above the cheering of the defenders and laughed loudly.

Back at the outer wall, the colonists were firing their weapons, killing the first arrivals. Caleb and Darius climbed to the top of the guard tower, just high enough to see what was going on along the side wall of the outer ward. The tuskers had indeed attacked on three sides, and were now filling in along the back wall as well. They were in a rage, trying to break through the barrier of sharp barbs, which were too tough to penetrate and too strong to sweep aside. Defenders on all walls were now firing into their massed ranks. At the rate they were firing, they would run out of projectiles long before they ran out of tuskers, but as long as the Spanglar held, they were safe.

Along the side wall, just at the edge of what Caleb and Chandy could see, a new wave of tuskers was gathering. They charged en masse right into the wall of crystals, the ones behind pushing them into the crystals where they screamed in pain. Others were beginning to climb over the impaled bodies at the wall and were in turn impaled. At the rate they were going, they would be able to scale the hedge in a matter of moments. Caleb carefully aimed his energy weapon and sent a beam of light directly at the edge of the outer gate tower. It exploded with a tiny impact that sent tile flying. Jonathan and the Keeper turned to see what was happening and Caleb pointed to the side wall. Quickly they realized what was happening and Jonathan barked orders.

Oil was sent streaming over the wall and down onto the Spanglar, drenching the dead bodies and climbing Tuskers. Torches were thrown and the central portion of the side wall burst into flames. Thick, oily black smoke rose amidst the screams of burning tuskers, and the smell of burning flesh was added to the air. The results were only temporary. After several minutes, the assault resumed and tuskers were quickly reaching the top of the wall. Darius was frantically screaming above the din and pointing the other side wall where a similar attack was underway. The outer ward would be overrun.

"Stand by the gate!" Caleb screamed, and six defenders rushed to comply. At the outer wall, defenders were now firing at tuskers coming over the parapets, setting up a deadly crossfire from two sides while defenders directly in front of the attack scattered toward the corners. Flames erupted on the other outer wall as oil was poured on the second mass attack, and Caleb watched helplessly, as great gaps began to form in the main gate where tuskers were breaking through.

The Keeper yelled something unintelligible from where Caleb stood, and the defenders began abandoning the walls. Tuskers replaced them on the parapets and began leaping into the ward, ripping and slashing at those defenders close at hand. Caleb nodded to the gate keepers and they instantly threw open the gates. Defenders from the outer ward streamed inside the inner walls and took up positions along the ramps. Jonathan and the Keeper were the last to enter, and just as they did, a single tusker leaped for the Keeper. Jonathan swung around and fired at the beast whose head exploded in mid air. He turned to come through the gate, but a second beast blocked his way. Shots erupted from the walls and the tusker literally fell apart in a series of tiny explosions, but others were coming from behind. As the gate closed, Caleb caught a final look at his father and four others, backs to the wall firing at the oncoming horde.

"FATHER!" he yelled. He sank to his knees and wailed mindlessly.

"Caleb!" Darius cried. "Not now, Caleb. We need you!"

Caleb retched, then heaved, trying to catch his breath.

"Caleb, they'll be through that gate in a minute!"

Caleb stood, sucked in a great gulp of air and looked over the tower. Tuskers were all around them, but the

space was too small between the wards for them to mass as
they had at the outer walls. The Spanglar fought them off
tenaciously, and they realized that their only entry was
through the gate. Caleb reached to his belt and produced
the bag of seeds. A small handful remained. The tossed
them over the wall directly into the entrance to the gate.
Milling Tuskers instinctively moved away, wildly shaking
those seeds that had landed on them. They screamed in
torment. Almost immediately, the seeds were taking root
and growing to cover the entrance. Oil was poured over
those tuskers still at the gate to drive them off, and the
hotter the fire, the more rapidly the Spanglar seemed to
grow. If the tuskers were going to breach this defense,
they would have to find another way.

The tuskers paced back and forth in a rage, snapping at
each other and wildly biting at the hedge with their tusks.
It only served to further frustrate them. The whole outer
ward was filled with them milling about and trying to press
forward. In the press, more and more of them were
becoming entangled on the hedge and again they were
beginning to climb over the bodies toward the parapets.
The defenders offered a withering fire wherever the tuskers
made progress. Hundreds fell dead or came apart in pieces
as the tiny explosive projectiles struck them, yet they still
surged forward. Then, as suddenly as they had charged,

they began to retreat, swarming back over the outer wall and through the outer gate. Caleb and the other looked on, dumfounded.

"Now what?" Chandy said wearily.

Darius began to laugh. He pointed out over the city walls toward the plain.

"Out there," he said. "Look at the lake!"

The lake lay shrouded in a dark, dense cloud. It roiled out of the forest and off the surface of the fens, swirling and rolling toward the town. Before it, the tuskers were in full retreat, but slowed by the exertion of their charge. Little by little, the cloud, now roaring on its own account, was overtaking them.

"It's the jack darts!" someone yelled. "They're swarming!"

Caleb looked at the scene absently. It all seemed surreal to him. His eyes weren't focusing well and the colors all seemed wrong. Everything was turning pastel and the harder he tried to see, the more difficult it became. Out in the fields, the swarm had reached the retreating tuskers and swept over them blindly, impaling most and shredding those in the lead.

"No wonder they retreated," cried Chandy.

"And we'd better do the same," answered Darius. "They'll be on us soon."

The Keeper stood at the edge of the tower and quieted the people, "Everyone to your homes! Those without homes will be housed with those who do! We have only a few moments before they reach the colony. Go!"
Chandy grabbed Caleb's arm, but he only stared back limply. He couldn't comprehend what was happening. None of it made sense.

"Darius, help me. We've got to get to my house!" Caleb started to say something but silently slumped to the floor instead. Slowly, the world faded away.

CHAPTER 31

C aleb slept for three days. The first two he was totally unaware of what was happening, the third was a mixture of deep sleep, restless dreams, and barely lucid ranting. Through it all, Kylie stayed by his side, feeding him when he would eat, bathing him each day, changing his clothes completely when he soiled them. He remembered none of this.

Finally, toward the end of the third day, he awoke and asked for water. This was followed by broth and a gentle massage by both Kylie and Jillian, who were determined to have him whole again. Of this he remembered being embarrassed by Jillian's touch, but grateful for Kylie's. After that, he slept again and didn't awaken until the fourth day.

Caleb sat up some time after dawn, steadying himself against the dizziness and nausea of being so long bedridden, slipped his feet onto the floor and tried to stand, shakily. A loud hissing sound surrounded him, mixed with the sound of voices, pleasantly talking and occasionally laughing across the room. He was sitting on the edge of a bed near the fire in the Crones' main hall.

At the table in the center of the room sat Chandy and Jillian, Darius, his mother, Donald Crone and, of course, Kylie. It was Darius who first spotted him and rose to help him to the table. Seating him between Kylie and his mother, Darius and Chandy settled in again. Caleb looked at his mother who was smiling at him gently.

"Mother, about Father..."

"Yes," she said softly. "We can talk later."

"I...couldn't save him. I couldn't do anything."

"I know, darling. Don't fret. It's done now, and you did all you could. Your father was a great hunter and a great leader. He led a wonderful life, one that he savored, and he was so proud of you, you know. You're so like him."

"I'm...so sorry."

"It's time to put grief aside. We have new beginnings to deal with," said Donald Crone with surprising resolve. "We have a town to rebuild."

Caleb looked at the man as if for the first time. Donald was very different. There was no trace of sadness about him now, and a new sense of purpose shown in his words. Caleb nodded but knew it would take a long time for his heart to heal from the loss of his father. He started to see that moment at the gate again in his mind, but before it could form, the hissing rose to a louder pitch and insinuated itself into his awareness.

"Is that the wind?"

"The windy season's come," announced Chandy, saying it like a great declaration. He was grinning broadly. "That means winter is coming and we can all snug in for three or four months and wait for the spring." He grinned ever more broadly and looked at Jillian, who studied her hands demurely.

"What about the tuskers? What happened? The last I remember there were jack darts swarming and someone pulled me off the wall."

"Oh, there were definitely jack darts," said Darius. "That was the biggest swarm I think I've ever seen. They went through the tuskers and annihilated them. Not one escaped. By the time they'd finished their work, every beast and a good number of jack darts were history. I don't imagine we'll have to worry about big swarms for years to come.

"None of them escaped?"

"Not a one. I went with the Keeper yesterday during the midday lull in the storm to the front gates. The wind and sand had stripped all the flesh from the bones and it's already started to break them down too. In another week, there won't be any trace of them at all. It'll be like they were never there."

"Until you look at the town and begin to count the dead," said Donald. He did not sound morose about it at all. It was just a statement of fact.

"How many died?"

"Don't know for sure," said Darius. "I think several hundred, mostly in the outer ward. Almost everyone made it to shelter before the jack darts came through the town. We're still counting heads. I've been working with Chandy and the Keeper to organize things. When the winds die down we'll have two good weeks before the ice comes and we can better distribute people. There are vacant houses in the outer ward that were virtually untouched. One thing's for sure, we won't starve this winter."

"How's the Keeper doing?" Caleb asked at last.

"Ask him yourself. He'll be here tomorrow during the lull. He's come every day to check in on his new Master of the Hunt."

"I'm not Master of the Hunt," Caleb said flatly.

"Actually, you are. It's been declared."

"I'm too young."

"Your father was a year younger than you are when he was given the post, Caleb," said his mother.

"I'm not experienced enough."

"After your defense of the inner wall? No one is going to believe that."

"But I don't want to be Master of the Hunt. I just want to be a hunter."

"No one asked you if you wanted it, Caleb," said Donald Crone. He spoke to him as his father would have, sternly and with kindness all at once. "Life gives us what we need, not what we want. It's your job. Get used to it."

"That's enough," said Kylie softly. Caleb felt her hand on his and turned to her. Her eyes met his tenderly. "My man needs to recover. This can all wait. He's had enough for one day."

He had enough indeed, he thought, and accepted Kylie's declaration without protest. She led him away from the table, but not back to the bed beside the fire. She took him to the settle, now further back from the window and outfitted with two large coarsely woven blankets in preparation for the winter. They settled in and he took her under his arm, holding her closely and loving her silently. After some time, he began to cry. She kissed him gently on each cheek, touching her tongue to his falling tears and whispered a quiet shush as he sobbed. He surrendered to her completely and continued to cry, more gently now, until at last he fell again asleep in her arms.

EPILOGUE

The windy season passed quickly for them all. Caleb remembered it only vaguely as he regained his strength and his sanity, and they all busied themselves daily preparing for winter. Fuel was gathered and distributed during the midday lulls, which became progressively longer as the winds began to subside, and food was inventoried for distribution. When at last the winds ceased, they organized the colony once again and Darius proved invaluable to Chandy and the Keeper in this process. At the end of the third week after the windy season, when the first frosts were forming on the feather grass out in the fields, they gathered on the plain for a ceremony to mourn the dead and give thanks for their deliverance. At the end of the service, the Keeper had said with great solemnity, "The Universe protects its own."

Like closing the last page of a book, Caleb completed his mourning. It was much the same with everyone.

When winter set in, Darius and three of his mates moved in to the Grant house. Caleb's mother came to share the Crones' house with Donald, Kylie, and Caleb. Chandy and Jillian moved in to the Keeper's compound and on the first day of the new year, they were married, as were Kylie and Caleb. They passed the long winter nights talking by the fire, playing winter games or making small items that would be needed in the spring. Caleb cleaned and repaired every rifle he could find and conferred with the metalsmiths on ways to improve their weapons for not only hunting, but also to protect them if the tuskers ever returned. He took to the post of Master of the Hunt more and more. The entire colony recognized his position and his wisdom for what it was, exceptional. He was happy with his new wife and their surviving parents. The time passed quickly and sooner than they expected, spring arrived.

It was when the ice was well into melt that Donald came to Caleb and insisted on a private conversation. They walked out into the soggy streets, replete with hoarfrost and melt and slogged their way toward the outer gate.

"I must discuss something with you," Donald said as they walked. He seemed nervous.

"Yes?"

"I want you and Kylie to move back into your house. Darius and his friends have already found another home in the outer ward. It's large enough for them, and from what Darius says, the closer he is to the wood, the happier he is."

"I...don't understand. Is there a problem?"

"Well, um, yes, but not like you think," Donald stammered.

"You'll be alone," protested Caleb. "I'm not sure you need that."

Donald stopped in mid stride and stared at Caleb. "I won't be alone, Caleb. Your mother and I are to be married. I hope it's with your blessing."

Caleb tried to hide the smile forming around the edge of his mouth. "Have you discussed this with your daughter?"

"I have. Kylie thinks it's a wonderful idea. It's you that concerns me. I've grown to love you like a second son. I don't want to jeopardize that, but our minds are made up. Your mother and I have grown very close over the winter. We both have wounds to heal and want to be together. I love your mother very much."

"Um, Okay," said Caleb in an offhand manner.

"Yes?" Donald said, taken aback.

"Yes," Caleb said, grinning. "And it's about time, too. When's the wedding?"

It was three weeks to the day from that moment that they were married and another week before the Keeper arrived at Caleb and Kylie's, now firmly entrenched in the Grant house. He had Chandy in tow, as usual, and after greetings and an offer of tea, politely refused, he took Caleb aside to talk.

"I have job for you. It's one that only you and Chandy can accomplish, and it is very important."

"Of course," Caleb said quickly.

"You and Chandy are about to embark on the adventure of a lifetime," he said grandly.

"Um, I thought we did that before the winter. That's about all the adventure that I can stand for one lifetime, Keeper."

"Ah, but once you hear, I think you'll want to go."

Caleb could feel something coming and he was not at all sure he was going to like it. "Go on," he said.

"That Spanglar seed that you found at the wall. I think that it was dropped purposely for us to find. Someone knew about the beasts and how to fight them. They came to our aid when we were in need, just as the Tower did generations ago."

"You're talking about that thing that went over the wall."

"That thing is a sentient being, Caleb. He's native to the planet, and he and his kind are obviously aware of us and our situation here. They've offered us aid and friendship. It would be unconscionable of us to not say thank you."

Caleb physically stepped back a pace. "And how do you propose that we do this?"

"By sending you and Chandy out of the valley. There must be a way out or our friend could not have gotten in. You are going beyond the valley into the world we live on. You're going to see what no one else among us has seen.

You're going to find what this world is really like, and you're going to find our benefactors."

"Ah... no. I'm happy here. I've got everything I want right here with Kylie.

"Ah yes!" called Chandy from across the room. "Think of it Caleb. It's the chance of a lifetime! We'll be the first to discover the rest of this world. If we're going to live here and our children after us, we owe it to them! It will be the greatest adventure ever!"

"Oh no. I don't think so," Caleb protested.

"Oh yes, my friend," said the Keeper gently. "and you leave in the morning!"

Finis

SNEAK PEEK

COMING JUNE 2006

There was a light rain was falling, which was unusual these days. Normally, it was either bone dry and brutally hot or chilled, with torrential downpours coming out of the north at odd moments during the day and night. The weather had been that way for years now. For the man staring through the window of his small bedroom, the light drizzle was just one more oddity in a long line of oddities that had inflicted him this year.

Three times he had found himself waking up to a nightmare not of his own making, a bizarre combination of events that left him puzzled, horribly frightened and totally unable to remember what had happened. He looked over at his left hand which was missing a ring finger and a pinky. That had been the first frightening incident in this macabre play. He had awakened as usual just as the sun was beginning to peak above the tops of the apartment buildings that filled this corner of the Southern Complex' central core. He remembered feeling particularly drowsy, as if he had been on an all night binge, but he remembered clearly slipping into bed about ten in the evening.

When his attention was finally drawn to the pain in his left hand, he discovered the missing fingers, the hand itself wrapped neatly in surgical bandages. Of course he had panicked, but somehow he couldn't bring himself to report the event or even seek medical help. He just noted his predicament, released a silent anguished scream from deep within his soul and gone back to sleep. That was the first time it happened.

The second time, he found that flesh had been taken from his right side, just under the arm, and that a large bandage covered the wound, some eight inches in diameter, all neatly wrapped with gauze and tape around his torso, like something out of an old war movie. Again he inexplicitly accepted the event with a terror that could not be voiced and in a very short time went about is business as usual. He explained to his co-workers at the newspaper that he had had an accident while climbing on a friend's roof to repair a leak and that in falling, he experienced some deep lacerations from a trellis on the side of the house. The accepted the explanation without comment.

Now the third incident had occurred only days before. This one was by far the most serious involving his right cornea, which had been surgically removed, leaving him blind in one eye. Again there was the scream, more insistent now but as silent as before, and no matter how much anguish he felt, he could not bring himself to call the authorities or seek medical help.

He stood looking out at the drizzling rain, wondering what was becoming of him and realizing that he was being taken apart piece by piece, but why? It was like that story of the guy who takes a vacation to Mexico or somewhere and wakes up in a tub full of ice with a missing kidney and instructions to call an ambulance immediately. He was living a horror story come true, and whenever it came to mind, which was almost constantly now, he would break out in a cold sweat and begin to shake uncontrollably. Yet for all his raw terror, he could not bring himself to call for help. Someday, he said to himself, someday I've got to call someone. Why haven't I called the police? He would reach for his com plate and begin to punch in the code for emergency help, but he would turn it off before speaking.

He turned away from the window in anguish, sitting on the edge of the bed, head in hands, and began to cry. At first he did it softly, but soon a flood of tears and wails poured out of him, all the built up frustration and fear bubbling over into the physical world.

"Mister Hayes?" called a voice at the door. Someone was pounding on his apartment door insistently. "Mister Hayes, are you in there?"

"Who is it?" he wailed.

"I've come to help you, Mister Hayes."

"I don't need your help!" he snapped and began to weep more softly.

"Mister Hayes, I believe you do. I know what's been going on, Mister Hayes. I know you are frightened and confused and that you've been badly abused. I'm here to see to it that all that stops."

He looked up at the door and calmed himself. "Who are you?" he said.

"A friend."

"I have no friends!" he snapped.

After a moment, the voice said, "You have more friends than you think, Magnus, and we want to help you. What's been done to you is inexcusable and we want to put a stop to it."

"How the hell do you know what's been done to me?" he screamed. "You can't know!"

"We know, Mister Hayes. We were there."

Magnus Hayes stared at the door in silence. He neither moved nor spoke. He sat very still, trying to make sense of what he was hearing.

"Are you still with me, Mister Hayes?"

"I'm still here," he said at last. "What do you want with me?"

"We told you. We want to help you, but we can't unless you let us in. We can give you all the medical attention you need and see to it that nothing like this happens again, but we can't do anything for you if you won't let us in."

Hayes stood. "Step back from the door," he said. After a full minute he crossed to the door and looked at the security screen beside it. Standing about four feet from the door was a tall man in a dark suit and wearing a tie. He looked as if he were on his way to a banquet or some other formal gathering. His com plate was propped against his right side in his hand and he was smiling, almost sympathetically looking back at the spy lens in the door. Hayes sighed and slipped the bolt on the door. He opened it.

"Hello, Mister Hayes," the tall man said. "My name is Anthony. I'm glad you decided to see me. There are two companions with me. They are around the corner and won't come out until you say it's all right. I'm fully aware of how frightening all this must be, and we do not wish to add to your fears. May I come in?"

"Um, yes. Tell the others to come in too," he said.

To his surprise all three of them men were so similar that they were almost mirror images of each other. They didn't look like brothers or as if they were closely related, but they were none the less mirror images. Each wore the same dark suit and each sported a red and gold striped tie that was far wider than the formal style of the day. They were the same height and build, and whereas the one called Anthony had nearly jet black hair, the other two were a sandy blond and a russet red. The red head had a splotchy, pinkish complexion while the other two were so pale that they were almost white.

They stepped into the room quickly and closed the

door behind them. While Anthony did the talking, the other two scanned the apartment, apparently looking for any surveillance devices or evidence that Hayes was not alone.

"What are they doing?" Magnus Hayes asked.

"Being sure that you are secure. You're in grave danger, you know."

"I know," he said, almost helplessly. "I know that very well."

"We want you to come with us to a safe place where we can protect you. I know that you must have endless questions, and we'll answer them all as best we can, but we must leave right away. Don't bother with packing. Just grab your personals and your com plate and come with us. There's no time to lose."

"Just like that?"

"Just like that, Mister Hayes. Remember the Mona Lisa."

Hayes' eyes glazed over when he heard this last phrase and he gathered those items that he always carried with him, his pocket knife, card to his apartment and his I.D. folder. He picked up his com plate and walked out into the hall without another word.

"What do we do about the rest of this stuff?" asked the red head, looking back into the room.

"Leave it. A clean up unit is on the way."

The four of them left through a side door and entered an alley where a single large van stood waiting. They hustled Magnus Hayes into the bay and drove away.

"Where too?" asked the driver, a burley man with curly hair and an odor laced with garlic.

"South," Anthony said, and take it easy. We've work to do.

Hayes was quickly stripped of his clothing and instructed to lie on a medical table which he did without comment. The three men took off their coats and ties and stepped into coveralls that enveloped them from head to toe. They donned surgical masks and soft protective helmets with clear visors. With a final glance at each other, they began their work.

Anthony began with the hands. He tied off the Magnus Hayes' wrists and picked up a surgical saw, severing the hand until he was through the bone and then grabbed the nearly separated hand with both of his and yanked, ripping it from the body. He dumped it unceremoniously in a plastic pail at his feet. He then proceeded to do the same to the other hand. The sandy haired man was simultaneously working on the head. He made neat surgical incisions along the base of the jaw from either side and separated the ligaments holding the mandible in place, finally ripping it away like some barbarian twisting a joint of beef free from a carcass.

"Watch the blood," Anthony said. "He can't die on us."

A spray was applied to the open wound, sealing it and the second man proceeded to the ears and eyes while Hayes lay perfectly still, not moving in spite of the lack of sedation, his tongue twirling grotesquely in circles as if searching for the missing jaw.

The red head monitored vital signs and occasionally injected this drug or that to keep the man alive, as piece after piece of human body found its way into the pail, each slab echoing with a resounding slap as it hit the growing pile of discarded parts. When they had finished, Magnus Hayes, now breathing heavily, lay on the table, each wound temporarily sealed, without hands, eyes ears testicles, penis, one of his feet or his nose.

Anthony bent over and bit his right cheek, sinking his teeth deeply into the flesh and ripping it away. The wound was a gaping hole that went clear through the flesh, exposing molars.

"Jesus!" snapped the red head.

"Orders. You get to take a chunk out of his leg." The man's reddish complexion was suddenly a pale green, but he did as he was told, wrenching a plug of flesh the size of a golf ball out of the man's left thigh and spitting it into the bucket.

"Now for the delicate work," Anthony said. "Scalpel, please."

Printed in the United States
51969LVS00001B/1-51